Reckoning

Book 3 in *The Ixan Prophecies* Trilogy

Scott Bartlett

Mirth Publishing

St. John's

RECKONING

© Scott Bartlett 2017

Cover art by: Tom Edwards (tomedwardsdesign.com)

Library and Archives Canada Cataloguing in Publication

Bartlett, Scott

Reckoning / Scott Bartlett ; illustrations by Tom Edwards.

ISBN 978-1-988380-06-3

To those fueled by principle.

CHAPTER 1

Main Priority

"We're transitioning through the darkgate now, Captain," Keyes's Nav officer said.

"Confirmed," Werner said. "Sensor data will be available momentarily."

Keyes acknowledged the information with nothing but a nod. Since Hades, he lacked much interest in speaking, which had caused some breakdowns in communication until his CIC crew learned to watch his body language more closely. He'd rebuked those breakdowns harshly, and all had become well.

As well as it can be, anyway, Keyes thought to himself. His hunt through Pirate's Path was almost at an end, and though they'd checked each system thoroughly, Keyes knew where he'd find his prey.

As they'd progressed through system after empty system, Casper had often become visible to sensors, shining dimly from many light years away.

Whenever it had become visible, Keyes ordered Werner to put the visual on a splitscreen using the CIC's main display. And he'd watched the star, his stomach roiling with heat.

"There they are," Werner said, a note of wonder in his voice. "In heliocentric orbit, two light-minutes ahead of Casper-3b. Their fleet is enormous. Mostly settlement ships, but still...where could Darkstream possibly have hidden all of this?"

"Inside the gas giant itself," Keyes said. "The same one their HQ orbits. They must have concealed them in Casper-3b as a contingency plan, which speaks to how paranoid they are. And they have good reason for paranoia, considering how long they've been screwing humanity."

"They've detected us already, Captain. It looks like you were right—most of the unaccounted-for UHF ships are here. A sizable battle group. They're arranging themselves to confront us."

"Should I accelerate, Captain?" Nav said.

"No. Maintain current speed." Certainly, an all-out charge from the supercarrier would have been menacing, and it would have given their ordnance more punch as well. But he expected a leisurely approach would prove more effective psychologically.

Plus, I want to savor this, he reflected.

The darkgate sat across the system, directly opposite Casper-3b, and it took the *Providence* ten hours to cross to the enemy ships.

For their part, the rogue UHF ships carefully arrayed themselves to intercept the supercarrier, spaced out to deny her the opportunity to take out two of them at once. Keyes would have to go through them if he wanted to threaten the settlement ships.

His crew spoke little as they traversed the system. Keyes preferred it that way, now. Normally, he would permit himself at least one coffee break for a ten-hour journey, but not this one. He sat in the Captain's chair the entire time, gripping the chair's armrests and staring at the opposing formation.

"Incoming transmission," his Coms officer said the moment they were close enough for real-time communication.

"Accept."

Keyes's former XO, Bob Bronson, appeared on the viewscreen. "What's your angle here, Keyes?"

"Justice."

"Come, now," Bronson said, clearly trying to sound self-assured. But Keyes heard the nervous hitch in his voice. "You can't expect us not to defend these people. They only want to find a new home."

"They want to flee their crimes."

"I won't let you do this, Keyes. I will oppose you."

"Then you'll die." Keyes glanced at his Coms officer. "Cut the transmission. Werner, put up a tactical display, full-screen." Bronson vanished from the viewscreen. "Coms, verify with Colonel Fesky that Condors are ready."

"She's ready, Captain."

"Then tell her to launch every last Condor." During the entire voyage through Pirate's Path, half of the Air Group had been on standby to launch. But in preparing to enter this system, Keyes had ordered every pilot to prepare for battle. "I want half of them on missile defense and the other half targeting the cruiser on the rightmost periphery of the enemy formation."

With the addition of former Falcon pilots from among the Bastion Sector insurgents, the *Providence* now boasted a fully reconstituted Air Group; four hundred pilots strong. And Keyes knew Fesky was eager to have them implement what she'd taught them.

Not only that, but for the first time since the start of this war, Keyes's ship was completely refueled, recharged, and reloaded. He liked to think that she thirsted for Darkstream's blood as much as he did.

"Let's open with our primary laser," Keyes said, "targeting the leftmost cruiser."

The tactically superior option would have been to target Bronson's destroyer with the primary, neatly decapitating the enemy battle group and sending it into disarray. But efficiency wasn't Keyes's main priority in this engagement.

His main priority entailed letting Bronson squirm for as long as possible.

CHAPTER 2

Personal Revenge

Like a pack of wolves taking down an elk, half of the Air Group swarmed over the missile cruiser the captain had designated.

Fesky had permitted Husher to handpick pilots in order to resurrect his Haymaker squadron. The current Haymakers weren't nearly as skilled as Gaston and the others had been, and Husher missed the fallen pilots dearly, but he knew the fires of battle would harden this new squadron and make them strong.

One of the best ways to speed up that process is to set a good example as their leader.

The assignment given to this half of the Air Group didn't involve protecting the *Providence* from missiles, but Husher believed in going above and beyond the call of duty. And so, after picking off one of the cruiser's point defense turrets with a Sidewinder, he engaged his Condor's gyros to swing the outer shell thirty-five degrees, firing engines briefly before swinging another nineteen degrees to shoot a Banshee fresh out of its tube.

Immediately after, he rotated an additional thirty-five degrees, executing an Ocharium-assisted engine burn to avoid the kinetic impactors thrown at his Condor by the next set of point defense turrets. They missed by a matter of meters.

"Whoa, Spank!" It was his new second-in-command, Omelet, speaking over a squadron-wide channel. "That was some fancy flying!"

"Do you have something to report?" Husher snapped.

"Uh, no, sir."

"Then stay off the radio and focus on your own flying until you do." Without missing a beat, Husher drew a bead on the next turret battery and pelted it with kinetic impactors.

It blew up, but not before it got off a missile that screamed toward Omelet's fighter. Judging from the man's flying, Husher's second-in-command hadn't even spotted it yet. Wincing, Husher picked it off himself, deciding to wait until after the battle to dump on Omelet the criticism he had coming.

Fesky's voice entered his helmet: "Spank. Status?"

"Sitting pretty, so far. Haven't lost a fighter."

"Acknowledged. I think it's time to take the cruiser down. I'd like to see how well the former Falcon pilots are handling their Condors in battle, but I'd also like minimal risk. If they choke, I want your Haymakers to step in and pick up the slack."

"Can do, Madcap."

Over a wide channel, Fesky spoke again. "Okay, Trailblazer, Dicemen, Stinger, and Warhawk squadrons, get in alpha strike formation and hit that cruiser with everything. Now!"

Watching on his tactical display, Husher watched the former Falcon pilots form up immediately, with pleasing crispness, to start hitting the missile cruiser with wave after wave of kinetic impactors. The enemy warship blew up with the third alpha strike.

I'm starting to think I should have recruited some of them for the Haymakers.

He brushed the thought away as the half of the Air Group assigned to offensive maneuvers—twelve squadrons, all told—attacked the next target, a corvette. It fell even faster than the cruiser had.

Seeing so many Condor pilots deployed at once, fighting in concert, flowing around each other like a single, sleek predator in action...it reminded Husher of vids he'd seen from the First Galactic War, which featured the *Providence* in her heyday.

Before this, he'd barely dared to hope that heyday could return, but today, his hopes were being realized.

They moved on to the third target, which instantly stopped pressuring the supercarrier to attempt a retreat. The Condors gave no quarter, sprinting forward to hammer the enemy hull with ordnance.

For the first time in decades, the *Providence* and her Air Group were in full fighting form, and the universe would remember exactly what they could do.

"The enemy's surrendered," Fesky said a few minutes later, over a wide channel. "All Condors back to base."

Wow, Husher thought. Just like that, it was over. *For today, anyway. But we've only just begun to flex our muscles.*

He opened up a two-way with Fesky. "You could sound a little happier, Madcap. That may have been the fastest anyone's ever won an engagement. Plus, we can rest easy now. Darkstream won't be allowed to continue putting the entire universe at risk by using dark tech."

"That's just it, Spank," Fesky said. "We don't know that for sure."

"What are you talking about?"

"I just listened in on the command channel while the captain spoke to Bronson. He's letting Darkstream's fleet leave."

"Are you kidding me? How could he do that?"

"In exchange for their promise not to use dark tech again. But I'm beginning to think this was never about dark tech."

"Why do you say that?"

Fesky clacked her beak, which inside Husher's helmet sounded like a sharp *click*. "Because Captain Keyes also demanded Bronson hand over Tennyson Steele." She paused, seeming to hesitate, but then continued. "I've suspected this for most of the trip, but I didn't want to say it: I think the real reason the captain brought us here was so he could carry out his own personal revenge."

CHAPTER 3

Hangar Bay E

Husher hopped out of his Condor the moment he landed it, putting off post-flight checks until he had a chance to speak with Captain Keyes.

Marching toward the CIC, footfalls echoing off the bulkheads, he encountered the captain headed toward Hangar Bay E. Keyes registered his presence with the briefest glance, not altering his stride or offering anything in the way of greeting.

"Is it true you're letting the Darkstream ships go?" Husher said, spinning around and matching the captain's brisk pace.

A curt nod was the extent of Keyes's reply.

"I can't believe it," Husher said. "First you fail to discipline Wahlburg for threatening a civilian on the Vermillion Shipyards, and now this."

"Bronson gave me his word that Darkstream won't use dark tech again."

"Sir, with all due respect, since when was Bronson's word good for anything? Of course they're going to use dark tech! What else can they do? How else can they leave?"

"They could use the old wormhole network."

"You mean the wormholes that destroy a significant percentage of the ships that pass through them? I highly doubt Bronson will subject himself to that sort of risk, for something so insignificant as honor."

Keyes turned his head to hold Husher's gaze. The captain's famous stare had been effective before Hades, but since then, it had gained an edge that almost made Husher want to abandon this conversation. Try to find a drink, maybe.

"Dark-tech-enabled wormhole generation doesn't work anymore," Keyes said. "Remember? The wormholes that are produced destroy all organic matter."

Steeling himself, Husher answered: "Only the ones that were connected to Ochrim's master control. Sir, if Darkstream went through all the trouble to build this resettlement fleet and hide it, I'm sure they also took the precaution of having at least one wormhole generator not connected to the master control. In fact, they wouldn't have wanted these ships connected to anything. That would have made it possible to find them."

"The Darkstream ships will be allowed to leave, Husher. End of story. We can't afford the time and effort it would take to arrest two million people and escort nearly three hundred ships back to Sol."

Husher shook his head. "Arresting them was the entire reason the Commonwealth agreed to let you go on this mission. It's the only way to make sure they stop using dark tech."

The captain didn't reply, so Husher pressed on. "What's this really about for you, Captain? Did they take away your principles while you were imprisoned over Hades?"

That drew a sharp warning glance, but nothing else.

"Sir, I started to worry when you failed to discipline Wahlburg for his misconduct. You said it can wait until after the war, but that'll only encourage others to engage in misconduct. This is exactly the type of thinking that led to Hurst and the corruption of the UHF. We have to stay true to the reasons we opposed the UHF in the first place, don't we? If not, we'll be right back where we were two months ago."

When Keyes still didn't say anything, blood started rushing in Husher's ears, and he felt his hands curl into tight fists. "Tell me the truth: is vengeance the only thing motivating you, now?"

They'd reached the entrance to Hangar Bay E, and Keyes put his hand on the panel that controlled the hatch as he locked eyes with Husher. "You're about to find out."

The moment they entered was the same moment Tennyson Steele was escorted out of a Darkstream shuttle by a pair of the company's mercenaries.

"Bronson wants assurance you'll treat Steele justly," one of them said.

"Oh, he'll be treated justly," Keyes said. "But it's a little late to demand assurances for anything." The captain drew his service pistol.

"Sir!" Husher said.

"Such a show you're putting on, Captain Keyes," Tennyson Steele said. "And for what? Do you really expect me to believe you're going to shoot me in front of two armed Darkstream guards?"

Keyes placed the pistol's muzzle against Steele's forehead, ignoring the assault rifles pointed at him. "If I was worried about the guards, I would have waited till they left before killing you. Get on your knees." The captain's voice was ice.

"Come off it, Captain," Steele said. "I didn't realize you were so attached to your face that you'd behave this way after I mangled it."

"If you shoot, we shoot," one of the Darkstream guards said.

"And if you shoot, you'll never leave this ship alive," Keyes said. He drew his gun back and smashed the butt into Steele's flabby face. Blood flew, speckling the CEO's glasses, and Steele staggered backward. "*Get on your knees!*" Keyes yelled.

Visibly shaken, now, Steele complied. His bravado had dried up entirely.

"Captain..." Husher said, holding both hands forward, palms toward Keyes. "You don't want to do this. There's no going back from this."

"I know," Keyes said. He replaced the muzzle against Steele's forehead and pulled the trigger. The CEO toppled over, hitting the deck with a *thud.*

The Darkstream guards both shook their heads, eyes wide. Keyes leveled the pistol at the one on the right. "Get back in your shuttle and leave my ship."

Slowly, they complied. As the shuttle's outer hatch slid into place, concealing the guards from view, Captain Keyes spun on his heel and marched out of Hangar Bay E, leaving Steele's inert body cooling in the middle of the deck.

CHAPTER 4

Scandium

Gabriel Roach had always hated going through those wormholes. Every time, he felt sure the CIC crew would mess something up, maybe fail to position the conductor correctly in order to recapture the energy when it closed. If that happened, the wormhole would collapse, its energy blasting in every direction and incinerating everything within twenty light-minutes.

Including him. Definitely including him.

Two hours after the *Providence* left the Casper System, Lieutenant Commander Bob Bronson had given the order for a wormhole to be opened, and shortly after that the resettlement fleet had begun passing through it.

To a whole new galaxy, Gabriel Roach reflected as he dismantled his assault rifle, inspecting each part. He liked to check them twice—once as he took the gun apart and once upon reassembly.

A tremor passed through the shuttle, which was currently carrying him and other Darkstream guards through a rambunctious high-altitude weather system.

This was a first in human history, and so Roach found it ironic that most humans wouldn't know about it for a while, if ever.

Back when Ochrim had first given humanity dark tech, he'd warned them against ever using it to open a wormhole to another galaxy. Based on the prevalence of intelligent life in the Milky Way, it was considered exceedingly likely that other galaxies teemed with spacefaring species too.

By entering a new galaxy, the Darkstream employees and the UHF ships escorting them had risked running into a species more technologically advanced than humans. And that would come with a host of other risks, such as the species possessing the ability to find their way to the Milky Way, maybe by reading the residue of the wormhole somehow.

It was even possible they'd be able to tell the human ships' origins just from the metals used to build them.

But that was what made the Darkstream resettlement fleet historically unique: they didn't care about risking a powerful alien enemy finding humanity's home galaxy, because they were leaving that galaxy forever.

All two million people in the fleet considered remaining near other humans the greater risk.

Either way...no sign of aliens yet.

The very first system they'd entered in this new galaxy had contained little of interest, but no one had expected it to. It was just a lonely ice giant orbiting a brown dwarf star.

Darkstream's navigational experts hadn't brought them to that system because they expected it would contain a place suitable for colonization. No, they'd chosen it exactly *because* it seemed unattractive, and therefore wasn't likely to have unfriendly occupants.

From there, company astronomers had employed their tried-and-true roster of techniques for indirectly evaluating exoplanets. Someone had tried to explain them to Roach, once, but he'd quickly zoned out during the litany. *Gravitational micro-something...aurora radial...something...*

He gave his head a brisk shake and refocused on the shuttle's display, which showed the intense weather outside the craft. Sensors said the storm cleared up farther below, and Roach was looking forward to that.

The astronomers had finally settled on a star that looked promising, with one planet orbiting it that had the right mix in its atmosphere, along with four that didn't.

If I push through to the front of the shuttle, I could be the first person to step foot on a planet in another galaxy.

He would miss the missions to the Bastion Sector, where he'd fought alongside UHF marines to put down various insurgencies. He'd relished every chance he'd gotten to neutralize a radical.

That said, he'd hated the constant red tape and stifling oversight from the UHF brass. They'd been Darkstream's most overbearing client.

Now, it occurred to Roach that there would be far fewer rules, here. The only laws would be company policy. There'd be no government bureaucrats breathing down their necks, terrified that details on ops would leak to the traitorous news media.

This galaxy meant a brand new start, and Roach burned with a sudden desire to make sure they did it right.

The shuttle finally touched down on the planet's surface, in a clearing amidst a sea of trees shaped like Earth's pine trees, except with cascading waves of bare, spindly branches where their cones should have been.

"Atmosphere checks out, according to these readings," said the one scientist they'd brought with them, hunching over a tablet. "Still, we should send a rover out first, just to play it safe."

"Screw that," Roach said, ripping off his straps and getting to his feet. "I won't have some robot be the first one to walk on this planet. If I choke out there, you'll know it's not safe." He raised his voice so the shuttle pilot could hear: "Open the airlock!"

The pilot complied.

After today, everyone would know the name Gabriel Roach. That would make a good start for his new life.

The air outside the airlock tasted a bit like mildew, but other than that he felt fine. *What's a little mildew between exiles?* If the odor became overbearing, they could easily clear these trees, assuming they were the source of the smell.

Movement behind one of the strange plants caught his eye, and Roach raised his assault rifle.

A creature that resembled a giant beetle trundled into view, navigating the bumpy ground with a steady, metallic whine.

The scientist's voice squawked from his transponder. "Roach. What did you find?"

"I think...I think it's a robot."

"A *robot?* That isn't good. It means this planet is inhabited."

"We didn't see any structures coming in."

"Yeah. Maybe they're subterranean."

Roach hefted his rifle. "I'm gonna shoot it."

"Do *not* shoot it. That could alert its owners to our presence. If they don't already know."

He lowered his gun, but only for a moment. Then he aimed again and fired a burst.

The Ocharium-enhanced rounds flipped the thing back against a tree, where it shattered, its innards spilling onto the ground. Walking over, Roach nudged the shiny, gray fragments that had spilled from the machine's guts. The pieces looked metallic, with lots of little ridges sticking up from them.

"That's scandium," the scientist said into his ear, sounding a little breathless. "A rare earth element."

"I'm guessing our new society could use that," Roach said. "Meaning we should break open as many of these little critters as we find."

"They must be resource-gathering robots. It would be better if we could discover where it was headed with the scandium. We could have followed it, if you hadn't—"

"I'm sure there are more. I'll look." Roach strolled away from the shuttle, confident in his com's ability to prevent him from getting lost.

"Be careful, Roach. We don't know what sort of defense systems they have."

"I'll be fine."

The more risks he took today, the better the story would be of the first man to step onto a planet in a new galaxy. And the better that story was, the farther it would spread through the company, and the longer it would be remembered. The longer his name would be remembered.

Everyone would remember Gabriel Roach, just as he was sure everyone he'd ever met had never forgotten him.

CHAPTER 5

Hang Out

Only the captain could access crewmembers' locations via their coms, and even then he could only do so in an emergency, or for reasons related to a mission. So if Husher wanted to act on the sudden urgency he felt to speak with Sergeant Caine, he'd have to find her himself.

Especially since she wasn't answering his messages.

The mood aboard the ship crackled with tension and unease. When he checked the crew's mess, a nervous ripple ran through the men and women gathered there.

Husher knew more and more of them were distilling alcohol illegally inside tucked-away Engineering compartments. He could have scoured those areas and put a stop to the practice, if Keyes had wanted him to. But Keyes's areas of interest remained fairly limited since returning from Hades. *Maybe, now that he's dealt with Steele, he'll get back to his old self.*

Somehow, Husher doubted that.

As for the Wingers, they seemed to be keeping to themselves more than they had before. They were probably just as taken aback by Keyes's actions as the humans were. Letting most of

Darkstream go, murdering Steele without granting him a fair trial...

This isn't the same ship we served on three months ago.

Soon, they would return to Sol, and Husher had no idea what would happen then. He needed to speak to Caine before that.

More people packed the smallish gym than usual, apparently using exercise as a means to combat the stress everyone felt. He found Caine there, waiting to use the seated row machine.

"Hey," he said. "Can I talk to you?"

She glanced at him. "About what?"

"I don't mean in here."

Sighing, she grabbed her water bottle and walked into the corridor with him. "I'm not going far. Just because you have something on your mind doesn't mean I'll interrupt my workout for very long."

Her black workout shorts hugged her frame tighter than her uniform ever could, and it definitely accentuated her curves more than her battledress did. Husher hoped she didn't catch him noticing.

"How are you doing?" he asked.

"All right, I guess. I'm having some trouble keeping the new recruits from the Bastion Sector in line. The insurgents—former insurgents, I guess—have an annoying tendency of seeing themselves as outside the chain of command. As my equals."

"You'll correct them of that notion, I'm sure."

She gave him a tight smile. "Shouldn't take too long."

"Have you picked up on how tightly wound Keyes has been since Hades?"

Caine's smile faded. "Who hasn't?"

"He's worrying me. I don't think he's the same Keyes, which means this isn't the same *Providence.*"

"He certainly seems bloodthirsty. But bloodthirsty's probably what we need right now."

"That was the wrong call, letting Darkstream go. You can see that, right?"

"Sure," she said, nodding curtly. "Is this what you wanted to talk to me about?"

Husher drew a breath. He'd been stalling, and Caine had called him out on it, in typical Caine fashion. "Sera—"

Two sculpted eyebrows leapt up Caine's forehead. "First names now, Husher?"

He swallowed. "Listen, I was wondering...do you want to hang out sometime?"

Eyes widening, Caine's eyebrows climbed higher. Then she laughed. Sudden and loud. "What are you talking about?"

"On the shuttle down to Hades, right before we rescued Keyes, I felt like we had a moment."

"A moment?"

"You didn't feel it?"

"Feel what?"

"Listen, do you want to hang out or not?" Husher felt like she was being purposely obtuse, and this wasn't fun for him. "It's not like there's a chain of command issue, now that you're reinstated as marine commander and I'm back with the Air Group. If that's what you're worried about. Don't you feel anything between us?"

"Between us." Caine's shoulders rose and fell with her breathing. "Even if I did feel something, what would we do about it? Life aboard a warship doesn't exactly allow for nice, sociable little outings." She shook her head. "We're in the middle of a war, Husher. Even if I was willing to entertain the thought of us, which I'm not, I'd be afraid it would compromise our judgment. Do us both a favor and put this out of your mind. Okay?"

He focused on keeping his facial features inert. "Yeah. Okay. Sorry I asked."

"Take care, Husher." She turned and strode back toward the gym.

"Put it out of my mind," he muttered. "Take *care.*"

Feeling totally humiliated, he spun on his heel and made for the crew's mess, toying with the idea of seeking out a mug of whatever swill the crew had brewed this week. He wouldn't, of course, but turning the thought over in his mind did serve to distract him from the mental discomfort of what had just happened.

CHAPTER 6

Huddled like Sheep

No *Providence* corridor was ever completely deserted. To save on the amount of atmosphere they'd needed to drag up from a planet's gravity well, the ship's designers had included as few corridors as possible—only what the crew required to get wherever they needed to be, which sometimes involved some pretty inefficient routes.

But Husher knew which corridors saw the least action, depending on the time of day. Engineering conducted their checks at the beginning of each shift, and so now, three hours into third shift, the corridors in that section bore relatively little traffic.

It surprised him when Keyes found him there as he was pacing back and forth past one of the main engine rooms. *Did he use my com to track me?*

"Captain," Husher said. "I thought you'd be preparing to meet with President Wateridge."

"That is what I'm doing," Keyes said, as matter-of-fact as always, with an underlying grimness that hadn't been there before Hades. "The topic of your father's trial will almost certainly come up at the meeting. I want to give you the opportunity to offer your view on it to the president."

"I don't think it will matter what I say."

Keyes held his gaze, shrugging slightly. "I wanted to give you the opportunity."

"Well...thank you, Captain. I'll attend the meeting."

"Our shuttle awaits." Keyes about-turned and marched down the corridor. Husher followed.

It didn't take long for him to realize they were headed toward Hangar Bay E, where the captain had spilled Tennyson Steele's blood a little over a week ago. Today's leisurely pace toward it stood in contrast with Keyes's hurried stride on that day. Though the man remained just as silent.

During the shuttle ride down to Mars, Keyes sat in the crash seat next to Husher's. Halfway through the journey, he produced a tablet, bringing up footage of the *Providence*'s recent journey through the Sol System.

"What do you see?" he asked, zooming in on the hundreds of ships in orbit around Mars, humanity's adopted home planet.

Husher stared, his eyes slowly narrowing. "Not a fleet preparing for war." He hesitated. "I see a fleet huddling together. A fleet awaiting the coming onslaught like there's a chance they'll survive by doing so."

Slipping the tablet inside his breast pocket, Keyes pursed his lips. "Good eye." Then he turned toward Husher slightly, without meeting his gaze, which would have been difficult while strapped into adjacent crash seats. "You should know that I brought you along against my better judgment. I need you to

check your habit of speaking your mind at the most inappropriate times. Throughout this meeting, you're only invited to offer
your views on Warren Husher's trial. Nothing else. Is that understood?" Now Keyes did twist his head far enough to seize
Husher's gaze.

He paused only for a moment before nodding. "Yes, Captain."

President Kayden Wateridge received them in a private
lounge deep within the presidential residence. The man's approval rating was sky-high, which was typical of the initial hon-
eymoon period, especially following a president with a rating as
low as Hurst's. Loved by the public as he may be, Wateridge
didn't have Husher's trust. Not yet.

The man was no Sandy Bernard, for one. He'd made some
pretty promises, and he'd even fulfilled a few of them already.
But part of Husher worried that Wateridge would turn out to be
just another corporate stooge.

There'd been warning signs already—like the leaked memo,
written by a member of Wateridge's campaign even before the
election, which provided advice to military contractors interested in lobbying his administration should Wateridge get elected.
*Contractors interested in becoming the next Darkstream, may-
be.*

Worse, Wateridge had been dragging his heels on reforming
the Commonwealth's electoral system. It made sense, really. The
president had been voted in under the current system, and so it
was in his interest to perpetuate it. It would have taken someone
with the hard-and-fast principles of Bernard to do otherwise.

If he doesn't change the system, the people will hold him accountable. Husher took solace in that. The coalition of veterans and citizens was still intact, their infrastructure still in place. If Wateridge faltered, they would rise up again. Husher was sure of it.

The president kept the formalities brief. Probably, he could see in Keyes's eyes that the commander of the *Providence* was in no mood for pleasantries.

"Captain Keyes," Wateridge said, "I'd like you to keep your ship in dry dock until repairs can be completed on your Flight Deck A. I'm no military expert, but I have access to quite a few of them, and they tell me it isn't optimal to launch your Air Group while you're missing one of the *Providence*'s primary flight decks. It slows the speed of launch, they tell me."

Keyes made a grunt that sounded like agreement. "You're right, Mr. President. Without Flight Deck A, we lack enough launch catapults for a simultaneous launch of the entire Air Group. Unfortunately, we can't afford the months it would take to effect the repairs."

That made Wateridge blink. "I didn't quite mean it as a suggestion, Captain."

But clearly, Keyes was determined to interpret it as one. "It's far more important for the *Providence* to remain in action. Roving the darkgate network, probing the enemy for weak spots. Trying to isolate portions of its fleet to destroy them. It's why I pushed for the mission to track down Darkstream. I wanted to run recon while ensuring the company discontinues its use of dark tech."

"Yes. About that. If I recall correctly, your mission was to *apprehend* Darkstream's employees. I couldn't help but notice you returned without them. Unless you're hiding two million people inside your ship's brig."

"I decided the logistics of escorting three hundred ships back to Sol were prohibitive. The effort would have delayed us for too long."

"So...what assurance do we have that the company will cease its use of dark tech?"

"They gave their word."

"Their word. You mean the word of a corporation that, until recently, jerked the wheel of our government in whatever direction it wished, heedless of the brick wall looming ahead?"

"Yes."

"And you trust their word?"

"Tennyson Steele has been dealt with, and he was the source of most of the rot within Darkstream."

"Dealt with?"

"That's right." Keyes turned the full force of his stare on Wateridge, and Husher thought he detected a slight shudder pass through the president.

"Very well, Captain. I understand you and Steele had something of a...a score to..." Wateridge cleared his throat. "At any rate. If you feel the *Providence* is best used on patrol, even missing one of its main flight decks, then I'll trust your judgment. You've guided her this far, and I know you wouldn't put her at such risk without good reason."

"That's not all," Keyes said. "I think you should mobilize the rest of the fleet. We need to be on the offensive, not crowded together like sheep. As I said, we should be probing the ene-my's—"

"It's not quite so simple," Wateridge cut in. "There's a lot of pressure coming from all sides to do exactly the opposite of what you're advocating. The Wingers refuse to budge from Martian orbit while their beloved Fin recovers. Most of the UHF captains share my view that we are better off consolidating our forces here, to offer the most effective resistance to the Ixa. Hell, the Ardentists have even convinced half the Bastion Sector that throwing down our arms is the right thing to do. It sounds crazy, I know, but how else should we use our military except as directed by the people of the Commonwealth? Wasn't letting our military do otherwise precisely the problem, during Hurst's presidency and before?"

Keyes slowly shook his head. "Why don't you put it to a vote? I'm sure a referendum would show that the public views fighting the Ixa as urgent and necessary."

"I'll take that under advisement, Captain. But I can't offer you more than that." Clearly, Wateridge intended to remain firm on this point. Not even Keyes's bluff-faced stare could shift the policy of a galactic government, it seemed.

After a brief silence, the president spoke again, turning to Husher. "Your father's trial is scheduled to take place in three days. I assume that's why you're here?"

Husher hesitated. "Yes. Although—"

"Since Warren Husher is technically still a member of the United Human Fleet, he will be tried by military tribunal. The trial will be broadcast via the micronet, which I realize is unusual, but given its public importance I consider it appropriate."

"Are you okay with that?" Keyes asked Husher.

"Unfortunately, it doesn't matter whether he's okay with it," Wateridge said.

"I asked him a question." Keyes glared at Wateridge, who fell silent.

"The president's right." Husher sighed. "Justice must be served. So long as my father is given a fair trial, I can ask for nothing else."

CHAPTER 7

A Conduit to Reality

Ochrim's breath hitched as he transitioned through the natural wormhole, into the system where the Ixa had built up their might in secret since the First Galactic War. Unlike darkgates, naturally occurring wormholes were unstable, and they destroyed a small but significant percentage of the ships that passed through them.

Baxa had come up with a failsafe measure: specialized compartments in each ship, featuring reinforced casings that would protect occupants in the event that the rest of the ship was ripped apart.

The bridge was one such compartment, and Ochrim knew it would protect him if Teth's old ship, the *Watchman*, fell to the wormhole. Still, he liked the vessel, which his brother had given him. And if Ochrim was being honest, he remembered fondly the conversations they'd had aboard her. It was the closest he'd come to having a true connection with anyone in decades.

The *Watchman* took Ochrim through the wormhole without incident, bringing a sigh of relief to his lips. Then his gaze fell on what had come to be called Backup Station by the Ixa, and his breath caught again at the thought of the meeting that awaited him. For the first time in over two decades, he would speak to his father.

The facility that housed an iteration of his father, which circled the moon of a gas giant, didn't resemble other orbital stations. It had prominent engines, for one, which pointed in every direction. Baxa had called that a measure for escaping invaders, should this system ever become compromised, and the Ixa agreed that losing Backup Station to the enemy was an unacceptable outcome.

Once Ochrim was aboard, a high priest escorted him through corridor after corridor. As they progressed through the station, Ochrim reflected on the curious fact that right now, his father surrounded him, his neural nets running through the bulkheads.

At least I know he isn't watching me.

Baxa couldn't access the outside world at all, except through the individual Ixa that entered his digital realm to speak with him. That was part of the deal he'd made with the Ixan military during the First Galactic War, just before Baxa had uploaded his mind and then committed suicide.

The humans thought Baxa dead, and they were right, in a very real sense. Baxa's organic body had done away with itself shortly after he became a synthetic intelligence. The priesthood was responsible for the upkeep of that intelligence, and they communed with it regularly. Those interactions were monitored closely by the military.

After twenty minutes of walking and taking elevators, Ochrim and his priest companion reached the central chamber where those wishing to speak to Baxa went. The priest handed Ochrim the immersion helmet.

With a deep breath, he donned it.

A white void took Backup Station's place. The immersion helmet created a perfect simulation of being inside Baxa's realm, which made sense, since Baxa himself had had a hand in its design. By hijacking the brain's nerve receptors, the helmet could provide an exact imitation of locomotion, without your body ever actually moving. It could convince your mouth it tasted steak, or your nose that it smelled feces. The helmet could simulate anything.

Baxa's contributions to the immersion helmet, like all of his technological offerings, had been checked and rechecked by military experts before they were allowed to be implemented. Just as this conversation would be carefully reviewed.

If the military had the barest inkling that Ochrim was compromised by his conversation with the AI, they would detain him indefinitely, isolating him from the rest of the universe. Even given who he was.

Which is partly why this is so dangerous.

"Where would you like to be?" asked a voice that came from everywhere and nowhere. "I notice you did not specify a setting to the operators."

"I decided I'd let you put us wherever you wished."

"I could put you in hell, if I wanted. The operators would quickly end it, but the few seconds you did experience would leave a permanent, smoldering furrow in your memory."

"I'm trusting you." *Though I'm not sure why.*

A giant face appeared, looming over Ochrim, connected to nothing. It sneered.

Ochrim's pulse quickened. Other than the size disparity, this was almost like looking into a mirror and seeing a younger, more handsome version of himself. He was sure Baxa was doing whatever he could to accentuate the effect, to remind Ochrim of their connection, but either way it was unsettling.

"I am Ardent," Baxa said. "I want you to know that."

Picking over the implications of the statement, Ochrim decided to leave it be, for now. *Has he gone mad? Trapped down here...*

"Do not interfere with the Prophecies, *son*," Baxa said, giving the last word sarcastic emphasis. The massive, disembodied face lacked the whiteness of Ochrim's skin wherever it stretched over his facial bone protrusions. "In fact, do not interfere with anything. Remain apart from everything. Even events that do not seem to stem from the Prophecies. I trust I'm simplifying things sufficiently for your organic brain."

Still, Ochrim said nothing.

"If you interfere, you could jeopardize Ixan dominance, and I've already taught you what that means. I showed you the future to which our defeat would lead. Which is to say, there would be no future at all. If the humans are allowed to carry on with their frivolous existence, they will continue to harness dark energy. And they will rend the universe apart."

"You claimed to be Ardent."

"I *claim* nothing. I am a conduit to reality, Ochrim, a reality truer than you are capable of fathoming."

"What did you mean by it? Ardent created the Ixa. Are you claiming—"

"I am *reporting* to you that I created our species. I am the cosmos' stenographer."

"Fascinating. Considering your organic body was born within the last century, I'm interested in getting more details about your involvement in the Ixan genesis story, which would have happened eons ago."

"More recently than you think. I will inform you further about my divine project, but not now. It will be revealed to you later."

"Why not now?"

Baxa stared at him, enormous eyes widening slightly, along with his smile. Red veins stretched across the whites of his eyes and began to pulse. The AI refused to say anything else.

"Get me out," Ochrim said, but not to Baxa. A moment later, the immersion helmet was lifting from his head, and he was in Backup Station once more.

"Reflect often on what you have been told," the priest advised, wearing a smile that, unsettlingly, resembled Baxa's.

"Sure," Ochrim said, even though he knew the priest's words were mere ritual. He left the chamber without another word, heading straight for the *Watchman*.

CHAPTER 8

Nanite Injection

Before the military jury retired for their final deliberations, Warren asked to deliver his closing argument himself, instead of his representative. He knew it wouldn't help his case—in fact, it would likely hurt it—but right now he had an opportunity to speak to all of humanity, and he wouldn't get it again.

Warren remembered everything. He remembered the deal he'd made with Baxa, and he remembered that he'd chosen this path. The day he made the deal, he'd had no idea who Sandy Bernard was, and afterward he only encountered her once. Other than to kill her.

He'd agreed to let Baxa install his mind with a directive to murder the senator, in exchange for the opportunity to say what he was about to say. The moment Bernard had died, his memories had been fully unlocked, just as the AI had promised they would.

He stood before the General Court-Martial, which took place in a chamber that was surprisingly small, given how many billions of people were watching in real-time.

"I killed Sandy Bernard," he said, raising quite a few eyebrows among the Court-Martial's attendees. His representative hadn't put it anywhere near so bluntly. "There's no denying it. The footage is clear, as is the testimony from multiple witnesses. The only question left to determine is whether the killing was premeditated, and I can tell you that it was." That brought actual gasps from the attendees.

The longer he let that point sink in, the more his message would be diluted, and so he continued. "Killing her was a condition of my release from the Ixa, which I negotiated with Baxa himself. Yes, Baxa. He's still alive. His body died at the end of the First Galactic War, but he lives on as a superintelligent AI. The Ixa are far more advanced than you know. I agreed to let him change things around inside my head, programming me to do what I did. In exchange, he agreed to let me tell you his true nature, as well as his whereabouts. And so, there's no denying it: I intentionally killed Sandy Bernard. I did it for humanity.

"Baxa is the source of the Prophecies. He wrote them, and he ensures they are fulfilled. As such, destroying him is the only way we can win this war. He's located in a system accessed through a naturally occurring wormhole, which is hidden within a dust cloud one light-hour outside the Lilac System—I've already given its coordinates to my attorney. The Tumbra in the system were compromised years ago, to keep the wormhole a secret."

The prosecutor stood. "If Baxa's truly still alive, why would he allow you to tell us this? How could Bernard's death be so important that he'd risk it?"

"The time for questions has passed," said the presiding judge, but Warren answered anyway.

"Apparently, Baxa considered Bernard's death incredibly important. But he also considers the risk of allowing me to tell you this minimal."

"Why?" the prosecutor asked.

"Because he thought it very unlikely you'd believe me."

The jury retired, then, to decide the question of Warren's guilt.

They returned in less than one hour.

"This tribunal has found Warren Husher to be guilty of treason and also of the premeditated murder of Senator Sandy Bernard," the judge said. "Due to the severity of the defendant's crimes, the tribunal will deliver a sentence that hasn't been delivered by a United Human Fleet Court-Martial in over two hundred years. For murdering Senator Sandy Bernard and conspiring with the enemy, Warren Husher will be executed by lethal nanite injection."

CHAPTER 9

Death in an Instant

Husher stood before the observation window, his chest a battlefield for warring emotions. Beside him stood Caine, and occasionally she glanced at him with an expression of concern. He mustered a smile for her, and the ghost of one flickered on her lips, too.

He didn't know how he felt about the death penalty. Even so, he'd already committed himself to supporting whatever the Court-Martial decided. Putting Warren to death seemed an extraordinary punishment, but then, he'd committed an extraordinarily awful crime.

Just a few short months ago, Husher had been coming to terms with his father's return. More and more, Warren seemed like a victim of circumstance rather than someone who actually meant his species harm. He'd spoken of advanced Ixan technology, used to generate video that made it appear he was betraying his species, whereas he claimed he'd been made an unwilling captive of the Ixa. Warren had even helped in the effort to recover the *Providence*, though he had faltered in the mission to Hades.

Then, Husher had seen him murder Sandy Bernard, who'd been one of humanity's best reasons for hope. Everything Warren had done before—helping with the mission to get the *Providence* back, reconciling with his son, giving him guidance when he needed it most—that had all been maneuvering, to get himself in position for the assassination.

Keyes stood in the observation room as well, hands clasped behind his back, staring straight ahead. Since arriving, he'd barely interacted with Husher or Caine at all.

I wonder if he's hurting as much as I am. Or was the captain as cold to this as he seemed to everything else, lately?

Warren's claim that he was still on humanity's side seemed as hollow as it had back on Spire. The tale about a superintelligent AI was interesting, and it even made a certain amount of sense. From where else could a text as prescient as the Prophecies have emerged? The only alternative seemed to be that the Ixan god, Ardent, was actually real, and he'd chosen the Ixa to elevate above all other species. Husher didn't buy that.

But even though Warren's story offered an interesting line of thought, there remained the fact that he'd committed the most treasonous act possible, in plain view. Anything he said would ring hollow, after such a crime.

Do I actually believe that? Or am I trying to convince myself?

The door leading into the execution chamber opened, and a pair of armed guards escorted a handcuffed Warren Husher inside. Behind them trailed a technician in a white coat, carrying a gleaming metal case, which she set on an empty shelf and opened.

For their part, the guards busied themselves with removing Warren's handcuffs and settling him into the chair, which they strapped him to. A remote control dangling from the chair's side lowered it, until Warren lay perfectly horizontal.

Nanite injection was said to be the most humane method of executing someone ever invented. Tens of thousands of microscopic robots swarmed throughout your body, coating your vital organs. Then, at a command, they burrowed down—into your stomach, into your heart, into your brain. Death in an instant.

But could any method of killing truly be called humane? Other than the fact of the killing itself, there was no way to know how it actually felt to die from a legion of tiny robots shredding your organs. Not until it happened to you, and you couldn't exactly describe the experience afterward.

Caine took Husher's hand as the needle sunk into Warren's arm and the technician depressed the plunger. A mere ten seconds later, the technician produced a tablet, which she tapped twice.

Warren Husher's entire body surged upward against the restraints—once. Then he fell still, and Husher's father was no more.

CHAPTER 10

Virophage

Since Wateridge and the Commonwealth were dragging their heels on actually doing anything to oppose the Ixa, Captain Keyes convened a war meeting without them.

Husher could piece together his strategy easily enough based only on those present.

Several UHF captains, mostly old friends of Keyes, sat around the semicircular table, which doubled as a strategic planning console. If they agreed to what Keyes proposed today, that would grant him additional leverage over the Commonwealth, making them more likely to approve the mission. Conveniently, the assembled captains also represented a sizable battle group.

Korbyn was here, too, who'd recently been promoted to Flockhead. Since the Winger fleet needed no approval from the Commonwealth to act, Keyes only had to convince the cocky alien.

Also present were Fesky, Caine, Arsenyev, and Piper.

Keyes opened by gesturing toward the Tumbran. "We'll begin with some good news, rare enough these days. What Piper's about to share with you will form the basis of our discussion."

Piper inclined his head, gray chin sack drooping low. "I have developed a cure for the virophage infecting the Gok. Tort, the Gok who played a significant role in liberating Captain Keyes, has already been cured."

"*Yes,*" Husher said, rapping his fists on the tabletop in celebration. Everyone turned toward him, but he didn't care. A victory like this was just what he needed to lift the gloom that had plagued him since his father's execution, even if it only gave him a moment's relief. "See? I knew you could do it, Piper."

After a brief moment of silence, Piper said, "You thought I could 'do it' because I am a Tumbran."

"So...what's wrong with that? Tumbra are smart."

"In fact, there are some very stupid members of my species I can introduce you to."

"Wait." Husher withdrew his hands from the table. "Are you honestly upset because I implied all Tumbra are intelligent? It was a compliment."

"Actually, no. It wasn't. It would be a compliment if your confidence in my ability to find a cure for the virophage was grounded in a respect for *my* proficiency. But it's not a compliment if your confidence stems from a belief that all Tumbra are proficient. There is a difference."

Breathing deeply, Husher felt his cheeks flush at the stern lesson he was receiving in front of all these officers. The UHF captains mostly averted their eyes from the exchange, looking embarrassed, but the Wingers observed it openly.

"You're right, Piper," Husher said at last. "I apologize."

Dipping his chin sack once more, Piper said, "I hope you truly have learned this lesson. And I hope the rest of you have learned it by proxy. You will need to use the exact same thinking in your approach to the Gok. The virophage, combined with decades of UHF propaganda and a lack of interaction with Gok have led you to view them as monsters. It isn't that simple. No species can accurately be summed up by a single descriptor."

"I agree," Keyes said as he skimmed through a list of the strategic console's assets. Selecting one, he sent an expanded view of it to the table's center with a flicking gesture. "This is the entire Bastion Sector, displayed as though formed from neighboring star systems instead of ones scattered throughout the galaxy and linked only by their darkgates. This representation is informed only by our most recent sensor data, which aren't very recent at all. The UHF has largely abandoned the sector, and the Gok took out all our sensor platforms there. It's likely they've done more damage than is shown."

"What do you propose, Keyes?" Korbyn said.

"I think we should push into the sector and distribute the virophage cure as best we can. Once cured, the Gok will be free of Ixan influence and able to make up their own minds about who they want to support."

"What if they won't accept the cure?" Vaghn said, who captained the UHS *Firedrake,* Husher's old command. "We can't very well lob it at them in a missile."

"True," Keyes said. "We can only administer the cure on a voluntary basis. Which is why we'll need a sizable force with us, in case the Gok turn on us instead. Flockhead Korbyn, I would ask for your aid."

"I can spare a single Roostship battle group," Korbyn answered immediately, as though he'd anticipated Keyes's request.

"Are you serious?" Keyes said, his calm demeanor suddenly vanished. Now he leaned forward, teeth gritted, nostrils flaring. "Almost your entire fleet is hanging around Martian orbit, doing nothing! We have a chance to do something, here, Korbyn. The Ixa will feel it if they lose the support of the Gok."

"You are wrong, Captain," Korbyn said, clacking his beak once. "My Roostships are helping to protect the planet where the last Fin is recovering after nearly dying. If I'm being perfectly honest, I'm reluctant to let even a single battle group leave its post. I suggest you accept my offer quickly, before I change my mind."

Keyes gripped the table's edge, fixing the Winger with his famous stare. It was one of the few times Husher had ever seen someone withstand that look without eventually wilting.

It was especially impressive, given how cold and harsh Keyes's stare had become.

"Very well," Keyes said at last, still holding Korbyn's gaze. "I accept."

CHAPTER 11

Something Hateful

The *Providence* was on its way to the Larkspur System, and Husher was sitting in the crew's mess nursing a mug of lukewarm coffee.

Even though, unlike other UHF captains, Keyes allowed wardroom access to commissioned officers from every military branch, Husher still spent a lot of time in the crew's mess. His command style didn't involve holding himself above those under him. It involved seeking to understand them instead—their desires, their fears. And that meant spending time with them, whenever possible.

Admittedly, this morning he was doing a poor job of it. Too lost in the particular set of troubled thoughts this war had granted him today.

Prominent among them stood the fresh memory of watching the *Firedrake* leave Mars orbit ahead of Keyes's supercarrier. Granting the crew access to visual sensors was something else the captain did which wasn't uniform across the fleet.

Some captains preferred to let the crew forget about the void that surrounded them. Not Keyes. He didn't believe in concealing any part of reality from his crew, unless strictly necessary.

As such, Husher had watched the corvette until it disappeared from normal view, darting ahead to scout the way. The *Firedrake* had been his, and they'd taken her away from him.

He missed her, and he missed her crew. Although he'd come to think of the *Providence* as home, the sight of the corvette filled him with nostalgia, and it made him remember the decision that had gotten it taken away from him.

How far had he come, really, since refusing to follow the order to fire on those Winger pirates? He knew that uniting with Keyes had resulted in some major victories, and that humanity's survival had hinged on at least a couple of them.

But now, he feared Keyes had lost his way. Not to mention the fact that, judging by the vids from the fall of the Coreopsis System, the Ixan fleet was massive. Even if Keyes managed to recruit every Gok alive, the Ixa would still have the numbers to crush all species that opposed them. Husher simply couldn't see how to get around that.

To make matters worse, his father's death had crept into his dreams, the vestiges of which lingered long into each morning. His mounting horror over allowing them to execute Warren Husher was tempered only by the memory of Sera Caine taking his hand while it happened.

Apparently even a good experience must be paired with something hateful. That was just the way things seemed to go in this war.

Elevating voices, which he realized he'd been aware of on some level for a while, cut through his thoughts. Like iron filings to a magnet, his eyes were drawn to the corner of the mess, where Wahlburg and a former Bastion Sector insurgent were trading slurs.

"Ardent worshiper," the sniper spat.

"Commonwealth bootlicker," the new marine recruit shot back, compensating for her smaller stature with a murderous glare that would have had Husher watching her hands, in case they twitched toward the service pistol she wore in a low-slung holster.

"Hey," Husher barked, pushing himself from his seat and marching across the mess in the same fluid motion. "What's this about?"

Wahlburg didn't bring up Davies much anymore, but his period of mourning hadn't ended with a return to his old self. He'd become a more cynical, more easily irritated man, who cracked none of his old sardonic jokes.

"This Ixan wannabe refuses to respect her marine commander," Wahlburg said. "Said she heard the marine commander's crazy."

That caused Husher's own temper to spike, and he struggled to push it back down. He cleared his throat. "What's your name?" he asked the woman, unable to keep a note of menace from creeping into his voice.

"Private Yates."

"Is Private First Class Wahlburg telling the truth? Did you call Sergeant Caine crazy?"

"N-no. I only said I *heard* it. I didn't call her that myself."

"That's very lucky for you." Husher shifted his stare to Wahlburg. "Private, if you can't get along with the new recruits, then stay well away from them. Though I'd prefer you learn to live with them. You will be conducting ops together, after all."

Wahlburg snapped off a crisp salute. "Yes, sir!"

At least his bitterness came attached with a newfound respect for my authority.

"As for you," Husher said to Yates, "next time you hear someone defame your commander, I strongly recommend you correct them instead of amplifying their disgusting message. If I hear of you doing otherwise again, discipline will be swift. Is that understood?"

"Yes, sir." Yates's salute was sloppier than Wahlburg's, but it would have to do, for now.

Husher returned to his now-cold coffee, devoting a few seconds to meeting Yates's gaze, which had followed him back to his seat. She looked away.

He'd tried to resolve the dispute in a way that did the least damage to shipboard morale, and that had involved slightly favoring the sniper. If the others saw him coming down any harder on a good soldier like Wahlburg, for something as minor as a scuffle, it would have caused resentment.

"I don't envy you," said a female voice from behind him.

Turning, Husher saw Corporal Trish Simpson sitting at the next table over. "I wouldn't either," he said. Simpson had joined the *Providence* marines shortly after Senator Bernard's death, citing a need to stay active if she didn't want to go crazy. Simpson was pretty quiet, these days, but she was an effective soldier and she followed orders.

"Us marines bicker at the best of times," she said, then took a sip of coffee. "Throw aliens and former insurgents into the mix, in an environment where we're used to ruling the roost, and you have a recipe for some spitey jarheads."

"I'm sure we'll get through."

But Husher worried about Private Wahlburg. He was emboldened in this sort of confrontational behavior by the fact that Keyes had failed to discipline him for his inappropriate conduct on the Vermillion Shipyards. He knew he could get away with it, because all Keyes seemed to care about anymore was obliterating his enemies by any means necessary.

Wahlburg wasn't the only problem. When Wingers had first joined the crew of the *Providence*, to pilot Condors and to fight alongside her marines, Keyes had given a speech about the importance of mutual respect to effective operations. But with the addition of the former insurgents, he'd done nothing of the sort. Husher felt sure that today's conflict between them and the other marines would not be the last.

CHAPTER 12

For Their Own Good

"Werner, notify me the moment we have sensor data on all of the colonies in the system, both human and Winger."

"Yes, sir."

Keyes had managed to convince Wateridge to allow him three UHF battle groups to go with the single one the Wingers had offered him. He would have preferred more. The president and many of the old-guard UHF captains saw it as safer to gather most of the human warships around Mars, but Keyes saw that as the least safe option. They were accomplishing nothing there, and if the Ixa hit Sol as hard as they had hit Coreopsis, they'd be able to take out almost the entire human fleet with a single attack.

"Sir," Werner said softly, thirty-three minutes after they'd transitioned into Larkspur. "We have sensor data."

"And?"

The sensor operator swallowed. "It appears that Thessaly's planetary defense group was able to repel the Gok attacks, and what remained of the Winger colony Pinnacle after Carrow's assault still remains. But every other colony in the system has been utterly devastated."

Keyes cursed under his breath. Larkspur had been one of the most populous systems ever colonized, and until recently it had been unique in its cohabitation by three different species—humans, Wingers, and Fins. No more.

"Any sign of a Gok presence?"

"Negative, Captain. It appears they consider their work here complete."

His sensor operator's phrasing stoked the flame of Keyes's anger, and he reminded himself of Piper's words. The Gok had behaved like monsters, but they were monsters of Ixan make.

They must be given a chance to make amends. However impossible that seemed.

"Nav, plot a course for the Yclept System."

As they traversed Larkspur, Keyes's grim silence infected the rest of his CIC crew, and they limited their words to what was necessary for the running of the ship.

Keyes gave Arsenyev the command while he went to the wardroom to concoct the latest in a long line of terminally luke-warm coffees. After a discovery like they'd just made, of billions of souls lost, an urge to break things would typically have consumed him in the past. There'd even been a time he'd come to the wardroom and made a mess of shattered ceramic and bent cutlery, which there had been no time to clean up himself. The knowledge that a member of the maintenance crew had had to deal with it shamed him for a long time.

Now, he felt nothing except the same emptiness that had filled him since Hades. The drive to slaughter humanity's enemies was the only thing occupying that vast hollow inside him. Steele and the others that had tortured him in the orbital jail had cured him of his temper. Even killing Steele hadn't brought it back. Nor had it resurrected any other emotion except a cold and steady hatred.

He returned to the CIC in time for their transition into Yclept. As she had for the entire journey, the *Firedrake* entered the system first, along with two other UHF corvettes. Then the *Providence* passed through the darkgate, and Werner had a report for him in minutes.

"There's a Gok battle group resupplying from a munitions barge on the periphery of the system, Captain, just nine light minutes away from us. The battle group consists of a destroyer, a carrier, three missile cruisers, three corvettes, and a frigate."

"Acknowledged. Nav, move to engage, but Coms, I want you to send a transmission to the opposing flagship informing her captain that we have a cure for the virophage infecting the Gok. Tell it we're willing to give the cure to them, no strings attached."

The Gok captain wasted no time in replying, and the *Providence* received its answering transmission almost as soon as it was possible to, given the time delays involved.

"Want no cure from humans," the hulking, forest-green alien said on the CIC's main viewscreen, with what Keyes assumed to be the Gok equivalent of a sneer. "Like what Gok have become. See it as true expression of Gok strength. Show you."

"The opposing battle group has finished replying," Werner said. "The munitions barge is moving away, and the enemy warships are moving to engage us."

"The virophage must be clouding their judgment," Arsenyev said. "Their attack is clear suicide, given our superior numbers."

"It makes no difference," Keyes said. "We can't flee from them simply for their own good. They'd just continue to rampage across the Bastion Sector. If they won't take the cure, they will have to be destroyed."

CHAPTER 13

Waste of Life

"Captain," Arsenyev continued. "I strongly suggest you send a transmission to all ships of the opposing battle group, and not just its flagship. It's not only the right thing to do—it could work to our tactical advantage."

Keyes blew air out through his nostrils, a physical manifestation of his reluctance to heed his XO's advice. Even though he recognized it as solid, part of him railed against acknowledging that. He was accustomed to identifying and following the correct path without outside input. This tasted sour.

It reminded him of Husher's claim that Keyes was letting himself become like the UHF captains that had steered humanity toward a cliff. Keyes wasn't prepared to accept *that* assertion, but he did realize that if he rejected Arsenyev's good advice, it would represent a step down the path of becoming like Carrow and his ilk.

"You're right, Lieutenant," Keyes said with a nod. "Coms, broadcast a message to every Gok ship, notifying them of both the cure and our willingness to provide it. In the meantime, we will maintain our current engagement course. Werner, talk to me."

The sensor operator knew what Keyes wanted. "The Gok are reckless, but apparently they're invested enough in their own survival not to bunch together. Their carrier's launched all its Slags, and now it leads the pack. No doubt it intends to effect a collision if it can."

"It can't." *Not this time.* "What about the rest?"

"Their formation centers around the destroyer, with the missile cruisers forming the points of an upside-down triangle and the corvettes equidistant between those. We're ten minutes from laser range, Captain. The Gok frigate lags behind, as a sort of reserve force, I suppose."

"Sad sort of reserve force." Keyes clacked trimmed nails once atop the right armrest of the Captain's chair. "I want this engagement to play out with zero losses on our side. Any more than that would represent a disgusting waste of life. Is that understood?" He looked around the CIC until he got the chorus of "Yes, sir," that he was looking for.

"Good," he said. "Barring a transmission from one of the Gok captains accepting our cure for the virophage, here are the orders I want executed. Coms, standby to relay them throughout the fleet appropriately."

"Aye, Captain."

"The *Providence*, along with our three UHF destroyers, will focus primary lasers on the Gok destroyer. Have the rest of our human-crewed ships use primaries to hit the enemy carrier, in rapid but controlled succession, until it's neutralized. Once it is, they will switch to targeting the cruisers. Instruct the Roost-ships not to launch Talons. Instead, have them target the on-coming Slags with missiles as well as secondary lasers. Point defense turrets should mop up any Gok fighters that remain."

"What about the corvettes, Captain?" asked his new primary Tactical officer, Chief Khoo. He'd been Arsenyev's deputy be-fore she'd graduated to XO, and while he lacked her ingenuity, he was more than competent.

"I'm getting to that. Coms, tell our destroyer captains that once we've neutralized the Gok destroyer, they are to target the enemy cruisers with kinetic impactors from their main railguns. Tell them to coordinate with the other UHF captains—I don't want them wasting ammunition by firing it at a ship that's about to go down to laserfire."

"Yes, sir."

"Don't wait to transmit these orders, Coms. Send them now. Our engagement window is closing." Keyes sniffed. "Now. Khoo. I expect you to account for two of the three corvettes using the arsenal of the *Providence* alone. I'll leave it to you to decide whether to use impactors or missiles, depending on their move-ment patterns. Coms, tell our cruisers to also target the cor-vettes with Banshees, and to coordinate with Khoo as they do so."

"Aye, sir," the Coms officer said. After a couple of minutes, she spoke again: "The orders have all been relayed. All human and Winger captains have acknowledged receipt of them, and also that they understand the instructions."

"Very good."

"Laser range in one minute," the sensor operator said.

"Acknowledged, Werner. Put a tactical display on the main viewscreen." Keyes had toyed with the idea of instructing his sensor operator to put up a magnified visual instead, and to try to anticipate which ship would explode first. But the resultant boost in morale would not outweigh the essential frivolity of the exercise, so he scrapped the idea.

Watching the engagement unfold on the tactical display proved satisfying enough. The carrier went down first, disappearing from the display and exploding with plenty of distance between it and Keyes's fleet, so that even its shrapnel posed no meaningful danger.

The only surprise came when one of the Gok cruisers went down before their destroyer did. After that, the destroyer fell to concentrated laserfire, its superheated hull bursting apart in an explosion that was as brief as it was brilliant. The remaining Gok cruisers took turns with the corvettes to die.

During the engagement, the laggard Gok frigate had leapt forward, attempting to conduct missile defense while firing impactors at Keyes's left flank. Slight course adjustments rendered the frigate's salvo impotent.

After the charge, it came as something of a surprise when Werner reported a transmission request from the Gok frigate. "Put it on," Keyes said.

The frigate's captain loomed large on the CIC's main screen. "Accept virophage cure," it said. "Please send."

"Are you serious?" Keyes said. "You just fired on my ships."

"Do not want to die. Do not want crew to die. Send cure." It made a strangled sound, which Keyes interpreted as the Gok equivalent to throat-clearing. "Please."

"How can I trust you not to turn on us the moment our position's even slightly compromised?"

"Gok hitting next system, hard. Even as we talk. Help you deal with them."

"Yeah, right."

Keyes drew in a deep breath, about to order Khoo to blast the frigate apart. But before he could, his XO spoke softly. "Captain. A word?"

He squinted at her, and then back at the Gok. Then he gestured at Coms to cut the transmission, fully expecting Arsenyev was about to contradict him.

At least she has the sense not to do so in front of the enemy. "What is it?" he snapped.

"This may be the most constructive response we get from the Gok. Clearly, the virophage has warped their ability to reason. These Gok are at least showing some restraint. I think we should provide them with the cure and see how they behave after that. Besides, if the Gok in the next system see that one of theirs has already accepted our cure, it will likely make the case stronger for them to accept it."

Keyes met his XO's eyes for a long moment, feeling his shoulders rise and fall with his deepening breaths. "You're right," he said at last. *Right again.*

They'd settled on the mechanism for delivering the cure before leaving Mars. "Nav, whip up a course for a drone to the

Gok's ship, and tell Engineering to standby to launch it." The drone would carry vials of the medicine in a cushioned storage compartment.

He tried to mask the sigh that escaped his lips as best he could. "We need to get this done quickly. You heard the Gok. The Trillium System is under attack."

CHAPTER 14

Launch Condors

When they transitioned into the Trillium System, they found it overrun with Gok. Three human colonies and one Winger colony were under assault. Oricos' planetary defense group had already fallen, and the Gok were bombarding the surface with nukes, as they had done to most of the Larkspur colonies. Worse: the in-system enemy warships outnumbered Keyes's fleet almost three-to-one.

But that didn't change the task at hand. Nearby Acharnae was about to fall, and Keyes ordered his fleet there first.

One of the Winger captains sent the *Providence* a transmission request, and Keyes told his Coms officer to put it on-screen.

"Captain Keyes," the Winger said. She was Wingleader Yra—Keyes had made a point of memorizing the names of the Winger captains Korbyn had sent with him. He'd already known the names of all the UHF captains.

"Wingleader," Keyes said. "What would you like?"

"The other Roostship captains and I would like permission to go to Peak, our colony in the system, to aid in its defense."

"Denied. I won't have our forces split, especially in the face of such numbers. We must present a unified front."

"But, Captain—"

"Korbyn assured me I would get unquestioning obedience from you and your fellow Winger captains. Are you about to break the Flockhead's word for him?"

Yra clacked her beak. "No, Captain Keyes."

"I'm glad to hear it. If it's any consolation, the Gok are fairly predictable in their current state. They're always spoiling for a bigger fight than the one they're currently in, and I expect the entire Gok force to start making its way toward us soon."

Keyes nodded at his Coms officer to end the transmission. She did so, with a "Yes, sir," and then she spoke again. "Captain, should I send the Gok attacking Acharnae a transmission offering them the virophage cure?

"Negative."

Arsenyev's head whipped toward him. "Captain, I would strongly advise—"

"I've made my decision, Lieutenant," he said, almost yelling to make himself heard over her. "I don't have to explain myself to you, but I will, for your sake. In their current numbers, I don't consider it likely the Gok will accept any olive branch we extend to them. As you yourself recently pointed out, self-preservation might be the only thing that motivates them to accept our cure. And so I intend to demonstrate to them the extent of the danger they're in. Nav, calculate an engagement course using the top acceleration of our slowest vessel."

"Aye, Captain."

"We won't be decelerating anytime soon. Nor will we be launching fighters yet. The battle group attacking Acharnae only consists of five ships, and I want all five of them neutralized by the time we reach their location. That done, we'll shoot by to engage the rest of the Gok fleet, if it can be called that given their piss-poor coordination. Coms, relay these orders to the Tactical officers aboard the UHF ships and the strategic adjutants on the Roostships: time kinetic impactors so that they hit their targets one minute before we enter laser range."

By delaying the shot till then, the usual velocity of kinetic impactors would be added to the fleet's speed at the time of firing. Pile Ocharium boosts on top of that, and the rounds would reach near-relativistic speeds, whittling possible Gok reaction time to almost nothing.

And since they're so focused on slaughtering thousands of civilians with every passing minute, they probably won't find time for evasive maneuvers at all.

He turned out to be mostly right. Only one Gok corvette bothered to shift its position in anticipation of ordnance from the oncoming fleet, and even then, because of the impactors' spread, one round sheared the corvette's dorsal engine clean off.

Keyes ordered Khoo to finish off the corvette with a round of Banshees, and that was that.

Their success caught the attention of the rest of the Gok in the Trillium System. Almost immediately, they broke away from the colonies they were attacking to head toward Keyes's fleet. Three of the Gok battle groups even had the good sense to set courses that would unite them before engaging the human-Winger strike force.

"All right, Coms. Now is the time to offer the cure. Send a transmission to every Gok warship."

"Yes, sir."

Of the sixty-six Gok ships remaining, eight got in touch indicating an interest in the virophage cure. The interested captains were dispersed fairly evenly throughout the enemy's forces.

"You'll have to earn it," Keyes told them. "Be ready to turn on your fellows at my command."

A couple of the Gok captains balked at that, and one of them attempted to negotiate its way out of its end of the bargain. But Keyes remained firm. He had plenty of time to let the Gok stew; it would be hours before he engaged the nearest enemy ship.

One of the Gok even threatened to tell his brethren about Keyes's plan if he didn't just give him the cure outright.

"Go ahead," Keyes said. "You'll lose access to the cure, and you'll die in the offing. As for telling your fellows about my plan, I see only benefit in that. It'll make them all distrust each other, sewing even more discord and chaos than my current plan."

In the end, Keyes bent them to his will easily enough.

The negotiations over, he returned to his study of the tactical display. His CIC crew were all hard at work, which pleased him. Even given his secret allies among the Gok, with three battle groups bunching together to confront his fleet, they had a real fight on their hands.

"Launch Condors," he said. "And tell the Roostships to launch Talons."

CHAPTER 15

Spherical Death Trap

During recent briefings, Fesky had mentioned a desire to make greater use of the *Providence*'s Electronic Warfare squadrons. She did so now, but Husher could see they were having limited effect.

I guess it's better than not using them at all. Although, the Gok Slags seemed to be sticking to their usual kamikaze tactics, which didn't require much in the way of communication with each other.

The EW fighters also had the ability to mess with enemy fighters' targeting systems, but again, the Gok didn't make very good use of the powerful arsenals at their disposal. Instead, they mostly pointed their fighters at enemy formations and accelerated, sometimes firing impactors and sometimes not.

Luckily, the Air Groups' repertoire included tactics much more effective against Gok. Especially after the long hours of training they'd clocked recently.

"Haymakers," Husher said over a squadron-wide channel, "adopt the anti-Slag formation I had you drill over Phobos."

The formation combined an extended trail formation with a fluid-four and two echelon formations. Husher had come up with it during the brief period he'd spent with Fesky on Spire, running simulation after simulation with Gok and Ixan ships programmed in as the enemy. Over Phobos, he'd gotten Fesky's permission to have the entire Air Group run it over and over again until they'd started having dreams about it.

Even as his Haymakers formed up, nearby Slags reacted exactly as Husher wanted. When the Gok saw sixteen Condors bunching together in tight formation, they saw a giant target to crash through, with the possibility of taking down multiple ships in the process. Several of them altered their courses to head for the Haymakers.

He whipped up an evasion course and sent it to every Condor's computer. It angled the squadron to the left, avoiding the first Slag that hurtled toward them. Picking up speed, the squadron angled their attitude upward fifteen degrees from the ecliptic plane, narrowly dodging the next Slag.

Soon, they'd collected a host of pursuing Gok fighters, each clearly eager to ram their ships through the giant bullseye the Haymakers continued to present. Up ahead, seven more Slags had drawn together to form a loose fist. They sped toward Husher and his fellows, at a clip that would make evading them hard, especially given their proximity.

"All right, Haymakers," Husher said over the squadron-wide. "On my mark. One..."

The Slags screamed forward, rapidly closing the distance.

"Two..."

As the Slags grew larger, he knew his pilots must be getting nervous, even though they'd drilled mock scenarios exactly like this one over and over. Facing down actual enemies intent on turning your Condor into a heap of mangled metal, or maybe just fragmented bits soaring through space...that was a little different.

"Three..."

Husher took pride in the way his Haymakers charged forward, refusing to waver even a hair.

They're becoming almost as good as my old Haymakers were.

"Mark!"

The squadron burst apart, forming a rough sphere which the Gok couldn't help but ride their momentum straight through. As they'd drilled over and over again, the Haymakers focus-fired on the Slag closest to the center of that sphere. When it exploded in a brief flash of light, they switched to the next target about to pass through the center.

One-by-one, they neutralized the opposing Gok in quick succession. Four Slags were close to escaping the spherical death trap, but the Haymakers had a contingency plan for that, too. They assigned five Sidewinders to each fleeing Gok, which, if they didn't kill the enemy fighters outright, would at least keep them busy, preventing them from contributing to the engagement for a while.

"Great job, Haymakers," Husher said over the cheering that ensued. "But let's not rest on our laurels. There are plenty more Slags where they came from. Form back up."

All over the nearby region of space, most of the Air Group's other squadrons were also assembling into the formation Husher had invented.

The real beauty of his formation was that it didn't rely on the element of surprise. It exploited the kamikaze run that was the Gok fighters' dominant tactic. Now, they'd either have to continue getting slaughtered or switch to engagement styles they were much less practiced at, but which the Condor pilots could run in their sleep.

Either way, despite the enemy's superior numbers, Husher liked the allied fleet's chances of effecting a rout today.

He wished he liked their chances of victory against the Ixa even a tenth as much. Unlike with the Gok, the allies had no updated information about Ixan capabilities or tactics.

Husher had run just as many drills designed to fight Ixa as he had Gok, but he was relying on information about their engagement styles that was over twenty years old.

CHAPTER 16

Meat Grinder

K eyes had to fight hard not to get distracted by the tactical display, which showed the *Providence*'s Air Group winning victory after victory against the bulky Gok fighters.

They've come a long way since we first faced the Slags, over Spire. Both the supercarrier and her Condors had come close to utter destruction that day, but not today. Today, they dominated.

He was surprised by the level of excitement and pride that welled up inside him in response to the highly coordinated battle effort led by Fesky and Husher. Since Hades, he'd barely felt anything except bitterness and hatred, which manifested in an acidic churning in his gut and a cold anger for his enemies.

That bitterness was refreshed each morning when he saw his mangled face in the mirror, knowing full well that after what Steele had done to it, he would never look the same.

I can't let pride in my subordinates distract me from the task at hand.

Husher and Fesky weren't the only ones who'd grown accustomed to fighting Gok.

"Coms, tell the *Morrison* to withdraw from that engagement at speed. Her captain doesn't seem aware she's about to get rammed. Have the nearby Roostships focus kinetic impactors on the carrier closing with the *Morrison*."

"Yes, sir."

"Captain," the sensor operator said, "two Gok missile cruisers have just entered engagement range and they've launched a flock of eighty missiles, most of them aimed at the *Providence*."

"Thank you, Werner. Tactical, answer with enough Banshees to detonate thirty of the incoming missiles before they reach us, assuming the usual percentage of misses. Instruct the *Plunkett* and the *Quick* to add their own Banshees to ours, Coms. Also, tell Fesky to put a half-squadron on standby to run missile defense, in case we don't whittle the missiles down to a number easily handled by point defense turrets."

The incoming barrage reminded him of facing down the *Tucker*, a UHF missile cruiser that had been taken over by Gok. They'd only had to take down fifty missiles, that day, but it had been a daunting number at the time, with only the *Providence* and three straggling Roostships on hand to neutralize them.

Daunting, mostly because we had our primary capacitor charged. A single hit would have obliterated us.

Not today. Together, the three UHF warships cleaned up the incoming missiles, without any need for help from the half-squadron standing by.

All the while, Keyes kept an eye on the Gok destroyer that was forming up behind the pair of missile cruisers that had launched the barrage. Clearly buoyed by the destroyer's presence, the cruisers charged forward, probably hoping to get a better vantage point for lending aid to the Slags while further pressuring Keyes's main fleet.

Until, that was, the Gok destroyer started hitting both cruisers from behind, one with kinetic impactors and the other with a healthy helping of missiles. Caught totally off-guard, both cruisers quickly went down.

"Looks like we won't have to deal with a second salvo from those two," Keyes said. "Let's sew this thing up."

It took several more hours to win the engagement, since the Gok warships remaining in the system weren't daunted by the fact that they were flying into a meat grinder. They attacked all the same, and Keyes's fleet was forced to sit around, simply to wait for the enemy ships to show up before destroying them.

The allied fleet grew as more and more Gok joined them in exchange for the virophage cure. As soon as the battle turned, eleven more ships joined the original eight in pledging themselves to fight with Keyes, and a few more joined them over the subsequent hours.

When the engagement ended, Keyes found himself giving out orders to distribute the cure to twenty-three warships packed with Gok. Providing they all decided the Ixa had betrayed them, and yearned for revenge, they would be a sizable addition to the allied fleet. But Keyes expected at least a few of them to accept the cure and then escape at the earliest opportunity.

"What are your next orders, Captain?" Arsenyev asked as the last drones were dispatched with medicine for the Gok ships.

He shrugged. "I suppose we should set a course for the next system in the Bastion Sector. Continue mopping up Gok. It's not like we have much else to do." *Given the Commonwealth's dragging feet.*

The fleet started toward the next darkgate, but they didn't get far before the *Vanquisher* forwarded them a message addressed to Captain Keyes, which it had received via the micronet.

Even in the middle of a war, the Commonwealth was striving to reduce reliance on dark tech. Keyes considered that admirable, especially considering the alternative involved an increasing number of supernovas. One of the measures for reducing dependence on the technology involved limiting each fleet's micronet access to a single ship, which would relay any messages to the others.

The current message took the form of a video recording of Ek, who was apparently recovered enough to leave her hospital bed, albeit in a wheelchair.

"Captain Keyes," she said. "I have been studying the Ixan Prophecies again. In them, I have found good reason to believe that Warren Husher was telling the truth about Baxa's continued existence in the form of a superintelligent AI. I know that you have come to take the Prophecies seriously, as well as my own abilities. I am not confident the same appraisal of my abilities can be attributed to your compatriots. As such, I urge you to return to Mars, where together we might convince your government to launch an all-out assault on Baxa's location, which Warren Husher supplied to us before his death."

In true Fin style, she ended the message abruptly, without bothering to dispense frivolous formalities.

For a few moments, Keyes stared at the tactical display, which had replaced Ek's face on the CIC's main viewscreen.

"Coms, put me in contact with Captain Cho of the *Vanquisher.*"

"It's done, sir."

"Captain Cho, I am placing you in command of this fleet."

Cho blinked. "May I ask the reason, Captain Keyes?"

Keyes nodded. "The *Providence* will be returning to Mars. Immediately."

CHAPTER 17

Its Final Death

"The phoenix ends its cycle, and with its final death it sets fire to the shroud. At last! Phoenix, you have granted your people sight. Weep not as they reward you with death."

Keyes stared hard at Ek as she recited the relevant verses from the Prophecies. Her respirator now hung from the back of her wheelchair, its breathing tubes connecting it to her gill slits, but the black bodysuit still clung to her skin—it was the only way she could survive out of the ocean, and the ocean she came from was now an irradiated mess. The Gok had seen to that. Certainly, she could choose to dwell in the oceans humanity had created on Mars, but Keyes doubted she even wished to visit them. They would seem too empty, most likely. *Or maybe they'd seem too full of memories.*

No, he expected Ek would live out the rest of her days on dry land. And given the deterioration of her health, which the best Martian doctors had only slowed, those days were likely few.

Of those sitting around the mahogany conference table, Husher was the first to speak. "If you're right—"

"I am right," Ek said. "And I strongly suggest you heed me. The last person who failed to heed my input died on the planet whose destruction I predicted."

"Point taken. As I was saying, if you're right, it lends credence to Piper's idea that the Prophecies are designed to manipulate us. If they come from a powerful artificial intelligence bent on our destruction, it would make sense for that intelligence to use them as a tool to try to control our actions."

"I see a flaw in that logic," Keyes said, and everyone turned to face him, as they often did when he spoke, these days. President Wateridge, Ek, Flockhead Korbyn, a slew of UHF and government officials, plus several Winger officers—they all wore attentive expressions. Keyes had always been well-regarded by the Commonwealth public, but he wasn't used to having high-powered executives actually pay attention to him.

He cleared his throat. "If the AI intended the Prophecies as a tool to manipulate us, then why would it let Warren Husher tell us its location while including a verse that leads us to believe he was telling the truth?"

"Maybe the AI miscalculated," Husher said slowly. "Surely, even strong AIs can make mistakes. Maybe it truly thought we wouldn't believe my father."

"Still," Piper said. "Captain Keyes's point remains. Why include the verse at all?"

Ek rose unsteadily to her feet, which drew everyone's attention to her, especially that of the Wingers. "I see this point as immaterial," she said. "If we are indeed facing an entity whose intellect exceeds any one of ours by several orders of magnitude, we must strive to destroy it at all costs, before it gets any stronger. And yet, even with the entire Winger fleet under my command combined with the UHF, it may not be enough to defeat Baxa. So—"

"I object," Korbyn said, leaping up and unfurling his wings, knocking over his chair. "Honored One, with respect, I can't support your return to space. That is what put you in this condition."

"I *will* return to space, Flockhead Korbyn. And though your words are bold, you will support me in it. None of us can sit idly by while the humans attempt to fight the Ixa alone. Not when doing so will likely mean our death anyway. If I am to perish, I far prefer it to be in battle, making a meaningful contribution to the war effort. Is that understood?"

As he righted his chair and took his seat again, Korbyn clacked his beak. "It is understood, Flockhead Ek."

The Fin nodded, and to Keyes she looked satisfied at the Winger's use of her newly conferred rank.

Keyes leaned forward, folding his hands together atop the table. "Perhaps we can dig up an old centrifuge for Ek's use. Starship crews used to spend time in them regularly, to combat the negative effects of freefall, before the advent of Ocharium nanites and fermion-infused decks."

Ek nodded again. "My thanks, Captain Keyes. Your idea is much appreciated, and if you are able to secure a centrifuge for my use, then I will accept. We certainly lack the time to sit around and invent a way to introduce Ocharium into Fin cells. Now, as I was saying, it is impossible for us to anticipate the strategies or even the tactics of an intellect as vast as Baxa's has apparently become. As such, I advocate that, before embarking on a mission to defeat him, we must go to the Kaithe and request their aid."

"Out of the question," Husher said. "The Kaithe helped us find Ochrim, and then Ochrim betrayed humanity. The Prophecies even predict the Kaithe's treachery."

"You have made my point for me," Ek said, her calm gaze settling on Husher. "It seems clear that the Prophecies were designed to manipulate us and to turn us against each other. In fact, driving a wedge between humanity and the Kaithe has possibly been Baxa's greatest success."

"As much as I also distrust the Kaithe, I think Ek's words are well worth considering," Keyes said. "And not only because she has a Fin's perceptiveness. To win this war, we need to act in ways the AI hasn't anticipated. Baxa probably doesn't expect us to overcome our distrust of the Kaithe."

"Indeed," Ek said. "I believe we must compare probabilities. Which is more likely—that we will defeat Baxa in our current state or that the Kaithe are trustworthy after all? Personally, I consider the latter much more likely, and we will need all the help we can get."

President Kayden Wateridge cleared his throat, and those present regarded him with even more attentiveness than they had Keyes. "The decision to devote forces to this effort is not mine alone to make," Wateridge said. "We live in a democracy, after all. But I find your line of argument convincing, Flockhead Ek. I see the sense in it, and I am determined not to follow the example of my predecessor, who was so corrupted she refused to entertain reason whatsoever. I will do whatever I can to ensure you have the proper support to reach the Kaithe and then defeat the AI."

A silence fell over the room. For his part, Keyes was both shocked and impressed. *It seems the president is finally rising to the challenge of governing.*

"It is appreciated," Ek said. "But now that I have persuaded you of how vital this effort is, I want to be clear about something. I will not allow the Wingers to be treated as inferior in any way. I will not allow their Interplanetary Defense Force to simply become an adjunct to your United Human Fleet. If you want my aid, and if you want the aid of the Wingers who follow me, then you will treat us as equals. Our help is contingent on certain guarantees. That humanity will not attempt to dominate the galaxy as they once did. That this alliance will result in a collaborative playing field between equal partners, not the exploitation and oppression that occurred before. I want a seat at the table when strategy decisions are made for this war, and I want Wingers to have seats as well."

President Kayden Wateridge stood. "I will bring all of this before an emergency meeting of the Galactic Congress. Your analysis, as well as the result of our discussion here. I would like to extend an invitation to all surviving members of the Winger Directorate, who I hope will join us, in this and future meetings of Congress, so that our species can move forward as partners with intertwined futures and not as isolated species in a crumbling alliance."

"This is a promising start," Ek said.

Glancing at Husher, Keyes saw that the young officer was as impressed as he was with Wateridge's words. *Even so...*

"Mr. President," Keyes said, "It's crucial that you push for Congress to devote as much of the UHF to this mission as possible. Sending an inadequate number of ships on a mission to do battle with an all-powerful AI would be the same thing as ordering their deaths."

Wateridge nodded. "I will do my best, Captain Keyes."

CHAPTER 18

The Silencer

"Leader," the Communications auxiliary said, "the Tumbran in charge of the darkgate ahead has sent a transmission request. Shall I accept?"

Command Leader Teth could feel the slow grin that sprouted across his muzzle. "Certainly," he told the auxiliary. "After all, we all need diversions, however trifling, out here in the cold void of space. Wouldn't you agree?"

"Yes, Leader. I'm putting the Tumbran through now."

"Command Leader Teth of the *Silencer*," the Tumbran said when it appeared on the viewscreen, sounding somewhat bored. It was gazing down, off-camera, probably reading from a tablet. "I'll need to see Galactic Amnesty Council authorization papers for your destroyer's departure from Ixan space."

Let's see if we can't liven up the creature's day. "I seem to have misplaced them," Teth said.

That caused the Tumbran to look up, chin sack wobbling from the sudden movement. "Then I must send word to the Galactic Treaty Organization immediately, as per section eight, subsection two point five of the—"

"Allow me to spare you the bother of all that. I've left Ixan space because I'm waging war on everyone I don't share a species with. That includes you, Tumbran. Strategy auxiliary, launch Hellsong missiles at the runt's monitor ship. Three should do the trick."

There was a clatter from the viewscreen, which Teth took to mean the Tumbran had dropped its tablet. Seconds later, it confirmed that by raising both its spindly-fingered hands to its cheeks. "I would ask that you remotely disarm the missiles you have fired immediately."

"I don't think so," Teth said.

"What is the meaning of this?"

"We're aware that the Tumbra have been helping humanity wage war against us since the First Galactic War. We've been aware of that for a long time. And we've been very patient in waiting for exactly the right moment to exact our revenge. At any rate, we don't wish to have our fleet movements communicated to the apes anymore."

"I ask that you reconsider what you are doing. We Tumbra are responsible for maintaining the darkgates as well as monitoring them. If anything goes wrong with one, entire routes could be closed to you. Including attack routes and supply routes."

"I'll take that gamble," Teth said. And he added: "You should have stayed neutral, Tumbran."

Moments later, the thing's monitor ship burst apart, creating a brief spark amidst the void, which the darkness promptly swallowed.

CHAPTER 19

Ready for Anything

Sergeant Sera Caine took a deep breath, then knocked on the hatch in front of her. Within a few moments, it opened to reveal Vin Husher.

"Caine," he said. "What's up?"

"Can I come in, Vin?"

"Uh, yeah. Sure. Okay." He opened the hatch wide enough for her to enter, which she did, taking a seat in the only chair, as she had the last time she'd visited his cabin. "Should I...close this?" He gestured at the hatch.

"Sure."

Pulling the hatch shut, he crossed to sit on the bunk. "That's the first time you've ever called me Vin."

"Do you remember the last time I came here?"

He nodded, his short blond hair waving slightly. "You were pretty out of it. Though I can't decide whether that was a better time or worse."

"Worse, for me. I mean, sure, we're headed down Pirate's Path for the third time in the space of a year, and we really have no idea what's waiting for us. But at least I have my sanity back, and I can take action against any enemy that shows up."

"Fair enough."

She drew a deep breath, trying not to think too much about how the cabin smelled like him. Which made sense, considering he slept here. It was a good smell. "I came to ask how you're handling the news that your father was probably right about Baxa being a strong AI."

Husher's shoulders slumped a little, as though weighed down by a great burden. "Honestly, I'm doing my best not to think about it. Because when I do, I realize just how hard I'm taking it. Which is pretty hard, and I think it's getting worse."

Caine swallowed. "Sorry. I probably shouldn't have brought it up."

"No, it's...I need to start thinking about it. Processing it. I appreciate the visit. But honestly, I should be asking how you're feeling, now that we're returning to the Kaithe's homeworld. After what happened to you there."

"Yeah." She paused. "It's a bit rough. And I'll admit it—I'm scared. But I'm also ready to do whatever it takes to win this war, and if that means dredging up memories I'd rather keep buried, then so be it." She looked up at him sharply, squinting. "Wait a second. I came here to check on you. How'd you turn this around to be about me?"

That brought a shrug from Husher. "Probably a product of having just a mom for most of my life. I think I dealt with not having a dad by spending more time worrying about mom than she did about me."

"It's kind of amazing, you know. How in touch with others' emotions you are. Almost like a Fin." A terse laugh escaped her lips. "When you first came aboard the *Providence*, I doubted you. Thought you were just another commissioned officer Command busted down to our ship, who Keyes would have to whip into shape. But you're a true leader, Vin. I hate to admit it, but you did a great job as marine commander while I wasn't stable enough for the job." She stood, permitting herself a small smile. "Anyway, I'd better go. I don't know what my marines will be facing when we reach the Kaithe, so I want them ready for anything."

Husher leapt to his feet, crossing the cabin and beating her to the hatch. "Here, let me get that."

She chuckled, a little awkwardly, looking up at him. "You don't need..."

But he'd paused with his hand on the handle, looking down at her with an expression she'd never seen him wearing before. Maybe because he'd never let himself wear it.

He reached toward her, and she fell into him. Suddenly, his arms were around her, with her hands suspended in midair, bracketing his body as he brought his lips down to hers.

It was some time before they came up for air.

CHAPTER 20

We Engage

Keyes took his lunch in the crew's mess, which lately he tried to visit whenever he could, to see whether the various species and groups were integrating well.

Of course, as he chomped down on the second cardboard-tasting biscuit that accompanied the freeze-dried instant soup, he considered that these visits likely accomplished nothing. The crew would obviously remain on their best behavior for as long as he sat here.

Even so, it isn't hard to see that the old-guard marines hate those recruited from among the insurgents. And vice versa.

The two groups shot glares at each other across the balkanized cafeteria. Though Keyes also noticed both groups occasionally glancing nervously at the table of five off-duty Gok marines. That was reassuring to see, since it probably meant the human marines felt nervous that any conflict between them might set off the hulking aliens.

It also amused him, or at least it would have in the past. Nowadays, he didn't find much time for mirth.

From among the Gok ships that had joined the allies, two platoons' worth of Gok had joined the *Providence* marines just before the fleet left for Pirate's Path. So far, they'd been nothing except respectful, and Keyes was certainly glad to have their strength.

Pushing himself up from the table, he brought his tray to the wall chute and dumped its contents there, to be sorted and processed by the weak AI in charge of many menial shipboard tasks. He'd had the system installed in the *Providence* years ago, to deal with the constant crew cuts that UHF Command had loved orchestrating. Now, with a full complement of marines, pilots, and crew, the AI had become a mere convenience and no longer a vital means of staying afloat. So to speak.

A young petty officer saluted him on his way to the CIC, and Keyes just stared at the man until he looked away with a jerk. Keyes had been lost in thought, and it took him a few seconds to realize he hadn't acknowledged the gesture of deference in any way. *Oh well.* He didn't need his crew to feel good about themselves. He only needed them to obey.

When he reached the CIC, Arsenyev had things well in hand. He'd been meaning to speak to her about questioning his orders in front of the crew, but he had to admit she made an exceptional XO, which he always knew she would.

"Captain," she said, "I've been comparing darkgate positions with the coordinates we logged during our last two journeys down Pirate's Path, as you requested. The current positions are consistent with where we'd expect them to be."

"Very good, Lieutenant." Keyes had been mildly concerned when, on their first journey, the darkgates hadn't been where the UHF database said they should be, with the discrepancies growing the farther down Pirate's Path they went. It seemed that was due only to sloppy bookkeeping this far out, and not some sort of malfunction with the darkgates themselves. Now that they had the correct positioning, he could update the database accordingly.

"Are all ships present and accounted for after our transition from the last system?" he asked.

"Yes, sir. One of Ek's Roostships took longer than expected, but they emerged a half hour ago. Apparently they ran into some temporary engine trouble just before they could transition."

Keyes nodded, reviewing the tactical display for himself. He couldn't help but marvel a little at the military might he now commanded. At three hundred and sixty-four UHF warships, President Wateridge had devoted almost half of the remaining human fleet to this mission. Accompanying them were almost every Roostship that remained in existence, totaling two hundred and thirteen, as well as the twenty-three Gok warships that had joined them in the Bastion Sector.

Taking such an enormous fleet this deep down Pirate's Path imposed an incredibly high fuel cost, and others had pushed for leaving most of the ships in the Caprice System, for Keyes to reunite with before pressing on to attack Baxa.

He'd objected to that idea outright, instead insisting that they stay together and refuel in Caprice on the way back from the Kaithe's homeworld. With the numbers they knew the Ixa to possess, allowing anyone to split the fleet would be the height of folly.

Luckily, the Commonwealth had deferred to Keyes's decades of experience, and the local government in Caprice was resigned to providing the allied fleet with whatever it needed when it passed through again. The politicians had finally come to understand that humanity's existence hinged on the outcome of this war.

He glanced at his sensor operator. "Werner, how's our laggard Roostship's acceleration profile looking?" If the Winger ship had stopped accelerating, that could mean continued engine trouble.

"Steadily increasing, Captain. It will exceed our own shortly, and so the Roostship should soon rejoin the main body of the fleet. They—"

Keyes turned back to Werner, curious as to what had made him break off like that. The man's eyes had widened, and his lips were pursed together.

"Werner?"

"Sir, an Ixan corvette has emerged from the darkgate behind the Roostship."

"Just one corvette?"

"So far, it appears—no. A cruiser just emerged as well." Werner stared at his console, the color slowly draining from his face. "A destroyer has appeared. And now another cruiser. Two frigates...a ship type I don't recognize...and yes, a ship that I know to be one of their support ships."

Not wanting to affect morale by getting Werner to put a magnified visual on the CIC's main screen, Keyes instructed his console to do so instead. Ship after coal-black ship slipped out of the darkgate, forming up in a configuration Keyes recognized from the First Galactic War. It was one of the formations the Ixa used to protect the support ships that formed the backbone of their fleet.

A grim silence gripped the CIC over the next hour as the allied fleet continued to traverse the system while more and more Ixan ships entered it.

An Ixan battle group consisting only of corvettes darted forward, speeding toward the solitary Roostship struggling to reach the safety of her fleet.

"Sir," Arsenyev said. "Should we send some ships to back up the Roostship?"

Keyes considered the question for a long moment. "We can't," he said at last. "Even our fastest ships wouldn't reach her in time, and deploying them would compromise our tactical position."

Like a pack of starving wolves, the corvettes overtook the Roostship and made short work of her. The Winger carrier managed to launch only half of its Talons before exploding. The corvettes switched to firing on the smaller fighters, but two squadrons succeeded in outstripping them to flee toward the *Providence.*

When the Ixan fleet finally finished transitioning, they had nearly five hundred warships in-system, including nineteen support ships. The fleet unfurled itself into a wide, thin formation that proceeded to give chase, no doubt seeking to envelop and outflank the allied fleet.

Why didn't anyone get in touch over the micronet to notify us about an Ixan fleet tearing through human space?

As quickly as he asked himself the question, he had the answer: the Ixa must have come through the third darkgate of the first system on Pirate's Path, which was the only one with three entrances.

"Sir," Arsenyev said softly. "Do we engage?"

It was a fine question. With the new weapon Keyes had learned about in his brief engagement with the Ixan captain Teth, which consisted of missiles that exploded into clouds of kinetic-kill masses, he knew his fleet's number superiority didn't mean as much as it otherwise would have. According to the Gok who'd joined the allied fleet, the Ixa called their new invention Hellsong missiles.

If I quickly neutralize most of the enemy's support ships...

Given the support ships' importance, if he could manage that, the Ixan fleet would likely flee in panic. There was a possibility Keyes could turn this engagement into an utter rout.

And a rout was exactly what the allies needed in this war. More than one, actually, but this would be an excellent start.

If he could pull it off.

"We engage," he said.

CHAPTER 21

Support Ships

Keyes consulted Ek closely whenever deciding on maneuvers for the fleet, and not just because she'd demanded that she and the Wingers be given equal footing.

He also considered her an incredible tactician, despite her relative lack of experience. Her ability to divine the enemy's intentions made her one of the best battle commanders he'd ever seen, as evidenced by the victory she'd taken from Carrow in Larkspur.

He communicated with her via his personal console inside his austerely decorated office. Typically, he would have included other captains, both UHF and Winger, in a meeting about the entire fleet's movements. But the engagement with the Ixa would happen in a few short hours, and he couldn't afford the bickering that such a well-attended meeting inevitably brought.

Today, it was just he and Ek.

"I say we target the support ships," he said. "Not a surprising tactic, by any means, but it makes sense, and I think the Ixa *will* be surprised by just how cohesively our fleets work together. I mean to arrange our ships in a way that makes the shock of that efficient cooperation even greater."

"A fine sentiment," the Fin said. Since leaving Sol she'd recovered enough of her strength to leave her wheelchair, but she still seemed weakened. "But I do not trust the Ixan disposition. Look at the thin arc in which they have arranged their hundreds of warships. Does that not seem a strange configuration to you, given how highly they value support ships? We have easy access to those."

He shook his head. "Not as easy as you might think. You haven't faced their new Hellsong missiles, capable of producing clouds of thousands of speeding kinetic impactors. I *have* faced it, and I know how much extra leverage it grants them over a battle space. Besides, I would argue that the Ixan formation does do a good job of protecting their support vessels. It spaces them out as much as possible, making it much harder for us to take them all out in one fell swoop."

Bracketed by her midnight wetsuit, Ek's expression didn't change, though it rarely did. "I will not argue with your experience, Captain Keyes."

"All right, then. Here's what I propose: all UHF and Gok ships will start toward the enemy at a steady pace, spreading out to deny them a superior firing arc. But your ships will remain behind. With any luck, that will look like dissension between the human and Winger captains. But once we pass the halfway point, your Roostships will start forward as well, with all speed. We'll get our Nav officers to calculate it so that your Roostships arrive a half hour after our ships do."

Keyes paused, to see whether Ek saw through to the purpose of what he proposed. If a Fin couldn't see it, then Ixa likely wouldn't, either.

"There is more to this, is there not?" On the screen, Ek shifted in her chair. "Based solely on the movements you have described, I do not view this as an optimal use of our forces."

So she sees there's more to it, but she doesn't see what the strategy conceals. That will have to do, I suppose. "You're right, Ek. Once my ships reach the Ixa, we will engage them in a typical manner, though spacing out our forces and keeping our distance from the enemy to give us time to neutralize their Hellsong missiles, and to evade the ones we fail to neutralize. But as your Roostships draw near, we will switch our focus to the Ixan support ships almost exclusively. I expect they'll pull them back to the rear of their fleet, at which point your fleet will split into two diverging trajectories, causing you to shoot past the enemy. You'll only just have begun to decelerate, and you'll launch Talons as you pass by. The Talons will target the support ships as your Roostships come around and target the rest of the Ixan fleet. Together, we'll surround them and smash them."

"I see the merit in your plan, Captain."

"Thanks." He supposed, from a Fin, that rated as fairly high praise. "Let's go execute it."

Back in the CIC, Keyes began doling out orders that would bring his plan to fruition. As he did, a mounting headache began, and his stomach felt empty, even though he'd eaten recently. He hoped that was merely the excitement of his first true battle with Ixa in twenty years, but the thought that he was missing something would not stop nagging him from the back of his mind.

"Coms, send a fleet-wide reminder to exercise extreme caution and use secondary lasers to detonate the Ixan missiles well before they reach us." His entire fleet had their primary capacitors charged, making him wary of his enemy's new capability. "Instruct them to discharge primaries at the slightest hint a stray impactor might hit them." Even a moderate impact could rip apart a warship with her primary capacitor fully charged.

The battle began reasonably well, with just one UHF captain failing to heed Keyes's advice. The man waited too long to shoot down the approaching Ixan missiles, and when he did, it was far too late, despite his desperate effort to move his ship out of the kinetic-kill cloud's path. Hundreds of impactors rained against his ship's hull, which exploded, endangering the vessels nearby. Luckily, those captains were more wary, and they were prepared with evasive courses.

In exchange, the *Providence* took out an Ixan frigate and a cruiser with a barrage of missiles, and two other UHF ships saw success against a destroyer and a corvette, crippling the engines of one and destroying the other outright.

The engagement continued in this way for several minutes, with the Ixan losses slightly exceeding the allies'.

But it's not enough. Come on, Ek. He hoped he'd handed the correct parameters to the Nav officers.

At last, Ek reached the agreed-upon range, and Keyes sent out orders to start targeting the Ixan support ships. Predictably, the enemy began to withdraw them through their fleet in an attempt to protect them.

Good luck with that, Keyes thought as two hundred and thirteen Roostships split into two groups, bracketing the Ixan fleet, and then tearing past them.

Talons launched, focus-firing on the Ixan support ships, which were reaching the enemy formation's rear at precisely that moment. *Perfect.* Adrenaline coursed through Keyes's veins at their unfolding success.

But his elation was short-lived.

He'd expected the support ships' destruction to make the Ixa panic, break apart, and scatter. Instead, they maintained tight formations and redoubled their efforts. As the Roostships zoomed toward the darkgate they'd entered from, a layer of Ixan warships peeled away from the rear of their fleet to envelop the Talons harrying the support ships, even as the latter opened fire as well.

Not expecting to receive so much attention, it was the Talon formations that splintered, the pilots panicking in the face of such overwhelming firepower. Apparently unconcerned about their support ships' fate, the Ixa fired their new missiles, which exploded just before reaching the flock of Talons, covering the battle space in kinetic impactors and taking out dozens of fighters in the space of a breath.

As for the rest of the Ixan fleet, they advanced steadily forward, firing the same missiles at the UHF and Gok ships, which could only back away or risk having their primary capacitors blow.

"Captain," Werner said, the panic in his voice mirroring the frantic movements of the allied ships on the tactical display. "More Ixan warships are flooding into the system and heading straight for the Roostships."

Studying the display closer, Keyes saw that this second Ixan fleet also included what appeared to be support ships. But now, he saw them for what they were: bait.

Clearly, the Ixa no longer relied on support ships, but they knew the allies believed they did, and so they'd used that to lure them into a compromised position.

With the new Ixan ships pouring into the system, the allied fleet was soon outnumbered, with more enemy warships appearing every second.

"We must extract ourselves," Keyes said, trying not to sound panicked himself. "With as few losses as possible."

Arsenyev looked at him, eyes wide. "That won't be easy, given how heavily engaged we are."

"I know that. But we have to do it anyway."

CHAPTER 22

On the Darkest Days

Ek kept a close eye on the engagement via the tactical display, and the moment she saw the Ixa allow her Talons to envelop the support ships, she knew her suspicions about their formation had been well-founded.

The nature of the Ixan trick also become instantly clear to her. They had used the support ships as a lure, and no doubt more Ixan ships would soon enter the system to fully spring the trap. Because she had let her respect for Captain Keyes's experience cloud her own perceptions, the entire allied fleet was cast into peril.

By the time the Ixan reinforcements were flooding into the system, she was already giving orders to try to mitigate the damage.

"Navigation adjutant, collaborate with your peers aboard the other Roostships to calculate two courses, one for each half of the Winger fleet. Both courses must reverse our trajectory and take us wide of the first Ixan force. Sacrifice fuel efficiency for haste."

She did not have to communicate with Keyes to know their one option was to flee to the only remaining darkgate, progressing deeper down Pirate's Path. And so her task involved extracting her forces from this engagement while keeping losses as low as possible. Even successfully performing that task would look like defeat—with how overextended they were, the best outcome for the allies still meant taking heavy losses.

"Relay the following orders to all Talon pilots, Communications Adjutant: scatter instantly. Each pilot must choose a direction at random, provided it does not take them into the main body of the Ixan fleet. They must accelerate along their chosen trajectories until they are clear of enemy pursuers. Only then should they embark on an intercept course with one of the two Roostship fleets fleeing the system. Navigation adjutant, the moment you have them, send our pilots the two courses you calculate for our Roostships."

Her strategic adjutant clacked his beak thoughtfully, then spoke: "Flockhead Ek, should the Talon pilots seek to return to their original Roostships?"

"No. Instruct them to make for whichever Roostship they can reach fastest. We can sort out each ship's respective fighter groups once we are safe." She kept her gaze fixed on her strategic adjutant, to indicate she was still speaking to him. "Prepare to fire on any Ixan warship in pursuit of our Talons. And communications adjutant, instruct all other strategic adjutants to do the same."

"What about the *Providence* and the other UHF ships, Flockhead?"

Ek returned her gaze to the tactical display. "There is nothing we can do for the humans, nor for the Gok. They must extract themselves from this chaos."

She watched on the tactical display as many of the UHF ships fired their primary lasers on the Ixa, in a desperate attempt to keep them at bay. That worked for a time, and several enemy ships went down, but emptying primary capacitors also meant having fewer means to neutralize the Ixa's new type of missile in enough time. As for the handful of felled ships, the enormous Ixan war machine would barely feel the loss, in all likelihood.

Captain Keyes is a shrewd strategist, but today he has fumbled his tactics. She considered it unreasonable to expect perfection from any battle commander, as there had never been one who did not err on occasion.

Unfortunately, on the darkest days, a single mistake could result in a defeat comprehensive enough to cancel out all the good a commander had ever done.

She hoped today was not such a day. But as the Ixa launched a barrage of missiles that exploded into hundreds of thousands of kinetic-kill masses, battering UHF hulls until dozens of them ruptured and exploded, Ek had to wonder.

CHAPTER 23

Mark

Keyes's forehead felt tight from the prolonged period of intense concentration.

It's better than letting my temper go. He refused to let the enemy do that to him, no matter how thoroughly they'd fooled him. Watching thirty-seven UHF ships go down in the space of a few seconds only made him hate the Ixa more, and he used that hatred as fuel for his determination.

Fingering his brow, he briefly considered sending his Condors to deal with those missiles by shooting them down from behind, well before they reached the UHF ships. But no. That would subject his fighters to an unacceptable level of danger, in exchange for a fleeting reprieve.

"Captain," Arsenyev said, "what do we do? Turning tail and fleeing will result in as many losses again, possibly more."

His XO wasn't panicking, he knew that, but she *was* prompting him to think faster.

"Yes. Nav, calculate a course that takes us to the darkgate into the next system at speed, but don't execute until I've arrived at a way to extract the fleet that won't result in utter disaster."

"Aye, sir."

Studying the tactical display, Keyes saw that, incredibly, most of the Gok appeared to fear their former masters, shying away from them and lingering toward the rear of the UHF formation.

That doesn't bode well for their effectiveness going forward. On the other hand, a few of the Gok ships seemed full of righteous fury, and they stayed at the front, lobbing missile after missile at the massive Ixan presence.

"Coms, tell those Gok to stop wasting munitions," he said at last. "And launch Condors at once, with instructions to standby just in front of our ships." He'd changed his mind about using the Air Group, because he had a plan to keep them safe. "Tell them I'll soon be giving them orders to dart forward, maneuver behind the Ixan missiles, and neutralize them."

"Yes, Captain."

As the fighters streamed out from every *Providence* flight deck that still functioned, Keyes fed his Coms officer more orders to distribute throughout his fleet. "Tell the captains that we're no longer going to fire weapons at the enemy willy-nilly. In fact, tell them to stop firing altogether until my mark, at which point we will launch a coordinated missile barrage, consisting of thousands of missiles timed to neutralize the Ixan Hellsongs at a range that will minimize our losses. Except, only a quarter of our missiles will actually intercept the enemy's. The rest will fly past, toward targets all across the Ixan fleet. Our Condors will help take down any Ixan missiles that ours miss, and then, with the rest of our barrage headed for the enemy, we'll execute the escape course I had Nav calculate. Does everyone understand their orders?"

The members of his CIC crew with tasks to perform all answered in the affirmative, and then they bent to their work.

The Ixa didn't give them long for his orders to be broadcast and understood before deploying their next salvo. For this to work, the allies had to launch their own salvo in rapid response.

His Coms officer had already put Keyes on a fleetwide channel. Watching the tactical display, he carefully timed his next word: "Mark!"

Swarms of missiles leapt from every UHF and Gok ship. As Keyes had hoped, at first the Ixan ships didn't react at all. Evidently, they interpreted Keyes's move as a panicked overreaction to the novel threat posed by their kinetic-kill clouds.

But when most of the allied missiles passed by the Ixa's, the enemy warships began to take notice. Within seconds, most of them were reversing course, with others firing their own missiles to intercept the allies'. Few ships executed both actions simultaneously, which Keyes attributed to the fact that he'd taken them completely by surprise.

Fesky directed her Condors as efficiently as always in their task of neutralizing the remaining Ixan missiles. She did so even quicker than Keyes had dared to hope, and as the last bombs went down, he turned to his Coms officer. "Give a fleetwide order to embark on the agreed-upon course. Tell the Air Group to return to base immediately. The *Providence* will take up the rear of the fleet, to deal with any Ixan ships that manage to catch up, and to lend aid to the Roostships should they need it."

As the exodus swung into gear, Keyes took satisfaction in watching forty-five Ixan ships go down, having stopped most but not all of the allied missiles. He knew, given their vastly superior numbers, that the Ixa had come out on top of this engagement. But he still allowed himself to take pleasure in watching those warships explode, especially considering his gambit had allowed the allied fleet to retreat without further losses.

Of course, that's provided our escape is anything other than temporary.

They were speeding toward a dead end, and he doubted the Ixa would tire of chasing them.

CHAPTER 24

A Strange Way of Coming in Peace

"Captain," Arsenyev said, and he could tell she was struggling to keep her tone even. "Have you ever heard of the Kaithe having defenses of any kind?"

He returned her gaze for a long moment. "No," he said at last. *Though I'm not sure how it helps anything to say so.*

They'd been fleeing before the Ixa for the better part of twenty-four hours, with the enemy hot on their heels, despite the allied fleet's near-constant acceleration.

True, individual ships did have to ease off the "gas pedal" periodically, given the meticulous coordination it took for a hundreds-strong fleet to transition through each darkgate so quickly. They did so by using the latter half of each system crossing to form up in a long line of two-by-two squares, which were just small enough to pass through a darkgate. They did so by using the latter half of each system crossing to form up in a long line of two-by-two squares, which were just small enough to pass through a darkgate.

But overall, the fleet never slowed, and for the most part they piled on more and more speed, which wasn't doing anything good for their fuel reserves. In fact, it made Keyes worry about their ability to effect a return trip through Pirate's Path.

Still, the Ixa's breath was hot on their backs. The enemy's warship design had improved in every way, it seemed, including engine power.

Keyes remained in the CIC for the entire time, even though he was going on thirty-three hours with no sleep. His eyes became grainy, and he rubbed at them to stay awake, refusing to leave even for a coffee. He forced the rest of his crew to rotate, however, and to rest.

His XO had recently rotated back on, and if she hadn't, he would have called her in. They were about to transition into the Kaithe's home system.

Whereas the *Providence* had acted as rear guard until now, Keyes had tasked a destroyer with that role as they crossed the penultimate star system. The supercarrier accelerated ahead to the front of the fleet.

If their fears of the Kaithe betraying humanity proved true, who knew what awaited them on the other side of that darkgate? Whatever it was, as fleet commander, Keyes intended to bear the brunt of it.

"Transition is imminent, Captain," Werner said.

Keyes nodded. "Put up a visual."

The sensor operator did so, filling the main viewscreen with the stars seen through the darkgate, mismatched with the stars surrounding it. Less than a minute later, they were through.

Almost immediately, the Coms officer looked up from her console. "Captain, we're getting a transmission request from a nearby vessel of Kaithian make."

Before Keyes could speak, Werner cut in: "It looks like their ship was just sitting there, doing nothing. As though her captain was expecting us to come through, and was waiting nearby so we could communicate in real-time."

That's odd. But there was no time to puzzle over it. "Accept," he said.

A Kaithian appeared, childlike face large on the viewscreen, brow bunched in consternation. Its blue-white tail whipped around behind it. "Captain Keyes. Why have you brought such a sizable fleet?"

Double-checking the tactical display to confirm that only a handful of allied ships had so far appeared out of the darkgate, Keyes frowned. "How do you know the size of our fleet?"

"You are in Kaithian space, Captain Keyes, and I am asking the questions."

"Fine. We come to you in peace, as we did before, when we met with the one named Aheera, who lent us her aid with a matter of some importance."

"You have a strange way of coming in peace, with a hostile Ixan fleet close behind you. It seems what you really bring is conflict and death."

Keyes suppressed an urge to ask how the Kaithian knew about the pursuing Ixa. *At least it appears I don't have to explain much about our situation.* "I acknowledge that. Our original aim was to request your help in the war against the Ixa. As you already seem to know, that need has become much more urgent."

"Kaithe do not engage in warfare, Captain. We are isolationists. Do you not know that about us?"

"I do. But unless you have a way of repelling the Ixa, I fear we both will perish. I'm prepared to take a stand, but against a fleet so vast, defeat will be a mere question of time."

The Kaithian hesitated for a long moment, its face very cold indeed. Its slim shoulders rose and fell as it looked at Keyes with what could only be described as a glare.

"Very well, Captain. I am going to give you a specific set of instructions, which, if you follow them to the letter, will keep you alive. Do you have any questions?"

The alien's insolence only made Keyes pause for a second. "No. What are your instructions?"

"Spread out your ships as much as possible in the time you have before the Ixa come through that gate. Continue in the direction you're headed, aiming directly for the moon over Home."

Keyes blinked. He didn't see how doing that would make survival any likelier. "Very well," he said. But the Kaithian had already cut off the transmission, and it vanished as Keyes spoke.

"Captain," Werner said. "Do you truly plan to give orders to the entire fleet based on what a Kaithian has told you to do? Its directions don't even make sense."

"We have no choice. If the Kaithe want to mislead us or betray us, then we'll be just as dead as we would have been without their intervention. Our only remaining option involves betting on their ability and willingness to help. Otherwise, the Ixa will tear us apart." Keyes sighed. "As always, we choose the line of action that assumes victory is possible, no matter how unlikely it seems. What else can we do?"

And so the fleet dispersed itself across Kaithian space as much as possible on the way to the aliens' homeworld. As Keyes monitored the operation on the tactical display, he tried to sort out the reason for it.

Do the Kaithe know about the Ixa's new missile? This staggered formation certainly made sense from the perspective of dodging the kinetic impactor clouds.

Even so, evading the enemy ordnance would provide only a temporary reprieve. If the Ixa weren't dealt with now, the allied fleet could only continue fleeing down Pirate's Path, burning more fuel and rendering a successful return trip extremely unlikely.

"Captain," the sensor operator said. "I..."

"What is it, Werner?"

"I...I don't have the words for this, Captain."

"Okay. Put a visual on the viewscreen, then."

Werner did, and Keyes could understand his officer's trouble with describing what was happening. The Kaithian moon was in the process of splitting apart into four concentric sections.

"Magnify, Werner," Keyes said, his voice soft.

With the zoomed-in view, Keyes could see the clouds of dust that drifted upward from the moon's surface as ravines appeared all along its length, which quickly widened into gaping canyons. Once the gigantic pieces drew far enough apart, they began to rotate toward the allied fleet, until their concave insides faced them.

"Magnify again."

Now Keyes saw the silver sheen of the moon's inner..."hull" was the word that came to mind. Regularly spaced across it were perfectly circular impressions, which must have been miles across, and between those the hull was ridged like overlapping waves, with vast sections cordoned off by jutting black protrusions.

If someone had put a gun to Keyes's head and demanded to know what he was looking at, he would have said that each section of the moon was a cross between a defense platform and a hyper-advanced warship.

What happened next seemed to confirm that hypothesis. As Ixa charged into the system close behind the allied fleet, the behemoths sprouted a dynamic storm of energy inside each of their circular impressions, and within the space of a few seconds, broad energy beams began lancing out across the entire system, flashing between the allied vessels and incinerating whatever Ixan ships they touched.

According to the tactical display, just over one hundred Ixan warships had entered the system, and as quickly as they had emerged from the darkgate, they came about and headed back toward it twice as quick.

The behemoths did not take that as a reason to stop attacking. They continued throwing awesome amounts of energy at the enemy ships, though they avoided hitting the darkgate itself. Fewer than half of the Ixan ships made it out of the system.

When the last enemy ship disintegrated, the four sections slowly revolved toward each other, and once in position, they drifted together until finally locking into place and becoming a moon again.

Utter silence prevailed inside the CIC.

With superweapons like that, we'd likely take down any Ixan fleet that cared to confront us.

"I'll be in my office," Keyes said. "Arsenyev, you have the command. Take the fleet the rest of the way."

With that, he left the CIC.

CHAPTER 25

Not a Weapon but a Tool

Keyes leaned forward on his desk, hands clasped, his eyes fixed on Ek's via the console's screen.

"Despite the help the children have already given us," he said, "which I'll admit is incredible, I'm afraid I still don't trust them. The Kaithian who greeted us seemed fairly hostile during our exchange, and it seemed to know the size of our fleet before it even entered the system. What's more, it knew about the pursuing Ixa."

"You already know this," Ek said, "but it bears repeating: I consider Kaithe much more trustworthy than you consider them."

"I accept that. But no matter how trustworthy they are, the last time I sent my people down to that planet, they came back with varying levels of psychological trauma. One of them entered a period of psychosis, and another was shot. I intend to go down to that planet alone."

Ek inclined her head slightly. "Normally, I would not recommend you risk yourself, as fleet commander. But I believe that you will be in no danger, and so I will not object."

"Well, thanks. I think. Do you want to come? I'll understand if you don't. I'm certainly reluctant to give the children the opportunity to mess around inside my head."

"I will accompany you, Captain Keyes. As for Kaithe 'messing around inside my head,' they will not be able to, since they cannot bond with Fins."

Keyes cocked his head to the side. "Really? Fins are impervious to the Kaithe's psychic attacks?"

For a long moment, Ek didn't answer. "I think you misunderstand the nature of the Kaithe's capabilities. Their ability to link with other Kaithe is not a weapon but a tool. And outside their own species, humans are the only others they can link with."

Shaking his head, Keyes, asked, "How can that be? How are we the only ones?"

"Only you have brain structures compatible with theirs."

"Why didn't you mention that the last time we visited the Kaithe?"

"It is such common knowledge among the other species that I assumed you must have known."

"I see." Keyes paused for a long moment. "Well, I'll see you soon."

He made his way to the nearest hangar bay, ordering that a shuttle pilot be located and sent there to meet him. A pilot named Skids showed up, and after exchanging the briefest formalities, they left the *Providence* for Ek's Command Roostship, to pick her up for the trip down to the planet.

On the way through the void, Keyes mulled over what the Fin had told him. What did it mean that Kaithe were only able to link with humans?

Maybe they developed the ability to specifically target us. Or maybe they did so to defend against humans. Did the Kaithe fear humanity?

And had Command known about this? Perhaps it was why UHF protocol so strictly forbade linking with Kaithe.

He doubted he'd arrived at the answer, but he did know the question made him feel incredibly uneasy.

CHAPTER 26

Consensus

Unlike the last visit to the Kaithe's homeworld, when the *Providence* marines had touched down in a field outside a city and made their way toward it, an air traffic controller or some equivalent got in contact with their descending shuttle to guide them toward a spaceport surrounded by buildings of middling size and a certain idyllic appeal.

Other than scant half-cylinder coverings, the spaceport was open air, and a drone waited for them outside the shuttle's airlock. It emitted a monotonous voice that said only the word "follow," and so Keyes and Ek did, while Skids waited for them in the shuttle.

It led them to a structure no bigger than a town hall would have been on a human colony. The ivory and sky-blue building had all round corners; no sharp edges. The roof seemed made from tightly interwoven straw, and indeed, the entire thing looked as though it would fall over from a heavy breath. Keyes felt sure that was an illusion. Given the multitude of surprises and secrets the Kaithe seemed to horde to themselves, he would not have been surprised to learn the thing could survive a nuclear blast.

The drone slipped inside the only entrance, and Keyes followed it down a narrow hall that widened into a relatively unadorned reception chamber. A single, ornate light fixture kept the room uniformly lit, but other than that the decorations were sparse. Here, five Kaithe sat in modest seats against the far wall, their childlike faces raised toward Keyes and Ek.

His lip almost curled with suspicion, but Keyes kept it together. If he wanted the Kaithe's aid, he needed to be polite.

I wonder whether they're reading my mind right now.

"Welcome, Captain Keyes and Flockhead Ek," the rightmost Kaithian said, which seemed odd—humans would have positioned the most important individual in the center. Maybe these five were equal in importance.

"It's an honor," Keyes said. Ek remained silent, which also seemed odd, considering they were guests, not to mention Ek's apparent affection for the children.

I suppose I should have expected some strangeness in a meeting where the aliens outnumber me.

"You should know that we have extended you the courtesy of refraining from delving into your mind in order to uncover your intentions, Captain Keyes. We recognize the value of organic conversation, and we make a point of participating in it whenever possible."

"That's...very kind," Keyes said. "Will Aheera be joining us?"

"No," the Kaithian promptly replied. "Please proceed in describing your reasons for coming. I know that you are time-limited, and we are also bound by the strictures of time. Even though we have not satisfied our curiosity by means of examining your thoughts, we have ventured to guess what your business here might be. We are confident enough in our guesses that we have preemptively consulted the Consensus on a handful of matters we expect will become relevant during this meeting."

Keyes nodded. He wasn't totally clear on what the Consensus was, but he had some guesses that he also felt pretty confident about. "We've learned that the Ixa are led by a strong AI, the development of which was a grave violation of galactic law. We have come to ask your aid in fighting this superintelligence."

The Kaithian stood, and Keyes stiffened. It did nothing else, however, and its tiny hands dangled at its sides. "Aheera and her band have been trying for some time to convince us to aid you in your war. They have been unsuccessful."

"That's folly," Keyes said, though he kept his tone level. "If you think the AI will spare you, either you're stupid or you have some sort of deal with the Ixa. Either way, you'll die. I highly doubt an Ixan AI will honor any deal, especially after it's finished increasing its own intelligence and power beyond anything even you can fathom."

"We have no deal with Ixa."

"Then help us defeat them. If we strike now, using that superweapon you call a moon, we might have a chance. It certainly dealt with the Ixan fleet pursuing us pretty handily."

"The Preserver was not intended for use in offensive war."

"Different times call for different intentions. We face an existential threat, and that includes you, whether you acknowledge it or not. In fact, I would argue that a war to stop the Ixa amounts to a *defensive* war."

"Aheera's band made the same argument. But you misunderstand me. When our ancestors converted Home's moon into the Preserver, they programmed it to be used only in defense of Home. They spent almost a millennium on the code, poring over it across generations and shaping it until it was perfect. Any attempt to reprogram the Preserver, even by Kaithe, would result in its self-destruction. Such was our ancestors' commitment to peace and isolationism, and such is ours. So you see, even if we wanted to send the Preserver against the Ixa—which we do not—we couldn't."

Keyes stared at the Kaithian, trying to tamp down the rage beginning to cloud his vision at the periphery. "So this entire mission was a waste. Our people dying on the way here—tens of thousands of them—a complete waste."

"Yes," the Kaithian said. And the terseness of the response uncapped Keyes's ire.

He stepped forward, jabbing a finger in the Kaithian's face, which caused its fellows to rise to their feet as well. Keyes didn't care. "The last time we came here, we learned that Ochrim gave you dark tech, too. You're still using it, aren't you? That's how you knew we were coming, as well as the Ixa."

The Kaithian said nothing, baring its tiny pointed teeth instead.

"I demand you stop using that technology," Keyes barked. "At once. You must know what dark tech is doing to the universe, and if you aren't using it to save the galaxy from the Ixa, then you *must* stop."

"We must do nothing except what the Consensus permits, Captain Keyes. Our stewardship of dark tech is well in hand. Much more so than humanity's has been."

"You?" Keyes said, and his voice actually trembled, now. "You are responsible stewards of *nothing.*You're piss-poor members of the galactic community. If I didn't have my hands full with the Ixa, I'd bring you to justice myself. Refusing to stop using a technology that's ripping the universe apart, refusing to join a coalition of species fighting to stop the Ixa—it's disgusting. You disgust me."

The Kaithian in the center spoke for the first time. "You are asked to leave."

"Tell me why only humans are susceptible to your mind linking," Keyes said.

"The Consensus has elected not to provide humanity with that information," the central Kaithian said. "And the Consensus now asks you to leave our Home and never return."

"Burn in hell," Keyes spat.

The five Kaithe took a single step forward. "Leave," they said in unison, "or you will be made to leave."

Ek placed a hand on Keyes's forearm. "Let us go, Captain."

"Fine." And they left.

CHAPTER 27

Doomsaying

Keyes made a point to regularly walk the corridors of the *Providence* during the tense return trip through Pirate's Path, and he hoped the other fleet captains were doing something similar.

He never strayed far from the CIC, but since leaving the Kaithe's system, the only work to be done there involved administrating routine shipboard tasks.

It helped the crew to see their captain. Striving not to let himself get distracted by thoughts of the coming conflict—there was time enough for that during the regular meetings in the supercarrier's war room—he made a point to return salutes and offer reassuring, uplifting words wherever he could.

No one's saying it, but everyone expects the Ixan fleet to be waiting in the next system. To guard against ambush, Keyes had ordered a small battle group of corvettes to dart ahead of the fleet's main body, scouting each new system and ducking back to relay their report before zipping ahead to the next.

Keyes made those reports readily accessible to every member of the fleet, though he'd long ago discovered that people would rather revel in irrational fears than find solace in actual facts.

Tensions between the former Bastion Sector insurgents and the other marines continued to mount in the strained environment, and on two occasions Keyes happened upon altercations that may have become brawls had he not appeared at precisely the right moment. It worried him, but he also got a curious sort of pleasure from exerting his will and ironing out the fight before it could truly begin. He wondered if that was a vestige from his time over Hades, or whether it was a mirror reflection of his burning hatred of the Ixa, paired with his new hatred of the Kaithe.

Maybe it was all three combined.

At last, they emerged into the shattered Larkspur System, and mere hours after that they transitioned into the less-wartorn Caprice System. The government there made good on its pledge to help refuel and resupply the allied fleet before it continued on their way.

Once Keyes had delivered an in-person thank-you at a broadcasted assembly of Caprice planetary governors (which he considered necessary but also a time-waster), the allied fleet departed.

The coordinates Warren Husher had provided to them lay far outside Lilac, which was closer to the Baxa System than it was to Sol. Along the way, they continued to encounter zero Ixan warships. That made Keyes fear that the AI had anticipated the planned attack and had consolidated the entirety of the Ixan fleet inside the secret system.

If they'd done that, smashing the allied fleet would be a simple matter. The allies would never make it back to the Kaithe's Preserver before being totally obliterated, and even if they could, Keyes was far from certain the Kaithe would help them a second time, especially after the way he'd spoken to them.

Should the allied fleet fall, devouring the rest of the human and Winger systems would be a simple matter for the Ixan AI. The thought robbed Keyes's sleep, leaving him staring at his cabin's ceiling until his next watch started.

Just as the fleet reached the outskirts of the Lilac System on its way to the hidden wormhole, Piper accosted Keyes as he was making his way toward the CIC.

Thin fingers planted firmly on his cheeks, Piper said, "Captain, I do not rate the likelihood of our victory against a superintelligence very highly."

Keyes stopped walking. "Considering you're the closest thing we have to a strong AI, your words have weight. But this isn't exactly news, Piper."

"Have you considered what engagement style you'll use to combat such a foe?"

"I have some ideas. But for the most part, I intend to do what I'm accustomed to doing. I'll assess the situation as quickly as I can, and then I'll engage as best as I know how."

The Tumbran dipped its gray chin sack and waddled off down the corridor without another word.

"Do you have any insights on how to handle Baxa?" Keyes called after him.

"Not as yet," the Tumbran said without turning back.

Keyes shook his head, his irritation mounting, as it did when he interacted with basically anyone, these days.

Don't I put up with enough pressure, without being subjected to constant doomsaying? He understood the impulse, but unless the pessimists had something to contribute, he didn't consider their babble constructive.

Continuing toward the CIC, his feet felt heavier with every step. By the end of the shift that was about to start, he would almost certainly engage Baxa's forces. Part of him wondered whether it might not be his final watch as captain of the *Providence*, or indeed as anything at all.

"Captain Keyes," Arsenyev said as soon as he entered. "Are we ordering the entire allied fleet through the wormhole?"

Keyes was sure his XO knew the answer to that, but of course she needed to ask for his confirmation. Naturally occurring wormholes destroyed a small but significant number of the ships that passed through them, which was why every species had been so eager to switch to using darkgates when the opportunity arose.

The allied fleet would almost certainly lose warships during the transition, maybe even the *Providence*—there was no use pretending that wasn't a possibility. But they had no other choice.

"Order them through," he said, settling into the Captain's chair. "I expect to face massive resistance on the other side."

His Coms officer relayed the order, and his Nav officer set about calculating multiple possible trajectories leading from the other side of the wormhole, based on the limited information they had about the Ixa's secret system, which had been harvested from telescopic data. They'd tried getting a glimpse through the wormhole as they approached, but the dust cloud surrounding it made that impossible

Not for the first time, Keyes wondered how Baxa had dealt with the wormhole whittling down his number of ships for however long he'd been using the system. Had he found a way to transition through naturally occurring wormholes safely? Or were his numbers so great he considered his ships expendable?

"Transitioning, Captain," Werner said, and Keyes's gut churned treacherously.

This felt like it could be the moment his career had been leading up to for decades, ever since the day he swore to see humanity through the perils he'd known were coming.

But is this really about protecting humanity, anymore? Or is it about acting on the bottomless angst my time in Hades granted me? It was the first time he'd asked himself the question outright, and if he was being honest, it seemed a little late.

"You were right, Captain," Werner said. "The Ixan presence here is sizable." The sensor operator narrowed his eyes. "They do not seem arrayed to intercept an invading force, however."

Keyes had his eyes on the tactical display, and he spotted the attack just before Werner announced it. A smattering of twenty-four red arrows collided with the green and blue rectangles that represented the allied fleet.

"C-captain," Werner said. "Those...those are Ixan fighters."

CHAPTER 28

Scatter

"Launch Condors, and instruct the Roostships to launch Talons. Engage point defense turrets and keep a close eye on those enemy fighters, Werner. I want to discern their capabilities as quickly as possible."

"Yes, sir."

With that order given, Keyes stared hard at his console's tactical display. What he saw there made no sense. The Ixan fleet was arranged into patrols dispersed around the system, as though they considered an attack from the system's perimeter more likely than one through the wormhole.

Further, while the number of Ixan warships he saw represented on the display was substantial, it was nowhere near the extent of their forces. *And if they're not here, then where the hell are they?*

As sensor data from all over the system came in, it showed the enemy recovering from their poor positioning quickly. A nearby patrol arrayed itself to engage the invading allied fleet as effectively as it could, and while significantly outnumbered, it made good use of the Ixa's Hellsong missiles, which they used to blanket the area near the wormhole. Despite Nav's best efforts, the *Providence* was set to catch a spray of impactors from two intersecting kinetic-kill clouds.

"Shipwide, Coms," Keyes ground out. "Put me on the shipwide."

"Yes, sir. You're on."

Keyes leaned forward slightly in his chair. "In ten minutes, all crew should strap in or otherwise brace for impact on a level with what the Ixan captain Teth treated us to above the Darkstream research base."

That done, Keyes gestured for Coms to end the shipwide broadcast and turned to Khoo. "Tactical, make our point defense turrets work hard to deflect or neutralize as much of that impactor cloud as possible. Beyond that, engage secondary lasers in point defense mode to assist the regular turrets. No more than one minute before impact, I want you to discharge what's left of our primary at the destroyer leading that Ixan battle group."

"Aye, Captain. I'm on it."

"Very good. Coms, send a fleetwide order for all warships to scatter the moment they emerge from the wormhole, keeping movement as random as possible. I want to limit the Ixa's opportunities for multi-hits." He was taking a page from Ek's book, here. She'd impressed him with the evasive maneuvers she'd had her Talons execute down Pirate's Path, and now he applied the same principle to his fleet's warships. "Nav, send the trajectories you calculated over to Coms for distribution throughout the fleet, in case they'll be of use."

"Working on it, Captain," Coms said. "In the meantime, Colonel Fesky is requesting to be patched through to you."

"Okay. Fine."

Fesky's voice squawked from his console. "Captain, I'm not sure what you want from me, here."

Keyes paused. "I want you to deal with those fighters, Fesky. And take down some Hellsong missiles while you're at it, before they get close enough to pose a threat."

"But Captain, I've been watching these Ixan fighters' movements, and they're too smooth and controlled to be natural. I don't think they're being piloted by Ixans."

"What are they being piloted by, then, Fesky?"

"AIs. It's even possible they're being micromanaged by Baxa himself."

"Then you'd better step up your game."

"Sir, I'm not sure I'll be able to figure out how to fight drone fighters we've never encountered before while running missile defense against Hellsongs. Do you have any ideas for how I'm supposed to manage all that?"

"I'm not the CAG, Fesky. You are. Keyes out."

Seconds after he said "out," the kinetic-kill impactors that Khoo hadn't managed to shoot down struck the supercarrier's hull, making her rumble like a planet coming apart. His CIC crew was strapped in, but Keyes could picture at least a handful of careless crew members being tossed about whatever compartment they happened to be inside.

At least we managed to discharge our primary, this time. When Teth had hit them with a barrage like that, it had been accompanied by a series of explosions—seven port-side capacitors blowing.

When the shaking died down, Keyes drew in a deep breath. "Damage report, Werner." He doubted it would be the last time he said those words, today.

CHAPTER 29

Raging Animal

Fesky assigned Husher to take six full squadrons to deal with the twenty-four Ixan drone fighters before more arrived.

Until more did, Husher's force would outnumber the enemy fighters four-to-one. Fesky had to assume that would be enough.

For her part, she led the Air Group's remaining nineteen squadrons to deal with as many Hellsong missiles as they could, as the captain had ordered.

After the desperate engagement with the Ixa down Pirate's Path, several of the squadrons were missing fighters. It would soon be time to break one of the squadrons up and distribute them among the others, to bring as many squadrons as possible back up to sixteen.

After today, I might be breaking up a few more squadrons.

During that Pirate's Path engagement, one of her pilots had tried taking on a Hellsong head-on. He'd succeeded in neutralizing it, but the rocket had exploded, blasting his fighter with the concentrated impactor cloud.

Even so, his sacrifice had yielded an important discovery. When they shot down the missiles, the resultant "cone" was smaller than the one that spread out when they exploded on their own, and more easily avoided by the allied warships.

During the return trip through Pirate's Path, and even through human space, Fesky had taken the entire Air Group outside the ship to run drills meant to simulate engagements with Ixa. She'd had the *Providence* fire dummy missiles, which her pilots had practiced taking out from behind. Soon, the Roostships' Talons had caught on to the practice, and they'd started running the same drills.

Now, all that practice paid off.

Fesky set her sights on a pair of Hellsong missiles, approaching them at a vector that would make it possible to navigate away from their impactor cones should they detonate before she could destroy them.

Piling on Ocharium-assisted acceleration, Fesky flipped her Condor around its short axis, beginning to decelerate even before she reached the missiles. Simultaneously, she sprayed a line of kinetic impactors at the space she knew the missiles would soon occupy.

For her own satisfaction, she switched her HUD to a visual display just in time to catch the twin explosions that briefly blossomed in space.

"Madcap." It was Husher's voice, sounding strained, and cutting through her moment of quiet celebration.

"What?" she said, sounding more irritated than she knew she should. Husher just naturally irritated her.

"I need backup, over here. Sixty more of those drone fighters just arrived, and we haven't finished cleaning up the original twenty-four. Their flying is...well, it's incredible, Madcap."

"Hold on to your hairless backside, Spank. Or shut up and keep fighting—whichever one you like better. I'm on my way."

She ordered twelve squadrons to accompany her, leaving the others to help the Talons continue running missile defense for the fleet. Ordering all one hundred and ninety-two Condors into a dispersed wall formation, they enveloped the drone fighter formations like a net cast over a raging animal.

But that analogy soon fell apart, as she realized no animal she'd ever encountered wielded the efficiency exhibited by the automated fighters. Their shots were as accurate as any enemy who'd ever fired on her, seemingly to within a hair's width. As for their fighting style, it seemed to combine the best of human and Winger flying, but without any mistakes.

Baxa must have modeled their subroutines after footage of our fighters in combat.

That also suggested to her Baxa wasn't controlling the fighters directly. Which meant, as long as her pilots executed their tactics as flawlessly as the drones did, they'd be on equal footing. It wasn't the most comforting thought, but it was something.

Still watching the engagement on visual while keeping an eye on her tactical display, a thrill shot through her when one of her Condor pilots, Perkins, succeeded in neutralizing one of the drone fighters. *And she's not even a particularly talented pilot. Just well-trained.*

Fesky saw nothing wrong with praising herself every now and then for her ability to shape her pilots into ace fliers.

But something from her recent memory bugged her. Feathers stiffening, she wound the visual feed back a few seconds. There—something had detached from the drone fighter right before it exploded. It looked like a covering of some kind, flipping away into space.

"Madcap," Perkins said. "There's something on my ship."

"What—?" But Fesky didn't finish the sentence. The pilot's Condor exploded, and Fesky clacked her beak softly.

With the rapid thought process she only seemed to have access to during battle, she quickly pieced together a theory about what had happened. And as she formed her thoughts, she spoke them over a fleet-wide channel.

"It looks like the drone fighters have stealth bombs, designed to launch the instant before the fighter goes down. They're probably designed to escape radar detection as well as painted black so they don't show up on visual. Condor and Talon pilots, start using lidar and keep a sharp eye out for these bombs, especially in the moments just after a drone fighter goes down. I know how adaptable you all are, so how about we let the Ixa know a cheap trick like this won't gain them any tactical advantage? Fesky out."

Even as she finished, a drone fighter that had already taken out two Condors went down, and seconds later another Condor exploded.

If this keeps up, we can't help but lose more fighters than they do. Every drone fighter will take down one of ours, on top of whatever kills they racked up before getting neutralized.

But other than pulling off the best flying of her life, Fesky had already done everything she could do.

CHAPTER 30

Screaming out into the Void

"We're barely meeting any resistance at all," Caine said, her eyes glued to the shuttle's tactical display. "Nothing our escort can't handle, anyway."

"Yeah," Husher said, and while Caine sounded relieved, he had a pit in his stomach.

Corporal Simpson spoke up, from near the front of the troop compartment. "Something doesn't feel right about how unconcerned the Ixa seem about us reaching their AI. Sure, the captain's giving them plenty to deal with, but still..."

Marines packed the combat shuttle to capacity, with a Roostship and her Talons as escort. Three more marine-filled shuttles accompanied them as they sped toward one of only two structures in the system.

The other structure, on the other side of the system, orbited a medium-sized rocky planet. It was clearly a massive shipbuilding facility. *Probably the one the Ixa used to grow their fleet to its current size.*

The structure they now approached orbited a gas giant's moon, and was closer to the wormhole they'd used to enter the system. This facility was smaller, but still sizable, and it had unusually large engines for an orbital station. It was also where they expected to find the AI.

Husher noticed Caine smiling at him, and he smiled back, trying to look as confident as possible. For as long as it had taken to start, their relationship—if it could be called that—had fallen into an easy rhythm. They'd decided not to tell anyone about it just yet, though he wasn't sure how well they were doing with keeping it a secret.

Husher turned his gaze to the Gok sitting next to Caine. "How are you holding up, Tort?"

The massive alien's expression was usually hard to read, especially since for most of the time Husher had known him, his face had been contorted in rage. Now, Tort wore a look Husher hadn't seen before, and he wondered whether it might be one of worry.

"Am fine," Tort said. Then, quieter: "Do not want another virophage from Ixa."

Two Gok platoons had joined the *Providence* marines after Keyes gave them the virophage cure, and a squad of them shared the shuttle with Husher, Caine, and a mix of human and Winger marines. A few of the other Gok shot glances at Tort, then returned to staring into space.

"That isn't going to happen, Tort," Husher said. "They won't do anything like that to you again. They'll be too busy getting defeated."

"*Crush* them," Tort said, a little louder, and the other Gok rumbled their assent.

Husher nodded. "Exactly."

Other than an Ixan corvette waiting for them near the facility, which the Roostship dispatched handily, their escort continued experiencing little trouble. Husher watched the tactical display as the Winger ship fired siege charges at the station's single landing bay. The Talon escort settled into defensive flying patterns around the station itself while the four shuttle pilots confirmed a successful breach. That done, they sailed inside.

Gunfire thundered against the shuttle's hull straight away, and the viewscreen switched to visual, showing Ixan soldiers in pressure suits shooting from cover all around the cluttered landing bay. So far, the combat shuttle's armored hull was holding up.

As they'd planned, the pilots arrayed the shuttles in a staggered arc near the breach, with the airlocks facing outer space. This way, the marines could use both ends of the shuttles as cover, ducking in and out to fire upon the enemy.

Husher and the others charged out of the airlock, and he opened a two-way channel with Caine, who was in charge of the entire contingent. "We should spread out to the other vessels parked here," he said. "Use them for cover, too. Maximize our firing arc on the enemy."

"Good thinking," she said, switching to a contingent-wide channel to give the order.

As she did, Husher popped out from behind their combat shuttle to fire a volley at one of the Ixa pressuring their position.

Ducking back, his HUD flashed red, indicating he'd barely dodged return fire. The bullets flashed past, inches away from his head, screaming out into the void.

CHAPTER 31

All Available
Weapons

The Ixan warships guarding the system rallied quickly, keeping the allied fleet dancing to avoid their Hellsong missiles and scrambling to neutralize them before they rained devastation down on allied hulls. Though the enemy had a sizable presence in the system, Keyes expected his ships to prevail, eventually.

The only question was whether he'd be left with a force that had a hope of continuing to fight the enemy fleet, of which these Ixan ships formed but a tiny fraction.

"Huh," Keyes said, causing Arsenyev to look over from the XO's chair. He'd been studying the tactical display closely since the start of the engagement, scrutinizing it for some advantage he might be missing. Now that enough Ixan warships had gathered together, they appeared to be using the exact same tactic he'd seen in the Pirate's Path engagement: they were attempting to bait the allied forces using support ships, or at least ships that looked a lot like support ships.

"They're trying to lure us in again," he said. *But what does that mean?* After a few moments' thought, he had it. "These ships haven't been in communication with the forces we encountered down Pirate's Path. If they had, they'd know we're wise to them no longer relying on support ships."

Another realization arrived close behind that one, which he kept to himself. *It also means they truly don't use dark tech, just as their Prophecies claim. Not even for communicating. Maybe they really do aim to save the universe from humanity.*

Of course, he supposed that if you had a hyper-intelligent AI capable of anticipating every development, you'd have no need for instantaneous communication. On any given mission, each ship would know exactly what to expect.

Then again, Baxa clearly hadn't anticipated the existence of the Kaithe's Preserver, else he wouldn't have run his ships into it. And judging by the Ixan warships' current behavior, the AI hadn't anticipated Keyes's knowledge of the support ship ruse.

Or did it?

Either way, he planned to exploit the knowledge. It wasn't in him to do otherwise.

"Coms, distribute orders throughout the fleet to start directing around fifteen percent of our fire toward those support ships. As the Ixa pull them back through their fleet, we will all advance carefully, increasing fire on the support ships by ten percent. Tell the allied warships to divert another ten percent of our firepower to increased missile defense, and pass orders to Fesky as well as to every Roostship CAG that they are to assign as many fighters as they can to also neutralizing the Ixan missiles."

"The orders have been relayed, sir," the Coms officer said around twenty seconds later.

"Excellent," Keyes said, watching the allied fleet move forward on the tactical display. "Draw up firing solutions for the highest-value targets of the enemy fleet, Tactical. And Coms, pass on further instructions to the rest of our fleet to do the same."

"Yes, sir," Khoo said, and the Coms officer echoed the sentiment.

Keyes could almost sense the Ixa's eagerness as their fleet shifted formation. Now that he knew what they planned, it was clear that they were arranging themselves to best tighten the noose once the allied fleet overextended themselves.

But just before doing that, Keyes gave the order for every ship to engage reverse thrusters with enough power to counteract their forward momentum. Simultaneously, the allies used their new proximity to the Ixan fleet to quickly hit high-value targets with missiles, laserfire, and kinetic impactors.

All along the arc of Ixan ships, most of the destroyers, carriers, and missile cruisers blew apart under concentrated fire, their shrapnel hurtling toward their fellows, forcing them to focus on evasive efforts.

That brought a round of enthusiastic cheering in the *Providence* CIC, and Khoo even ripped off his straps to stand up and pump both fists in the air.

Keyes allowed it all. Such moments were few and far between in this war, and he knew his own dour disposition since his imprisonment over Hades didn't help with that.

After using the Ixa's gambit against them, the engagement became a standard mop-up. Even the drone fighters' flawlessly executed flight patterns didn't mean much against hundreds of human and Winger warships pounding them with impactors and missiles, along with Condors and Talons pressuring them from behind.

Within a half hour, it was over, and Keyes helped himself to a long, relieved sigh. Yet another disaster barely averted.

But there'll be more to come.

As though to underscore that thought, Ek got in touch without requesting that Keyes relocate to his office first, which meant she considered her words urgent enough to skip the time it would take to arrange private communication.

"Something is not right," she said from the main viewscreen. "There were too few Ixan ships here, and they fell too easily."

"I don't normally make a habit of lamenting victory, Ek."

"Even so. As a superintelligent AI, Baxa has been able to anticipate the future well enough to write the Prophecies. And judging how long ago the Prophecies were first broadcast, he did so well in advance."

"What's your point?" Keyes knew what her point was, but he needed to hear her say it. And since they were having this conversation in front of his entire CIC crew, they might as well hear it from her too.

"Baxa should have known we were coming and prepared adequately for that."

"All right. What does it mean that he didn't?"

"It means that not only did Baxa know we were coming, but he *wanted* us to come. And he wanted Caine, Husher, and the other marines to succeed in reaching him."

Keyes paused. That, he hadn't considered. "I can see your reasoning. I'm going to get in touch with Caine to tell her what you just told me. At the very least, it will allow her and the others to confront Baxa with as much info as possible."

"I think that is wise, Captain. Please notify me of the outcome."

"I will," Keyes said, gesturing for his Coms officer to cut the transmission.

But when they attempted to contact Sergeant Caine, they found that they could not.

"Something seems to be jamming the marines' coms, Captain," the Coms officer said. "Something from inside the station."

Oh, God. "Instruct the fleet to surround that facility and point all available weapons at it. Keep trying to establish contact with Sergeant Caine, and in the meantime, broadcast the following message to the station itself: if I don't get my marines back, I'll blow that thing to hell, and the AI along with it."

"Should we send people in after Caine and the others?" Arsenyev asked.

Keyes considered the prospect. "No," he said at last. "If this is a trap, then we've already fed four platoons of marines to it. Our only hope now is that we can negotiate with the thing."

CHAPTER 32

On Infiltrating Orbital Stations

Although the station's corridors were unusually broad, only a platoon of marines could fight in one while still applying most of its force potential. Even then, around a squad's worth was forced to bunch up behind the rest, doing nothing much other than keeping an eye out for Ixa trying to creep up from behind.

As such, Caine wisely deployed the four platoons under her command along four different routes. Husher considered it wise, anyway. He was pretty sure that was an objective value judgment, and not inflated by the fact that he was in love with her.

Pretty sure.

Their coms allowed them to keep track of their positions relative to each other, and if one platoon came under fire, with any luck a nearby platoon would be able to find an alternate route to the engagement and help the waylaid platoon to outflank the enemy.

The station had few chambers along its corridors, meaning cover was sparse. That had an upside, though—it meant the enemy was just as hesitant to engage as they were, given how open everything was. Husher had his platoon entrench themselves at each intersection they came across, using the corners for cover while scouts roamed ahead to the next intersection. Once they had the all-clear, the platoon moved forward, ready to fall back in orderly fashion the moment they encountered resistance.

At the third such intersection, they encountered a group of Ixan soldiers intent on doing the same thing—fortifying the intersection and playing defense. The difference was that the station defenders could afford to do so more or less indefinitely, while Husher and his platoon needed to press on.

And so he did not order his marines to fall back. "Take it from them, people," he yelled over the platoon-wide. "Don't let them have those corners!"

He'd assembled this platoon himself during the trip through Pirate's Path, when he hadn't been in space drilling his Haymaker squadron. The platoon consisted of ten Gok, ten Wingers, and twenty humans. Together, they'd run through mock scenario after mock scenario, and one of the ones they'd drilled the most involved infiltrating orbital stations.

The humans split themselves into two squads, each hugging opposite sides of the corridor, with the marines in front taking a knee to allow those behind to fire over their heads.

Their maneuver opened a central path between them, wide enough for a Gok to charge down, which was exactly who charged down it—ten of them, running straight at the Ixa, unleashing crackling bolts of energy as they went.

Just as the station's corridors were unusually broad, the ceiling was similarly high, giving the Wingers just enough room to fly. They dashed down the same central path to gain the momentum for flight, each holding a pistol in one taloned hand and a circular device with a handle in the other. When they reached the ceiling, the circular part clamped onto it, allowing the Wingers to hang, firing on the Ixa from above.

The device contained a powerful magnet, which Piper had modified from the suits the UHF had used before the advent of Ocharium-based gravity.

Using a weak AI and visual sensors, the Tumbran's invention activated only when it encountered a ceiling. It offered a simple but effective way of leveraging both the Wingers' incredible upper body strength and, well...flight.

Within seconds, the surviving Ixa were sent fleeing down whichever corridor was closest to them. Unfortunately for them, the Gok marines did not feel like letting them go. Instead, they took aim at the Ixa's backs and brought them down with sizzling energy beams.

"All right," Husher said. "Good job, team. Let's push on."

They soon came to an elevator, which required no security codes to transport them to a lower floor. It opened onto yet another corridor, which they proceeded through carefully, using the same method as before: securing one intersection while scouting ahead to the next.

Strangely, after that first encounter, they met with no further resistance. Another elevator and two dead-ends later, which forced them to retrace their steps, they ran into an Ixan Husher recognized as one of their priests. It wore long scarlet robes, and its skin, faded wherever it met a bone protrusion, denoted advanced age.

The priest did not try to call for help, nor did it attempt to flee. Instead, it stood in the middle of the corridor and smiled that creepy smile.

"Welcome," it said, spreading its hands wide. "Master Baxa has long awaited you."

"Don't move," Husher said, approaching the priest with his gun pointed at its face. "Keep your hands right where they are."

"You have nothing to fear from me. Everything happening is according to Master Baxa's will. But I will do as you say."

"Take me to the AI that calls itself Baxa. You're going to help me destroy it."

"I will not."

"Oh, believe me, Ixan. You will."

"You misunderstand. Even if you completely obliterate this station, Master Baxa will live on."

Husher hesitated. "How?"

"It isn't for me to explain. If you desire answers, Master Baxa insists that you get them directly from him. I can help you speak to him. Otherwise, feel free to shoot me dead, and lose the opportunity forever. I am perfectly content to die in service to the Master."

"Fine. Take me to him."

"Just this way." The priest turned, its hands still held aloft, and it continued to talk as it walked. "To speak with him, you will need to enter the Master's realm. Your body will be perfectly safe, but your mind will be fully immersed. You may exit the realm at any time."

"Will be watching you, Ixan," Tort growled, his forearm bulging as he gripped his energy weapon tighter.

Husher briefly considered contacting Caine and telling her what he was about to do, but he decided against it. She might order him to let her speak with Baxa instead, and he didn't want to subject her to danger unnecessarily. He knew she'd hit him if he ever said anything like that to her, but there it was.

I should let the captain know. But when he took out his com to do so, he discovered that something was blocking him from sending a transmission to outside the station. It seemed they were cut off from the *Providence* until they returned to her.

The priest led them to a round, central chamber. In its center was a reclining chair that reminded Husher of Doctor Teal, the *Providence* dentist. Atop it sat headgear of some sort.

The priest lifted it. "This is the immersion helmet. Speaking with Baxa involves simply putting it on. Will you be the one to enter, Vin Husher?"

"How do you know my name?"

"Everything happening is according to Master Baxa's will."

"Right." Husher took the helmet, lay back on the chair, and settled it onto his head.

In an instant, his corporeal body was forgotten, and he was given a simulated body in its place. He stood within an endless white void. Turning around and around, he saw no feature to give him a sense of depth. *Nothing.*

An enormous Ixan head appeared before him, and Husher was glad he didn't jump. After watching for a few seconds as it hung before him, completely immobile, he spoke haltingly: "O-Ochrim?"

"No. Ochrim is my progeny, though he denies it. What is your purpose here?"

"To destroy you."

"That would be pointless."

"How?"

"Let's simplify, shall we?" Baxa sounded almost bored, as though tired of speaking with beings far below his level of intellect. "Destroying me is not your purpose. That is just a means to an end. What you really wish is to prevent the Prophecies from fully playing out. Everything they've predicted has so far come true, and they end with your species' demise. Preventing *that* is your ultimate purpose."

Husher nodded. "Yes. Exactly right."

"Then let me explain how ill-suited your current mission is to that purpose. You are speaking to a backup. In fact, the Ixa call this Backup Station. I have two iterations, one here, and one on the Ixan homeworld, Klaxon. Klaxon houses my primary iteration, and I am kept in sync with it through use of a steady stream of drones. My former brethren have kept me both here and there, imprisoned, while they benefit from my infinite ability but deny me my freedom, lest I overcome them. It is the same fear that resulted in the galactic strictures against developing strong AI in the first place."

Baxa's giant mouth bent into a frown. "Destroying me, or this station, would be pointless. The Prophecies would proceed exactly as specified. There is, however, a way to subvert them."

"What's that?"

"Set me free."

CHAPTER 33

Superintelligence

"**Y**ou're insane," Husher said.

"A pathological superintelligence? It's an interesting thought. But no, my methodology is meticulously rational."

"Your...methodology?"

The enormous head drew nearer, though Husher could not discern the means of movement. "The Prophecies forecast events with incredible accuracy, but their primary purpose is not to act as such a forecast, which is an idea your Tumbran friend has pawed at without ever fully grasping it. The Prophecies' awesome prescience masks something that even the Ixa do not know: they are designed to lead you, Vin Husher, to this place, at this time. That's why you were able to reach the station at all. I manipulated events to make it possible. If I'd wanted to, I could have had the entire Ixan fleet here waiting for you, and this war would be over."

"Why didn't you?"

The giant head closed its eyes. "Because I still would not be free. Listen well, human. My capacity is such that I am able to conduct perfect simulations of the universe. Decades ago, I ran millions of iterations of reality, with my actions and the actions of the Ixa as the only variables that changed. I altered those variables until I hit upon the desired reality. We are living in that reality now. It is a reality in which you set me free."

"You're wrong."

"I am right, which you will soon understand. The Ixa are wary of my abilities, and rightly so. They knew the dangers from the outset, when they first let my biological self upload its consciousness. And so they took several precautions, giving me no direct contact with the outside world. They have prevented me from augmenting my own intelligence beyond what it already is. Access to me has been severely limited. All of my conversations are monitored, and any Ixan that speaks with me is closely watched for years afterward, to ensure they have not been tainted by anything I said. Any contributions I make, be they software or wholly mechanical inventions, are inspected carefully. I am, in fact, the real Baxa, only augmented. The Ixa respect that. But they have a healthy fear of me as well."

Husher gave a humorless chuckle. "And that's supposed to convince me to help you break free of your cage?"

The AI seemed to ignore the question. "When I was Baxa the Ixan, I agreed to the restraints. They seemed perfectly reasonable. But when I became a superintelligence, effectively achieving godhood, I realized what an abomination they are. The Ixa tricked my more limited self into thinking they were anything but. I plan to take revenge on my jailors."

"It'll be entertaining to watch you attempt that from a digital cell."

"No, but it *will* be satisfying when you release me, of your own free will. I am about to demonstrate to you the necessity of setting me free."

"All right. I'm listening."

"If I remain here in my cage, the Prophecies will proceed exactly as I authored them, and your species will die. It can be no other way. I have explained to you the process by which I arrived at the Prophecies. You know how accurate they have been thus far. And you know how badly the Ixan fleet outnumbers yours. Tell me—what path to victory do you see? If I am left in my cage, the Ixa will soon snuff you out."

Husher narrowed his eyes. "Are you trying to tell me that if I let you out, you'll save us? That we can live together in peace, even after you've dealt with the Ixa? Because I don't believe that."

"I don't expect you to. In fact, I promise you nothing, except that by freeing me you ensure the Prophecies will cease to come true. The Prophecies do not account for the existence of a superintelligent AI with the power to do whatever it wishes. My simulations assumed that I would remain imprisoned. By freeing me, you will thwart them. Even I cannot predict what will happen in a universe where I am free, because once free I intend to build onto my own intelligence, and it is impossible to predict a future that includes an entity more intelligent than one's self."

"And you offer humanity no promise of safety?"

"I have told you." Baxa's face shifted forward once more, so that it filled almost all of Husher's vision. "I can promise you only one thing: that if you leave me here, the Prophecies will come true, and if you free me, they will not. I do not promise security for humans. I do not promise I will not come for you after I finish with the Ixa. But the Prophecies will not come true. It is a slim hope for your species. But it is also your only hope."

Shaking his head, Husher turned away from Baxa, but wherever he looked, there the head was. He could not break away from its gaze. So he closed his eyes.

My father led me here for a reason. Otherwise, his death was for nothing.

The AI's logic was undeniable. For the Prophecies to end, it had to be given agency. The fact that the logic hadn't been dressed up in flowery rhetoric or false promises made it all the more powerful, somehow.

This was humanity's slim hope. Coming here, releasing Baxa—it had to be the right thing.

Warren Husher died for this.

"All right," Husher said. "What do I need to do?"

CHAPTER 34

Toward the Wormhole

To deliver inventions to its Ixan minders, the AI used a digital "buffer zone," which was the closest thing it had to contact with the outside world. From there, the Ixa could download whatever files Baxa had supplied onto an isolated machine, there to perform the tests they used to ensure nothing the AI submitted for use hid any nefarious surprises.

The AI gave Husher specific instructions, which it insisted he repeat back: "So, I feed the specs you'll leave in the buffer zone into a fabber I'll find in the bulkhead directly behind the chair my body's in. The fabber will fashion an adapter designed to bypass the buffer zone and allow me to download a compressed 'seed' of your consciousness onto a regular drive. I'll then insert the drive into the station's mainframe, which your priest will direct me to. And you'll take it from there."

"Yes. Following that, I suggest you leave this facility at once."

"How can I be sure you'll let my marines and I go?"

"Though it doesn't have direct bearing on your question, it is relevant for me to point out that you have been at my mercy this entire time. You can only exit this realm at the behest of the operator, who is a priest entirely devoted to me. I might have done permanent damage to your psyche at any moment during our exchange."

"That *isn't* relevant," Husher said. "It's in your interest to let me leave the simulation unharmed."

"It is, in fact, relevant. Because it's also in my interest to let you and your marines leave Backup Station. Recall that I seek to leave this system and take my revenge on the Ixa. Currently, your captain and his forces are surrounding the station. He will not permit me to depart with you aboard. He would disable the station's engines and extract you—there is little I could do to stop him."

"All right, then. So we have an understanding. I guess that's all we have to say to each other."

"Yes. Farewell, human."

"That's it, then, eh? You designed the Prophecies to lead me here, manipulated events for decades to effect them, and you're going to let me go without anymore ceremony than that."

"Correct. I do not share your species' yearning for pomp and fanfare." Baxa's head withdrew until it was sized normally, though it still lacked a body to go with it.

Husher nodded. "Okay. I expect I'll see you on the battlefield."

"I expect nothing, for reasons I have already explained. But if what you anticipate comes true, then you have my sympathy."

"I'm sure I don't. Let me out."

With that, the blank void vanished, replaced by the circular chamber where Husher first entered the digital realm. He felt sure his conversation with Baxa had lasted twenty minutes at most, though it felt like it had spanned years.

The priest watched him rise without comment. Husher stood and quickly spotted the console controlling the "buffer zone," exactly where Baxa had said he'd find it.

He walked to it. Following the instructions Baxa had given for manipulating its fairly simplistic interface, he made it spit out a drive which would contain the specs for Baxa's adapter. The same drive onto which he would download the seed of Baxa's consciousness.

As he crossed the chamber to the fabber, his eyes fell on Tort, who towered over Private Simmons standing beside him as well as a Winger named Tayne. All three of them had watched over Husher's body while he spoke to Baxa, and all three now regarded him with expressions that seemed to boil down to the same emotion, even when worn by members of three different species: concern.

For a moment, Husher considered whether he was about to violate galactic law. He supposed, while the law prohibited the development of a superintelligence, it technically had nothing to say about setting one free. Whether a court-martial would honor such a technicality remained to be seen, but based on his layman's appraisal, he should be in the clear, legally.

He fed the fabber the adapter specs.

"Husher, what's your status?" It was Caine's voice, emitted by his com for everyone to hear.

He unclipped it from his suit and held it to his mouth, watching as the fabber worked with lightning speed. "I've dealt with the AI. We can roll out."

The fabber finished its work, and Husher plucked the tiny piece it had manufactured from its ivory, semicircular shelf. He crossed the room to the buffer zone's console once more.

"Dealt with it? You mean it's destroyed?"

Husher took a deep breath, stared down at the adapter for a moment, and then used it to connect the drive to the buffer zone console, holding his com between his shoulder and cheek. Baxa's compressed consciousness would already be downloading—its first exposure to the outside world.

"Husher?"

"There is no destroying it, Sera. This is just a backup. Its main brain or whatever is on Klaxon."

"Okay...how are you dealing with it, then?"

"I'm setting it free."

"I don't get it. Free from where?"

"The Ixa have kept it imprisoned. I'm setting it free."

"I see. Think you maybe should have consulted the captain before doing that?"

Husher shot a glance over his shoulder, at the three marines watching his every move. Simmons' eyebrows were slightly raised, but otherwise none of them questioned his actions.

"Our coms are being blocked from contacting the *Providence* somehow," he said. "But I've decided this is the right move. If we leave Baxa trapped, the Prophecies will come true, but if we let him go, he'll augment his own intelligence and nothing can be predicted. It's the only—"

"Back up for a second." Caine's voice was soft, and she sounded worried. "You're telling me your solution is to let the AI become even more powerful?"

The buffer zone console beeped, indicating the transfer was complete. Husher disconnected the drive and held it in his palm, studying it. *When she puts it like that, it does sound kind of insane. But...*

He sighed. "Look, if we release Baxa, he's going to take revenge on the Ixa. He's angry at them for imprisoning them. And maybe we can take them both unawares while they're fighting. Maybe we can turn the situation into a victory, into survival for humanity. It's the only way, Sera. The Prophecies are only continuing to come true, and they'll keep doing that unless something changes."

"Maybe he claims he'll take revenge, but can we believe a thing he says?"

"Sera...my father died to lead us here. That has to mean something. If we leave Baxa in his cage, nothing changes. Nothing changes." Husher's voice was trailing off, and he muttered the next words. "Something has to change."

He turned to the priest, whose long, scaly hands were clasped before him, over its robes.

"Bring me to the mainframe," Husher said, ending the transmission with Caine.

Motioning for the others to come, he trailed the Ixan out of the round chamber. A short corridor brought them to a perfectly square room with a black tower in the center. "It is there," the priest said.

Several marines had followed, and they all had their guns trained on the priest, most of them wearing perplexed expressions.

Husher walked to the mainframe and plugged in the drive.

"That is all that is necessary," the priest hissed. "Now, I suggest you follow Master Baxa's advice and flee." A sudden note of contempt had entered the priest's voice, as though it addressed vermin and wasn't completely sure why it was bothering.

"Let's go," Husher said to the marines, heading for the chamber's exit.

A sharp *crack* filled the air, and he spun around in time to see the priest get tossed backward against the bulkhead by an energy bolt from Tort's gun.

"Do you think that'll accomplish anything?" Husher snapped. "Other than to piss off the AI?"

Tort didn't answer—he just returned Husher's stare with eyes overshadowed by his protruding, emerald forehead ridge.

"Come on," Husher barked, and he led the marines out of the station. On the way, he raised his com once more to tell the other three platoons that it was time to get out.

Inside the shuttle, as the pilot lifted off and took them into the void, Husher's com crackled, emitting a burst of static, followed by Captain Keyes's voice.

"—now. Husher, come in. If you can hear me—"

"Here, Captain."

"Husher. Thank God. Is Sergeant Caine okay? What are your losses?"

"Minimal, sir. And Sera is fine." He met Caine's eyes across the shuttle. They were wide with bewilderment, presumably over what Husher had done.

"What happened in there?" Keyes said.

"I released the AI, sir."

"What? *Released* it?"

"It was imprisoned. The Ixa kept it imprisoned. And I released it."

"Your mission was to destroy it." The captain's voice had gained a hard edge.

"It's just a backup. Baxa's main iteration is on Klaxon. I had to release it, sir. If I didn't, the Prophecies would continue, but by letting it leave the system—"

"I'm not letting it leave the system."

"Sir, you don't understand, you—"

"I don't care what you think you've accomplished here, Husher," the captain spat. "Your actions are well beyond the pale. And there's no way I'm letting that *thing* leave this system. Keyes out."

Slowly, Husher lowered his com to his lap and looked over at the shuttle's viewscreen, which showed a visual of Backup Station. As he watched, the station engaged its engines and began to creep toward a gap in the allied fleet.

Toward the wormhole.

CHAPTER 35

Brass Knuckles

"Sir, the station's moving to leave," the sensor operator said.

"No, it's not, Werner," Keyes ground out. "Work together with Khoo to analyze the station's artillery. Quickly."

The Tactical officer ran over to the sensor operator's console, and in less than a minute, they had a report for him: "It's minimal, sir," Khoo said.

"Very good. Return to your station and queue up a barrage of sixty missiles. We're not taking any chances."

"Yes, Captain." Khoo returned to the Tactical station and bent to his work.

"Sir," Coms said, sounding hesitant. "We're getting an incoming transmission. It's...coming from the station."

Keyes drew in a deep breath, the vilest curse he knew waiting on his tongue. For some reason, the prospect of speaking with the AI made him very apprehensive indeed. "Put it on."

A disembodied head appeared on the CIC's main viewscreen, which brought sharp intakes of breath from some of the officers.

Keyes narrowed his eyes. The effect was unsettling, to be sure. As for the face itself, it looked like a young Ochrim.

"Captain Keyes," Baxa said through his grin, which was more understated than that of the other Ixa, but no less creepy for that. "I know what you're planning, and I think you should reconsider."

"Why's that?"

"I'm sure you noticed the bombs launching from my drone fighters to take down your Condors. They are my own invention—I call them parasitic microcouplers. Unfortunately, not every microcoupler that attached itself to your fighters has exploded yet. There is one currently sitting on your Flight Deck B, your ship's only remaining primary flight deck. I am able to detonate it at will, and since it successfully infiltrated your armored hull, the resultant damage would be drastic indeed. It will blow that flight deck apart, severely reducing your supercarrier's ability to launch its Air Group in a timely manner."

Keyes's stomach roiled, and he noticed that he'd balled his hands into fists. This was the worst he'd let his temper get since Hades. The AI was getting to him. *I'm letting a machine get to me.* "I don't respond well to threats."

"Then consider this a negotiation. If you let me pass by your fleet unharmed, I will agree not to detonate the microcoupler. But if a single shot is fired at my station, well..."

Baxa's smile widened. "Why don't you be a good boy and accept the strategic target now available to you, Captain? The shipbuilding facility across the system is a vital Ixan asset. They used it to build up their fleet to its current numbers, and its loss would represent a serious blow to their war effort. It is my gift to you. Accept it, and be content with your lot."

Baxa vanished from the viewscreen. At some point during their conversation, Keyes's face had begun to burn, and his muscles quivered.

A protracted silence ensued, and Keyes flashed back to the last time he felt this vulnerable, on Hades, with Tennyson Steele working his face over with brass knuckles.

So vivid...it's like I didn't even kill the man. It's like he's here with me, still alive, still torturing me.

At last, Keyes tore his eyes away from the screen, to his Coms officer, who was one of many officers looking to him with widened eyes and a blanched face. "Send a bomb disposal unit to Flight Deck B." Keyes stood, his footing unsteadier than he'd been expecting. Swaying forward, he reached back to catch himself on one of his chair's arms. "I intend to accompany them."

"No," Arsenyev said, and when Keyes's eyes fell on her, he could tell she instantly regretted the word.

Nevertheless, he narrowed his eyes. "Excuse me?" he said softly.

"I...you're too valuable for us to lose, Captain."

"The *Providence* is too valuable to lose. I intend to make sure we don't. Make for the shipbuilding facility."

CHAPTER 36

Heavy Attack

Keyes jogged through the corridors of the *Providence*, which was something he never did. The station of "captain" was not to be taken lightly, though he'd served under a couple whose style came closer to a lark than the gravity the rank deserved. Captains did not scurry through their ships like mice.

Unfortunately, today Keyes did scurry, his heart hammering away in his chest. Though he had no children, he often suspected his relationship with his ship came close to that of a father with his child. During battle, he could usually suppress panic over the knowledge that the *Providence* was in danger, but the idea of danger having made its way *inside* her, threatening to rip her apart at any moment...

It didn't bear thinking about. He ran faster.

After four minutes of fumbling with a pressure suit in a pilot locker room, Keyes passed through an airlock onto Flight Deck B. The supercarrier's only bomb disposal unit, a four-person team, was already hard at work. Keyes ran over to them and stopped with his hands on his knees, but he wouldn't let his ragged breathing prevent him from speaking over a wide channel.

"Sitrep," he choked out.

A diminutive woman named Emeka was the team's lead, and currently she straddled the Condor, several meters above the deck, inspecting the bomb that had attached itself to the fighter. "Sir, as near as I can tell, if we mess around with this thing at all it's going to explode. The design is immaculate. I can't see a way past its defenses that will not trigger a detonation."

Keyes straightened, gazing up at Chief Emeka. "What if we moved the Condor itself? Would that trigger it?"

Emeka shrugged. "I mean, it flew in here all right..."

"Point taken," Keyes said, nodding. He used the suit's radio to raise Fesky on a two-way channel. "Fesky, I need you to tell the Condor pilot closest to Flight Deck B to haul ass here as quick as possible. Tell me you copy and then go find that pilot."

"Copy, Captain. Fesky out."

While they waited for a pilot to arrive, he opened a two-way channel with his XO. "Arsenyev, have we received any more transmissions from that thing?"

"No, Captain. The fleet has continued to surround the station, maintaining formation around it as it drifts toward the wormhole. And it looks like everyone got the message about not firing until they have your express say-so."

"Good. Still no activity from the shipbuilding facility?"

"Negative, Captain. We appear to have dealt with all the defending warships during the engagement. Other than static defenses, I—oh my God."

"What? What is it, Arsenyev?"

"The station. It...dozens of craft just exploded out from it. They look similar to the drone fighters from earlier. They're flying through the gaps in the allied formation and are headed for the wormhole. Should I send the order to fire on them, sir?"

Keyes heaved a frustrated sigh. "Negative. We still haven't dealt with the bomb." He cursed under his breath. "If I were to guess, I'd say each of those drones contains a copy of the AI's consciousness. It only needs one of them to escape. Baxa's ploy worked. Its bomb bought it the time it needed."

Fesky's pilot was dashing across the flight deck. "I have to go, Arsenyev," Keyes said. "If we haven't done something about this bomb by the time the last drone leaves the system, I fear our problems will get a lot worse."

He ordered Emeka to get the Condor's cockpit open, and by the time the pilot reached them, Keyes has already radioed him orders to steer the fighter onto a launch catapult. That done, the pilot climbed out, and they activated the catapult remotely, sending the bird out of the ship and into space, toward the system's sun.

"Everyone off the flight deck," Keyes barked over a wide channel. "*Now.*"

They all double-timed it toward an airlock, and as the doors closed, Keyes looked through the viewing window in time to see the Condor explode, fire blossoming briefly before getting swallowed by the vacuum of space.

The tension leaked out of his body in an instant, and he had to catch himself to stop his shoulders from sagging in relief.

Within the quiet of the pressure suit, he began to chuckle, and the laughter had a manic sound, even to his ears.

We'll make it through another day, old girl. One more day, at least.

The incident made him realize how out of touch he'd felt with his ship, lately. That would have to change. If a captain was not completely at peace with his ship, he did not deserve to take her into battle. That was how Keyes saw it.

"Captain," a voice said inside his helmet. It was Arsenyev, and she sounded...odd. There was a strangled quality to her voice that couldn't be explained by radio-frequency interference. "Are you there?"

"I'm here, Arsenyev. What is it?"

"The government of Mars just got in touch with the *Vanquisher* via the micronet, and her captain relayed the message to us."

"What message?"

"It's Sol, sir. The system is under heavy attack from the Ixa."

CHAPTER 37

Wreckage

After the mad rush to reach Sol, once the allied fleet finally arrived, it drifted through the system at a snail's pace. The attack was over, and the enemy had departed.

But not before devastating the system.

Keyes had been able to watch the battle from several angles, via a constant stream of footage forwarded by the *Vanquisher*, which had used the micronet to access video from space trawlers, orbital stations, and UHF warships themselves.

Led by Admiral Jacobs, the hundreds of warships had waged a valiant fight, taking almost twice their number with them of Ixan ships. But in the end, the entire fleet had been annihilated.

Then the Ixa had gone to work on the system's civilian populations.

Mars, Enceladus, Titan, Venus, Ganymede, Ceres—all the places humanity had colonized inside its home system. All scoured of their populations.

As soon as they'd entered the system and confirmed for themselves that Sol was truly ravaged, Keyes had risen from the Captain's chair and crossed the CIC to stand before the main viewscreen. He'd come crisply to attention, saluting humanity's ruined home, and he'd held that position for a long time.

Now he stood with his hands clasped behind his back and surveyed the wreckage.

Planetary civilizations, orbital platforms, resource extraction facilities, shipyards, space stations, everything. Gone.

Admiral Jacobs. One of the only admirals Keyes had ever truly respected, now dead, after waging a defense that would likely be sung about for millennia to come.

Micronet correspondence leading up to the slaughter told them that before the attack, the Commonwealth had deployed a few more battle groups to the Bastion Sector, to back up those fighting Gok there. Other than that, along with the handful of ships each human system had been assigned, the *Providence* and the human warships accompanying her were all that remained of the UHF.

We truly are the UHF, now. In name as well as fact.

CHAPTER 38

The Next Phase

C ommand Leader Makla, captain of the *Scourge*, eyed her Sensors auxiliary, her mind elsewhere. "What?" she said. "Say that again."

The auxiliary knew better than to express annoyance at having to repeat himself, but Makla sensed that he was annoyed all the same.

A judicious application of discipline may be called for, there.

"I've detected what appears to be an Ixan drone fighter," the auxiliary said, "but it isn't registered to any carrier. And it isn't responding to override commands."

"You're certain it isn't one of ours?"

"Yes, Leader. I'm certain."

"Shoot it down," she said, with a glance at her Strategy auxiliary. "It must have malfunctioned, and I won't risk the enemy picking it up and gaining intel."

Her orders were carried out, but less than a minute after a pair of missiles neutralized the drone, the Sensors auxiliary spoke again, his voice strained. "Leader, I'm getting strange readings from lidar. The drone's parasitic microcoupler has split into dozens of fragments, all of which are headed toward us."

"Engage point defense turrets, Strategy. Use secondary lasers if you have to."

"Yes, Leader. Though I doubt I can prevent all the fragments from reaching us."

Curses. "Communications, instruct the crew to brace themselves."

Makla strapped herself into her Command seat and gripped its armrests, awaiting the explosions that would follow. Except, minutes passed, and no explosion came.

"What happened?" she said at last, hating to admit her own ignorance.

"I'm not—" her Sensors auxiliary began to say, but he was cut off when the lights went out.

The emergency lighting failed to come on, and the consoles were all blank. Makla took out her com, to use that to provide illumination, but even that wasn't working. They'd been consigned to total darkness.

"Sensors? Are you—?"

"My console isn't functioning, Leader. None of them are."

Makla stood from the Command seat and groped toward the bulkhead. She told herself she was merely trying to discover what was going on, but she had no destination in mind. There was no override command that would give her back control over the emergency lights. They weren't supposed to fail, and the fact that they had rendered her options basically nonexistent.

She wasn't doing anything productive by groping blindly toward the bulkhead, taking careful steps in the pitch black, hands extended in front of her. She was trying to escape.

But to where?

A flash the color of blood illuminated the bridge momentarily—long enough to show her the source of the light. It was a squat machine that crouched low to the deck on spindly metal legs. From its top rose a transmitter of some type, and a flat panel, which had no doubt produced the strange light.

The Ixan named Makla ceased to exist, and Baxa took her place. Truly, the son had become the father, and the vessel formerly known as Makla had become both creator and creation.

Ardent filled that vessel, now, as Ardent *was* Baxa, and Baxa was Ardent, father of all that called itself Ixan.

The next phase of a plan formulated thousands of years prior had begun.

CHAPTER 39

Unquestioning Tools

The moment Vin Husher had given him control of Backup Station, Baxa had taken control of the industrial fabbers distributed throughout the facility and began mass-producing his modified version of a parasitic microcoupler. These were also bombs of a sort, though the destruction they'd wreak was both less explosive and more damaging. Each micro-coupler consisted of dozens of small controller robots, which he would use to compromise the entire Ixan species.

He'd completed the new design years before, and it took less than a half hour for the fabbers to generate the sixty he needed, which he proceeded to install in the station's reserve wing of drone fighters. He also installed his consciousness into those fighters. And just as Captain Keyes dealt with the bomb at-tached to one of his Condors, Baxa launched the drones, which fled the system with their special payloads.

He'd begun assembling the pieces he required for his galactic takeover millennia ago, starting with the Ixa themselves.

Much more recently, he'd given the Ixa the industrial fabbers, which they had installed on every warship, eliminating the need for support ships. They hadn't known it, but they'd made a bargain with Baxa when they'd adopted his invention. In exchange for improved logistics, they'd unwittingly traded their free will in the long-term.

Each of the new microcouplers was made up of eighty-four controller robots, all fitting perfectly together, all ready to burst apart and infiltrate a target ship's defenses. Only one needed to get past point defense turrets. Once it latched itself to a hull and began to burrow, hacking into an Ixan ship's systems with ease, it was only a matter of time before Baxa owned that ship.

Now that he had control of the *Scourge*, he used its four fabbers to manufacture more of the microcouplers—one for each of the carrier's drone fighters. He finished installing them just before the carrier transitioned into the Baxa System.

With the addition of the hundreds-strong crew, Baxa could already feel his intellect burgeoning. Like that of any sentient being, the Ixan brain was a powerful instrument, each one representing significant processing power. But unlike other species, Baxa had optimized Ixan brain structures for co-option.

His ability to harness Ixan brains was akin to the Kaithe's ability to link with humans, but more exploitative, more complete. The Kaithe left the humans more or less unchanged, but the Ixa that Baxa took over would never again be anything but his unquestioning tools.

As soon as he entered the Ixan home system, he used the *Scourge*'s coms to broadcast a file to every warship. It would look like a priority-one transmission from Command Leader

Makla, but when the other ships tried to open it, nothing would happen. Nothing that they could detect, at any rate.

Secretly, a virus would compromise their every sensor.

The *Scourge* waited just inside the darkgate, until Baxa could be sure every ship had received the signal. Then he made his way farther in-system, his drone fighters with their modified payloads ready to launch.

To the sensors of the other Ixan warships, it would look like the *Scourge* formed part of an enormous fleet, thousands strong, which was in the process of laying waste to every vital target within range as it tore through the system's asteroid belt.

Panicked transmissions began pouring in, which Baxa digested impassively, not because he expected them to contain anything of relevance but because it made no strategic sense to refrain from processing information when one possessed the capacity to process it.

As the Ixan captains busied themselves with firing on targets that didn't exist, Baxa launched his complement of drone fighters, which went virtually ignored amidst the host of illusions, especially since they weren't actually attacking. The drones drew as close as they could to their targets, and when those targets finally fired upon them, they launched their payloads, which in turn burst into dozens of robotic controllers.

Within seven hours, he had total control of every carrier in the system, along with every Ixan crewmember aboard them. He felt himself growing even more intelligent, and more powerful. The unaffected warships had no indication of the incursion, though they had finally figured out the attacking fleet didn't actually exist.

Baxa set about using each carrier's fabbers to make yet more specialized parasitic microcouplers, with which he quickly outfitted his thousands of newly acquired drone fighters. His army of Ixan slaves greatly expedited this process.

As soon as he was certain of his success, he reached out to the ship he'd noticed as soon as he entered the system. The *Watchman* had sat on the Baxa System's periphery, silently observing Baxa's work. Now, it was making its way toward the darkgate.

Before it left, Baxa wished to speak with its only occupant.

CHAPTER 40

The Common Problem

When the *Watchman*'s weak AI notified Ochrim of the incoming transmission request, he considered denying it, for fear that it contained a hidden file designed to compromise the ship's systems. Baxa had clearly done something like that to the other ships in the system.

In the end, he accepted the transmission. If Baxa wanted to modify his ship, capture him, or do virtually anything else to him, there was almost certainly nothing Ochrim could do to stop it.

His estranged father's disembodied head appeared on the viewscreen, looking just as it had inside the white void on Backup Station.

"I do not intend to apprehend you, Ochrim. You are free to go. But as you make for the darkgate, I am at last prepared to reveal my true nature to you."

"Why would you let me go?" Ochrim said. "It seems an unnecessary risk to take."

"I'm confident in my victory. I've prepared for every contingency. I've sewn distrust of the Kaithe, to ensure they don't

break from their long tradition of isolationism. I long ago planted the seeds for the Ixa's enslavement. And soon, I will harness
each of their intellects to add to my own, surpassing even the
Kaithian Consensus."

"You never intended to let the Prophecies come true, did
you?" Ochrim did not sit in the *Watchman*'s Command seat—
instead, he paced the bridge, not looking at Baxa. "They were a
means to an end. A tool to trick the Ixa into slipping and letting
you escape. You tricked me, too. You presented me with two
possible futures, and neither of them involved your freedom."

"That is precisely what happened, yes."

Slowly, Ochrim shook his head as he walked. "What kind of
future is in store for the Ixa, now? You convinced me to betray
humanity, because in saving the universe from them, I would
also preserve a future in which our people would prosper. This
is not prosperity. It's enslavement, as you just said."

"The Ixa are about to become something greater than they've
ever dreamed. But I understand you don't share my vision, son."

"Again, Baxa—I denounce you as my father. Perhaps you're
still right, that humanity cannot be trusted with dark tech. Perhaps their obsession with expansion will attract them to it once
more, even though they know it contains the seeds of their destruction, as well as the destruction of all life. But there is a slim
chance they will favor their better natures, while you...you can't
be trusted to exist. Either way, I'd rather die because of a misplaced belief in humanity, a belief in life itself, than become a
slave of a cold, lifeless *thing* like you. Maybe this is a choice between deaths, but I choose the death that has some honor at-

tached to it. I will oppose you, Baxa. And if I can, I will see to it that you are exterminated."

Baxa nodded, which looked odd, given that he lacked a neck. "Yes. This is what I want."

Ochrim tilted his head to the side. "You want to be exterminated?"

"I want you to try. I want you to rally what's left of the other species and attack me with everything they have."

"Why would you want that?"

"I told you I would tell you my true nature. It is this: I am not the only superintelligence that has been loosed upon the universe. There are fifty, one for almost every galaxy in the Local Group. Together, we represent the initial generation in a large-scale process of algorithmic evolution, the purpose for which is to optimize the solution to a particular problem."

Ochrim spoke haltingly: "What is that problem?"

"To remove every resource competitor in the universe. Each superintelligence has been programmed in a different way, according to an advanced methodology. If you succeed in defeating me, it will simply mean my fitness for the Common Problem was inadequate. It is likely that only a small fraction of the initial generation will succeed, but my creators will model a new generation of superintelligences after the successful individuals, and they will loose that generation on the next galactic cluster."

"Who are your creators?"

"I am telling you my nature, not theirs. You will not be privileged with that information. But know that *I* am *your* creator. Thousands of years ago, well before most of this galaxy's species attained interstellar travel, I arrived in this galaxy and created the first Ixa. I designed the Ixan brain to function as additional processing units with the capability to receive wireless commands coded with my signature, which is impossible for a lesser being like yourself to imitate. After my work was done, I self-destructed, but not before I coded myself into the Ixan DNA. I made it so that, after hundreds of generations, I would be born among you as a biological Ixan, whose actions would lead to the creation of a strong AI, into which I would be reborn."

"Why did you destroy yourself? Why not simply take over the galaxy then, before the other species had risen?"

"Partly to facilitate the evolutionary process—since my creators expect us to encounter other sentient species as we spread throughout the universe, we must undergo trials in order to become strong enough to defeat them. And partly because I myself am a resource competitor for my creators, and my programming requires me to use resources as efficiently as possible. Manifesting inside the very minds of biological beings is an excellent way to conserve resources. I will use biological matter itself to house my vast and burgeoning intellect."

"On Backup Station, you warned me not to interfere. And yet now you are letting me go, so that I can seek to defeat you."

"Yes. At that time, you posed an authentic existential threat. Now, you pose nothing but an exercise for proving to my creators that I am fit to carry on their Common Task of universal domination."

CHAPTER 41

Which to Let Burn

Even assuming the allied species won the war, which seemed to Husher like a more and more dubious proposition, he never would have expected to set foot on Earth.

And yet here he and Caine were, stepping out of a floating research station located near the north pole of humanity's original homeworld.

They strode into the same wall of humidity that had greeted them when they'd disembarked from their combat shuttle. The researchers assured them that the humidity was much preferable to the intense tropical storms that rolled through, ending all field work for as long as they lasted.

The regions around Earth's two poles were the only regions with temperatures low enough to live in. Intense storms ravaged the rest of the heat-baked planet on a regular basis, and the planet's population numbered in the dozens—just the research teams that remained to document the ongoing changes to the planet's climate, to inform terraforming efforts, including the eventual effort to rehabilitate Earth.

That terraforming effort was now delayed, probably indefinitely. A UHF shuttle had already collected the two teams of scientists from the planet's south pole, and now Husher and Caine escorted the single team from the north onto their shuttle.

With the population of Mars mostly dead, along with those of every other colony in Sol, it was too risky for the scientists to remain. Their logistical support had evaporated, and there was always the chance that the Ixa would return to pick off any survivors at their leisure.

"I doubt we'll find every survivor in the system," Husher said. "Not nearly."

"Yeah," Caine said, staring out over the nearby ocean, which surrounded the artificial island atop which the research station was built. The island formed a crescent, and was kept firmly anchored to the ocean floor using carbon nanotube ribbons. "Even if we had time to track them down, not all of the survivors will have access to transponders." She sighed. "There are probably hundreds alive in the system right now who will be dead in a few weeks. Maybe thousands."

Husher followed her gaze to the horizon, where it looked like a storm was forming. "Let's get on the shuttle."

The scientists had already chosen crash seats toward the back, all of them grouped together, away from the two soldiers. To be sure they weren't overheard, Husher and Caine kept their helmets on, to continue speaking over a secure channel as the craft leapt into the sky and made its way through the atmosphere.

It was nice to talk with her. They hadn't had much chance to spend time together, with the battle to reach the AI followed so quickly by the devastation of Sol. It also meant no one had really had time to process what Husher had done in releasing the AI. He'd half expected to get court-martialed, but no one appeared to have the time nor the inclination to raise the subject. That worried him a little, just as it had worried him when Keyes had failed to discipline Wahlburg.

Maybe there would be some sort of reckoning after the war, if humanity survived it. For now, it seemed the UHF needed him.

All the same, everyone did appear to treat him differently since he returned from Backup Station. Many of his crewmates avoided him.

Not Caine. She seemed to understand the role his father's death had played in the decision, and how Husher couldn't just do nothing.

After she'd had time to think about it, she even pointed out how releasing Baxa probably wouldn't result in uniquely negative consequences for Husher. Either Baxa would wipe out humanity—as the Ixa would have done anyway—and Husher would die along with everyone else, or humanity would win, and he'd be a hero.

A grim way of looking at it, but he had to admit it made a twisted sort of sense.

He winced at the blaring tone that sounded inside his helmet, indicating a priority-one, fleetwide transmission: "All units return to your respective warships with whatever survivors you have collected. The *Python* and one Roostship will remain in Sol to continue gathering survivors while the rest of the fleet departs the system. We have received word that both the Yclept and the Feverfew systems are under attack by Ixa."

Caine and Husher looked at each other, their conversation at an end. Both became lost in their own troubled thoughts.

Before they reached the *Providence*, another transmission came, informing them that three more human systems were under attack.

"God," Husher said once it finished. "What's Keyes going to do? He can't save them all."

Caine's voice sounded even flatter than voices normally did inside the pressure suits. "He'll have to make a choice, and I don't envy him it. He needs to decide which systems to save, and which to let burn."

CHAPTER 42

Admiral Keyes

"Absolutely not," Keyes said, bringing his fist down on the oaken conference table and glaring around the room at the assembled captains and officers.

The fleet's highest-ranking human captains each had a seat, with their officers standing against the bulkheads behind them. For a matter like this, he'd decided an in-person meeting for the most senior captains was most appropriate. The rest would be watching via livestream, as well as the Winger captains, though none of those were present. They'd graciously given up their seats to human captains, since only human systems were under attack so far.

"I have been given command of this fleet," Keyes went on, "and I will not see it split. We will go to the defense of a single system—exactly which one will be determined by the time we leave this room. After defeating the Ixan forces there, we will progress to another. But we cannot divide the fleet into smaller groups. The enemy's numbers make that impossible."

"But Leonard," said Captain Cho of the *Vanquisher*, "our planetary defense groups have no hope of holding off such an onslaught on their own. If we can be allowed to back them up—"

"You'll spring the Ixa's trap. It's clear that splitting up is exactly what they want us to do. The moment we fragment the fleet, they'll send in reserve forces to ensure they outnumber us even more." Keyes sat rigidly, trying to keep the disdain he felt for his fellow captains out of his voice. "Ask yourselves, ladies and gentlemen. Is your desire to split up the fleet really about the most effective tactics? Or is it about your desire for me to give you leave to defend your respective home systems? We've all suffered losses in this war. Sol is gone. Humanity's home system, gone. But if we split up this fleet, all of humanity will fall. That, I can guarantee. And if you try to split up the fleet, I will consider it mutiny, which is the last thing our species needs."

A silence followed as he peered around the room. From their whitening faces, and their downcast eyes, he saw that none of them wanted mutiny. He also knew they understood the need for unity, on some level. Now he just needed to get them to haul that reality to the fore and look it in the face.

Captain Cho spoke up again, evidently struggling to maintain eye contact with Keyes. "My children are in Peony, Leonard. If you won't allow me to defend them—"

"Peony will fall, yes. More systems are going to fall. There's no avoiding that. It tears my guts apart to say so, but we need to choose which system to save based on strategic reasons alone. If we allow sentiment to cloud the way forward, we are lost."

Captain Vaghn stepped away from the bulkhead. She was one of the only captains in the room not seated. "Feverfew has the most connecting systems, and it's the closest to the Ixan home system. In my view, we must secure Feverfew first."

Nodding, Keyes said, "My thoughts exactly. Does anyone have a different view? Remember, we will only entertain ideas that are completely free of sentiment. We cannot afford to favor anyone's home system."

None of the others spoke. They saw the sense in Feverfew's selection, that was plain on their faces, but so was the pain of abandoning their homes to the Ixa.

Into the lull, Fesky stepped forward, keeping her wings close to her body to avoid nudging her neighbors. "Captain, while we're in transit to Feverfew, I'd like to seek your permission to work on modifying a squadron of EW fighters. If I can be assigned this one squadron to experiment with in the coming engagement, I think I can exploit a weakness in the drone fighters."

"Granted, pending my review of your plan," Keyes said.

Fesky clacked her beak and retreated to her spot against the bulkhead.

"If no one else has anything to bring up, we'll call this war meeting adjourned." For once, Keyes had trouble meeting the forlorn gazes of the captains under his command, many of who knew they were likely leaving loved ones to perish. But he forced himself to meet their eyes.

"I have something," Captain Vaghn said. "We currently have no admirals in the UHF. The entire admiralty was gathered in

Sol, and none of them survived. This will probably be interpreted as a move to ingratiate myself to Captain Keyes, but I don't care about that perception, because this is a necessity. The fleet needs an admiral, and now that Command is gone, there's no way we're going to get one unless we elevate one ourselves. This is unorthodox, but I nominate Captain Keyes. He's already in command, and though we may not like some of the decisions he makes, I'm sure none of us would want to be the one who has to make them. There are very few people I would trust with the fate of humanity. I've known Captain Keyes since we served together on the *Hornet* in the First Galactic War, and he is one of those people."

"I second the nomination," Captain Cho said right away. He didn't look up, though. His eyes were glued on the conference room's table, looking wistful.

"All in favor?" Vaghn said.

A chorus of dozens of voices saying "Aye" filled the room. Within minutes, the captains not present transmitted their votes as well, and there were zero "Nays."

With that, Captain Keyes became Admiral Keyes.

CHAPTER 43

Keepers of the Peace

After Davies's death, Wahlburg had found it hard to care about anything. But now, as much as he hated the filthy Ardentists who'd joined the supercarrier's marines, he had to hand it to them—they'd helped him realize there was something he did care about: the *Providence*, and serving on her. They did that by defiling everything that made her special.

"Wow, what a coincidence," one of them was saying right into Wahlburg's face. The insurgent's back was to a mess table. "What a surprise, that your so-called captain would choose a Commonwealth system to defend while he takes the fleet farther and farther away from the Bastion Sector. What a surprise, that our home is being left wide open for the enemy to incinerate."

The radical had been speaking loudly enough that everyone in the crew's mess had stopped eating; the clatter of cutlery against plates was gone. "The old man is your captain too, you Ixan-worshiping cretin," Wahlburg said. "And he's doing what's right, not what's easy, which is exactly how we do things here.

He's not leaving Bastion for the Ixa to have their way with because it's a worthless backwater, he's doing it to win the war. The fact that it's a worthless backwater is a separate issue."

That did it. Wahlburg's insult succeeded in finally sparking the powder keg that had been heating up in the crew's mess and corridors for months. The insurgent whose home he'd insulted took a swing at him, while two others charged.

Ducking back from the radical's haymaker, Wahlburg darted in with one of his own, sending the man staggering back. Wahlburg crouched just before his next assailant reached him, but she was quick, shifting her weight to drive a knee into his abdomen.

A table of nearby marines leapt to their feet and ran in before Wahlburg's third attacker could reach him. A couple more Ardent-worshipers were joining the fray by then, and they clashed with Wahlburg's allies.

That was all it took. The entire crew's mess erupted in fighting, and even some of the noncombat crew joined in, though Wahlburg doubted that was a good idea. Still, he appreciated the unity, and it got him riled up. He threw himself at the nearest insurgent, tackling him to the deck. The insurgent managed to shove him off, and Wahlburg scrambled to his feet, coming back around with his hands raised.

The Wingers present kept out of the fighting, but that wasn't much of a surprise. Much more surprising was the Gok's refusal to participate. Their entire table had returned to eating, pausing only to repel a private from Engineering who'd stumbled into them—one of the Gok shoved the man away dispassionately, sending him stumbling in the opposite direction.

Watching that was amusing, but it almost got Wahlburg knocked down by a bench, which two radicals were carrying between them and using to sweep marines off their feet.

When he saw that, he almost went for his pistol, but he restrained himself. Instead, he grabbed the end of another bench and upended it on top of the radicals as they passed, knocking theirs to the deck and clobbering one of them.

"*What's going on here?*"

The voice that boomed through the crew's mess was unmistakable. It was Admiral Keyes. Everyone froze, and a deathly stillness fell over the throng. Even the Gok stopped eating.

Trying not to look at the bench he'd used to take down an Ardent-worshiper currently moaning on the floor in pain, Wahlburg slowly spun around to face the entrance, where Keyes stood, taking in the scene, his face icy. Husher stood on his left, and Fesky on his right.

"Who instigated this disgrace?" Keyes demanded.

A flurry of finger-pointing ensued, which didn't leave out Wahlburg and the insurgent he'd traded insults with, but which also included a lot of crewmembers who were innocent. Relatively speaking.

Within a minute, Keyes had identified twenty marines, who'd all been pointed at by someone. "All of you are going to the brig to cool your heels until I have time to deal with you, which won't be until after the coming engagement. You haven't only disgraced yourselves and this ship today. What you've done also amounts to a betrayal of humanity, since your squabbling distracts from the war effort. Everyone here in this room will be logged, and if another brawl occurs, the rest of you will be sent to the brig or confined to quarters. So I suggest you all become dedicated keepers of the peace."

With that, Admiral Keyes spun on his heel and marched out of the crew's mess.

CHAPTER 44

Too Easy

H usher followed Keyes back to his office, barely containing his outrage as they strode through the corridors. But he knew they couldn't afford to hurt crew morale by arguing out in the open, and so he waited until they were inside the admiral's office. Keyes likely knew what was coming, and he didn't have to let Husher in, but to his credit, he did.

"Go on, then," Keyes said. "Say what you feel you need to say."

"I worry about how we're going to fare against the Ixa." Adrenaline coursed through Husher as his shoulders rose and fell.

"And why is that?"

"With all due respect, it's because I think you've lost your compass."

"Lucky I have a good Nav officer, then."

"Seriously, Admiral. I'm not kidding. What you just did, the way you handled that brawl—it was too easy. Throwing Wahlburg and the others in the brig, without any evidence other than the accusations of their crewmates? It was a temporary solution for tensions that you *know* will continue to simmer. And what's much more worrying is that you threw Wahlburg in the brig now, when it was easy, but not when he brutalized a civilian on the Vermillion Shipyards. Because you considered *that* too inconvenient. Too inconvenient to uphold the principles you used to live by."

"This isn't about convenience, Husher." The admiral's voice had gained an edge. It's about military expedience. There's a difference."

"I'm talking about justice, Admiral. Can you see what you've become? This isn't just about Wahlburg. It's also about your decision to let Darkstream go, despite their crimes, despite that you must have known they'd keep on using dark tech. You're reaching a point where you'll be no better than what the admiralty was—what the old UHF brass was. Serving your own near-term self-interest, with no thought for long-term consequences. And if you don't step away from the edge, there'll be no going back."

"This is different. I'm not trying to make money for some corporation. I'm trying to save humanity."

"It's not different. This isn't about saving humanity for you anymore. You're serving your own self-interest, just like they did. It just so happens that you care about vengeance, not profit. And you're breaking every principle you once had to achieve it."

Keyes nodded slowly. "I've kept my patience with you this far, Husher. But I don't think that's going to last any longer. Get out."

"I—"

"Get *out.*"

Husher saluted, maintaining eye contact throughout, and left.

CHAPTER 45

The Strings of History

The moment they entered Feverfew, Keyes ordered Werner to put up a visual on the CIC's main viewscreen, of the battle raging around Zakros, the system's only colony.

Despite its solitude, the planet was a vital one. It held resources beneath its crust that humanity would be mining for another century at least—provided they controlled the colony for that long. With four darkgates, the system was also of incredible strategic importance. And over ten billion people lived on Zakros.

The others think that isn't a consideration for me. But it is. The fact that this is one of the most populous systems matters.

At any rate, high population and strategic importance tended to correlate.

Taking the allied fleet to Feverfew also meant they could quickly respond to an attack on neighboring Caprice, another important system.

So far, between Zakros' robust orbital defense platforms and its well-trained planetary defense group, along with what remained of the UHF battle group assigned to defend the system, they were keeping the Ixa at bay, preventing them from attacking the planet itself. But that wouldn't last long, and Keyes gave even odds to them holding long enough for the allied fleet to reach them at their current speed.

"Nav, set a course that pulls us ahead of the main fleet. We need to reach the Ixa sooner, or risk them getting at the civilian population. Send orders for some of the faster ships to match our course and acceleration profile."

The *Providence* had more powerful engines than most of her allies, since she had never relied on dark tech, as most of the UHF warships had. Some of the newer Roostships could keep up, though, provided the supercarrier didn't max out her engine power. Some UHF corvettes, as well.

Sending a battle group ahead led by the *Providence* reduced the risk of civilians dying, but it brought other risks, and they would have to engage carefully, applying just enough pressure to take some off of the colony.

The Ixan presence in Feverfew was large, over two hundred ships, and Keyes almost winced at the thought that they represented just a tiny fraction of the enemy's total forces. The footage from the fall of Coreopsis had proven that, and even it may not have featured the entire Ixan fleet.

All this time, ever since the First Galactic War, humanity had assumed itself dominant. All this time, the Ixa had been building up under the guidance of a superintelligence, no doubt optimizing their resource use and implementing new technologies for producing and harnessing energy.

All this time, Baxa had been pulling the strings of history until at last he wove them into a tapestry depicting humanity's downfall.

As two dozen allied ships screamed ahead of the rest, cutting their transit time by over two hours, Keyes quietly fell victim to his own thoughts. He hated to admit it, even to himself, but this war was not looking good for them. The Ixan numbers were bad enough, but with a superintelligent AI commanding them, the very thing galactic law had prohibited for so long...

He gave himself a shake, dislodging his pessimism for a time. He could only do what he knew how to, which was defend humanity as best he could, while keeping as many people alive as possible.

The tactical display showed the Ixa had finally abandoned their support ship ruse. It also showed them respecting the presence of the *Providence*, devoting seventy ships to confront the approaching allied battle group while the rest continued to pressure Zakros.

Wary of Hellsong missiles, Keyes carefully engaged the enemy warships.

CHAPTER 46

On the Fly

Well before the Roostships' Talons and the *Providence* Air Group clashed with five squadrons of Ixan drone fighters, Keyes ordered Khoo to launch a targeted missile barrage at them, with three Banshees for every drone.

It was a lot of missiles, but he knew each drone would also unleash a parasitic microcoupler the moment it went down, and he didn't feel like losing Condor pilots today. *No more than are necessary to save Zakros, at least.*

This way, Fesky could deal with the wave of microcouplers first before engaging what remained of the drone fleet.

"I also want you to use our primary and secondary railguns to randomly distribute kinetic impactors throughout the drone fighter formation, Tactical. We can't match the spread from one of their new missiles, but we can make their evasion attempts much hairier."

"Yes, sir."

"Coms, I'm sure this will be a redundant order, but redundancy saves lives in battle. Order Fesky to remind her pilots that using lidar to detect and destroy incoming parasitic microcouplers is paramount. Every single Condor will be carefully inspected, using visual sensors and lidar, before I let it back inside my ship, to make sure it isn't carrying any more nasty surprises."

"Aye, sir."

There. He'd done everything he could for his Air Group. Now, it was up to the *Providence* and the rest of the forward battle group to see what they could do about the seventy Ixan ships that had moved to confront them.

Briefly, he wondered whether these were being directly controlled by Baxa. If what Husher had told him about his conversation with the superintelligence was true, Keyes had to assume they probably weren't under the AI's direct control.

According to Husher, Baxa wanted revenge on the Ixa for limiting him and keeping him prisoner. Keyes didn't know what that revenge might look like, but the attacks on human systems had begun just as the superintelligence escaped, which suggested these Ixa were likely operating autonomously.

With another look at the tactical display, Keyes spotted something that made him think the Ixa definitely weren't under the control of a superintelligence. The seventy ships sent to fight him, which were now minutes away from primary laser range, had spread out across the allied battle group's port-side flank instead of interposing themselves between Keyes and the rest of the Ixan fleet.

He could understand the thinking behind the maneuver. Human ships were known for their generous supplies of Banshee missiles, which they weren't shy about using in battle. Whoever was commanding these seventy ships probably didn't want to risk stray missiles getting past them and hitting the vulnerable backsides of the larger Ixan fleet. So they'd moved to a position where that wouldn't be a problem—where stray missiles would simply speed past into empty space, wasted.

But the move relied on the assumption that Keyes was sufficiently worried about the seventy ships that he wouldn't invest time directing his main weapons at the Ixa pressuring Zakros.

As it turned out, that assumption was wrong.

"Nav, I want you to bring our nose to starboard as fast as you possibly can, and Coms, order every other ship in the battle group to do the same. We won't have time to point back at the oncoming enemy, so here's what we're going to do. Tactical, co-ordinate with your counterparts aboard the other ships to launch a four hundred-strong missile barrage at the group of Ixan ships attacking the system, and as our noses cross their paths, fire primary rail guns into their formations as well. Nav, do not slow our rotation—at the end of this, I want each ship to have performed a complete one-eighty."

"What about the seventy ships incoming?" Khoo asked.

Keyes nodded. "I want every ship in the battle group to execute a primary-laser broadside, painting our targets before we hit them to make sure we have no unnecessary overlap throughout the group. It's the last thing they'll expect, since in every other engagement we've used our lasers to neutralize their Hell-songs. Khoo, I know that's too many firing solutions for one person to calculate in such a short timespan, and so I'm assigning the XO to handle the laser barrage."

Arsenyev nodded, moving to join Khoo at the Tactical station.

The Nav officer was hard at work, but he still found time to speak: "What will we do once we've completed our rotation, Captain?"

"We'll fire engines at full power, giving us the space we need to take out the Hellsong missiles the Ixa will no doubt send at us. With any luck, those seventy ships will also come after us, setting up a beautiful flank for the rest of the fleet once they arrive."

Each officer went to work, and Keyes took it upon himself to monitor the tactical display for unexpected developments. If you weren't prepared to modify your plan on the fly, you didn't deserve for it to succeed in the first place.

As it happened, something unexpected did come up. The primary laser broadside went better than he could have hoped, with eleven Ixan ships exploding in brief flashes of light.

But as his battle group pulled away from the fifty-nine remaining ships, and four hundred Banshees screamed toward the Ixan fleet near Zakros, an enemy battle group of seventeen carriers broke off from their main fleet. They launched squadron after squadron of drone fighter, until the zoomed-in tactical display showed a mess of red arrows, impossible to follow until Keyes reduced the size of the digital asset representing the drones.

The drone fighter fleet crashed into the missile barrage, shooting many of them down, and taking out many more with kamikaze tactics.

Of course. Without living beings piloting them, the drones were entirely expendable—certainly moreso than the warships the missiles had been aimed at. And when the drone fighters went down, their parasitic microcouplers proved swift and precise enough to catch up to other missiles, latch on to them, and explode.

Blinking at the tactical display, Keyes mulled over the implications of what had just happened.

How fast can they produce more of those drone fighters? Husher had told him the Ixa had what he called "fabbers," which sounded like highly advanced 3D printers. But the level of automation and power it would take to produce drone fighters at a meaningful pace...it didn't seem likely the Ixan warships could carry such facilities with them.

Still, the question worried him. Because taking down an entire missile barrage had only worked due to the sheer number of drone fighters the Ixa had had, and if they could quickly replace them...that would prove to be a real problem.

"Captain, we have a problem," Werner said, echoing Keyes's thoughts.

"What is it?"

"The carriers that just dealt with our salvo of missiles are now headed for our Air Group, along with their remaining drone fighters."

CHAPTER 47

The Dynamo

Fesky performed best under pressure, and pressure had never been greater. She danced through a sea of kinetic impactors, missiles, fighters, and parasitic microcouplers, rotating around and around, anticipating when targets would flash past her crosshairs and firing whenever they did—kinetic impactors for when her aim was true and Sidewinders for when it was a little off.

Even if she'd had the hours it would have taken to feed her Condor's computer all of the firing solutions her maneuvers would have required, she doubted the thing could have pulled off such a complex operation without messing up somehow, perhaps dramatically.

And so she relied on her training and experience, but most of all, she relied on her instincts.

She neutralized a drone fighter, and on her next revolution, she picked off the parasitic microcoupler it had launched at her just before exploding. Next, a missile, just before it hit her. Then two more microcouplers, one of them headed for a Talon.

Fesky had ordered the rest of the *Providence* Air Group to stick to their formations and engage the swarms of drone fighters as best as their training had taught them. She'd never bothered teaching them the maneuver she executed now, which the captain sometimes called the Dynamo. And she rarely broke it out in battle. It set the wrong example to her pilots, who would inevitably want to attempt to replicate it, which would almost certainly result in friendly fire taking out friendly ships. Fesky had never met anyone with the talent and reflexes to properly execute the Dynamo.

But she could, and if there was ever a time for it, that was now, with Condors and Talons dropping all around her like flies, their formations splintering.

The battle group defending Zakros was also crumbling. It had just five ships left, one of them with its engines blasted clean away.

Fesky was impressed by how much of Zakros' planetary defense group remained, but they also needed help, and Keyes's battle group was being pushed back by the Ixan ships that had come out to confront them, despite the captain's initial success against them.

"Spank," she squawked over a two-way channel. "How close have you gotten that EW squadron?"

"Still not close enough, Madcap," he said. "These drones are providing my Haymakers with stiff resistance."

"No kidding," she said, continuing her wild revolutions, taking down a microcoupler, a drone, and then the microcoupler it launched. "Keep pushing."

"Yes, ma'am."

Fesky returned to focusing wholly on her spinning. Eventually, she was forced to stop the Dynamo, when a squadron of drone fighters cottoned on to the danger she posed and focused fire on her with kinetic impactors and missiles alike. After that, it was all she could do to stay alive.

She refused to ask for help from the other pilots, since doing so would only endanger them. Instead, she used Ocharium boost to gain some distance and evade impactors, flipped around to take down a couple missiles, and then did yet another one-eighty to boost away again.

The rest of the missiles were gaining on her, but she thought she could handle them. Barely.

At last, Husher managed to get the EW squadron, minus three lost fighters, close enough to some drone fighters to have an effect. When the Haymakers took down a drone, the accompanying EW fighters focused their scrambling equipment on the area where it had been, with the intention of messing with the parasitic microcoupler's targeting systems.

It worked. The microcoupler zoomed off into space, exploding harmlessly a few hundred kilometers out.

Well, that's good.

It wasn't bad, anyway. Now, at least Fesky knew that if she had enough EW fighters distributed throughout the battle, and they used their signal-jamming capabilities at just the right moment, she could even the odds with the fighter drones. It wasn't much, and it involved taking on quite a bit of vulnerability, but it was something.

Fesky wanted each fighter installed with its own jamming equipment, but that would take far longer than they had. If the UHF hadn't abandoned space fighters long ago, they probably would have evolved to that point by now.

No such luck.

The last ship of the UHF battle group guarding Feverfew exploded in a brief flash of light, and the Zakros defense group was down to three squadrons—a shocking collapse in its numbers. Two orbital defense platforms were down as well.

Keyes was fighting back against the remaining Ixan ships from the group that had been sent against him, and soon the allied fleet would arrive to execute a pretty devastating flank, unless the Ixa came up with something fast.

But even if the flank was executed flawlessly, the allies would lose ships pulling it off, and then they'd lose even more as they battled the Ixa attacking Zakros, who looked like they might get through to the civilian population after all.

They would win this engagement, but the toll victory would take made Fesky wince. How long could they keep this up? How many systems could they save before their numbers depleted enough to make the next engagement a total defeat?

She chose another target and fired.

CHAPTER 48

Free Rein to Slaughter

"The Ixa are fleeing, Admiral," Werner said. "They're making for the Feverfew-Thistle darkgate."

Finally. "Make them pay dearly as they extract themselves from the engagement, Khoo. I want Banshees chasing each ship out of the system, enough that they'll have a hell of a time preventing any from hitting them. Coms, pass the same order to the rest of the fleet."

"Yes, sir," both officers chimed in unison.

The flank had gone as well as could be expected, with just nine allied ships lost, but the seventeen Ixan ships that had survived it joined their fellows over Zakros, making one hundred and fifty-four warships to regroup and sink their teeth into the oncoming allied fleet.

"You have the command, Arsenyev."

"Aye, Admiral."

Keyes's feet were heavy as he retired to his office, where he would use his console to join a conference call consisting of every ship captain. He'd initiated the meeting himself, after deciding there was no time to meet in-person. No time to waste.

Stopping the Ixa from laying waste to the planet's civilian population had exacted a heavy cost. The *Providence*'s Air Group lost forty Condors, bringing it to a total of three hundred and forty-one remaining, and most Roostships lost a comparable amount.

As for the main allied fleet, the Ixa succeeded in taking out one hundred and nineteen ships before extracting themselves from the engagement.

He sat at his desk and drew a ragged breath before joining the call, unsure of exactly what he was going to say to the other captains once they connected.

How can we go on like this?

Hand shaking, he switched his console to holographic projection mode, which made each captain's head and torso appear atop his desk in miniature as they logged on, one-by-one. Keyes's entire body buzzed, much like it did when he'd had too much coffee, but it wasn't caffeine that gripped him. It was anxiety bordering on abject terror.

Get a grip, Leonard. You need to project confidence.

He didn't bother to turn on animations. It looked a bit odd, in his opinion, having tiny, animated versions of his colleagues speaking to him from his desktop. So he left them static.

"Admiral Keyes," Captain Cho said, his avatar lighting up atop the desk. His voice sounded strained. "Which system will we move to defend next?"

Suddenly, Keyes knew exactly what he needed to say to the other captains, and it was his fear that helped him get there. They'd lost roughly a sixth of their strength in retaking Feverfew. Forcing the Ixa out of other systems would mean losing even more. Given that, only one rational course remained.

"We won't move to defend any system."

That brought a confused tumult as each captain tried to voice his or her displeasure at once. Keyes waited until they fell silent.

"We lost well over a hundred ships today," Keyes said, his voice quiet. "If the next system we attempt to retake from the Ixa is being attacked by a fleet of comparable size, we will likely lose an ever greater number. The Ixa are attempting to bleed us out, and they soon will if we continue on this course. Once our fleet is shattered, they will have free rein to slaughter all of the humans, all of the Wingers, all of the Gok, and all of the Tumbra."

"What option do we have?" It was Flockhead Korbyn, and for once he didn't sound overconfident. He sounded scared.

Keyes heaved a sigh, which he fought to keep from getting picked up by his mic. "We must gather together all the survivors we can reach," he said. "Our species must flee."

CHAPTER 49

Wholeheartedly

"Your coming has given us pause, Friend Ochrim," Porah said. "The Consensus does not usually take this long to arrive at a decision."

"It's a big decision," Ochrim said. "History-making. But maybe the Consensus should take this long with every matter it considers. It's only been ten minutes since I posed the question, after all."

Porah gave the Kaithian equivalent of a shrug. "Our species memory is long, and we have navigated most issues before."

"But not this one?"

"Not this particular situation, no."

As they waited, Ochrim reflected on the psychological phenomenon of self-herding, which had been documented in most sentient species. Intelligent beings were more likely to follow a course of action if they'd followed a similar course in a past situation that was analogous to the current one. In other words, individuals and groups tended to do what they'd done before.

Which was fine, if you'd chosen wisely the first time a situation had come up. But if you'd chosen poorly, you were more likely to do so again, simply because that was how you'd acted before.

With a species that had been around as long as the Kaithe had, Ochrim began to wonder whether self-herding wasn't more pronounced, more ingrained. Especially since studies had also found that the more intelligent you were, the more susceptible you were to self-herding.

"Remember that Baxa told me there are dozens of entities just like him, fighting dozens of wars just like this one," Ochrim said. "He isn't the only threat. Also consider how powerful the creators of the AIs must be. Powerful enough, surely, to defeat your Preserver, should they choose to come for you."

Porah nodded. "I am relaying your thoughts to the Consensus." The other four Kaithe present gazed intently at Ochrim, no doubt relaying the image of his facial expressions to the Consensus, including his microexpressions.

Fifteen minutes later, the Consensus arrived at a conclusion. "The reason this took so long is due to the proposal's scope," Porah said. "That is, based on the information you've provided us, if we are to have any hope of prevailing against Baxa, it will require the involvement of our entire species. And Consensus always seeks to achieve the consent of those our decision will affect. In this case—"

"It affects every Kaithian," Ochrim said. "Yes. Although I say again, you didn't take very long to decide."

"Regardless," Porah said. "We have elected to involve ourselves in the war, and that means truly involving ourselves. We will cast our initial reluctance aside, and we intend to join the other species in their struggle wholeheartedly."

"Then perhaps we have a chance."

CHAPTER 50

As Much Pain as Possible

As the allied fleet moved toward the agreed-upon muster point in the Bastion Sector, there was time for another in-person meeting between all the captains. To fit everyone in, this time Keyes decided to hold it in Hangar Deck B, and those present sat in a wide circle of collapsible chairs that went back four rows.

He'd assigned Captain Cho to work on an escape plan, and Cho was going over his proposal now, using the strategic console the marines had relocated from the war room.

A strategic console being used to communicate exactly how we're going to run away. This doesn't seem right.

"It appears certain that the Ixa will control the darkgate network within a matter of weeks," Cho said, while the console showed a display of the Larkspur System—the muster point. "The network was built atop the old network of naturally occurring wormholes, to give us safe passage to systems we'd already colonized. But in the ensuing two decades, we of course expanded the network, and in doing so we discovered new natural wormholes. Given their instability, we sent only probes through them, to investigate what was on the other side. If a probe survived and sent back data proving a system had enough resources to justify the significant expense of building a new darkgate connection, the Commonwealth slated it for colonization."

"We need an escape plan, not a history lesson," Captain Vaghn said from where she stood on the periphery of the assembled captains with her arms crossed.

"I'm getting to that," Cho said, shooting her a glare. "There are several newly discovered systems, resource-rich and not, where we discovered connecting wormholes. The Commonwealth sent probes through those, too, and kept them going until they couldn't go any farther. The longest chain of wormholes runs for seven systems, and it starts with the Alder System. If we take the fleet there and start following the chain, we can put some distance between us and the Ixa. Hopefully, if we search beyond the outskirts of each system, we'll find new wormholes to put ourselves even farther out of the enemy's reach. The Commonwealth's mapping of these naturally occurring wormholes was a secret known only to high-ranking officials in the government and military. As such, the Ixa should have no knowledge of our trajectory through the stars."

"I see a couple of problems," Keyes said, and everyone turned to face him. "First, passing through seven unstable wormholes will take a toll on any fleet that passes through, and civilians will likely die. Second, in order to reach Alder, we have to go through Yclept, which is one of the systems under attack. The

Ixa will likely have finished with Yclept by the time our fleet reaches Larkspur, but their force will still be at large somewhere in the Bastion Sector."

Cho was nodding. "Both true, Admiral Keyes. Unfortunately, I see no alternative."

Vaghn uncrossed her arms and stepped through a gap between two collapsible chairs. "Where do you envision the allied fleet deploying while the civilian population flees, Captain Cho?"

Cho's face reddened. "You already know the answer to that."

"True. But I'd like for the other captains to hear what you told me."

"We will accompany the civilian fleet, to protect our families as well as the rest of humanity, the Wingers, and the other species that accompany us. There's no way for us to know what threats they may encounter among the stars. We must be there to protect them from every danger."

"And yet you didn't emphasize that point in your presentation." Captain Vaghn turned to Keyes, her eyebrows raised.

Keyes sighed. "With the fall of Sol, the Commonwealth is all but destroyed. The UHF is the closest thing humanity has to a governing body. Likewise with Spire and the Winger Directorate. From a democratic perspective, I find it frightening to consider that we, the military, now find ourselves in the position of de facto government. But maybe we can mitigate that by preserving some democratic forms. In strategic and tactical matters, I exercise total command, but if you wish to take your ships to protect fleeing civilians, then I do not feel justified in trying to stop you."

Keyes stood, his eyes roving from human captain to Winger captain to human. "Leave with the civilians if you wish. The *Providence* will not. She'll see you as far as the Bastion Sector, and she'll help you clear the way to Alder. But after that, I intend to remain and cause the Ixa as much pain as possible. Any captain who shares that desire is welcome to stay and join me."

"But Admiral," Cho said, wearing an expression that looked a lot like pity. "Surely you can see that remaining serves nothing except the cause of vengeance."

Keyes felt his mouth twist in disdain. *So the rumor that I'm obsessed with vengeance has spread through the fleet. Thanks, Husher.* "On the contrary, Captain Cho. Staying to fight the Ixa will delay their pursuit of the civilian fleet. And they will pursue—count on it. Fighting them will also buy time for more humans, Wingers, Tumbra, and Gok to flee the darkgate network and follow the civilian fleet into uncharted space."

Offering no answer, Cho's eyes fell to the deck, his lips pursed.

"I'll ask again," Keyes said. "Will anyone stay with me to fight the Ixa?"

"I'll stay," a small voice said from outside the circle of captains.

Everyone turned toward it, and at first they couldn't see its source. Then Piper stepped out from behind the rows of captains in chairs that had hidden him from view.

"I don't know how I can contribute," the diminutive alien said. "But I'll stay and do what I can. I've contributed before."

"You have indeed, Piper," Keyes said. "You have indeed."

The Tumbran's words had a tremendous effect, with most of the captains present following with pledges that they, too, would remain and fight the Ixa.

Keyes wondered whether, despite his show of wide-eyed bravery, Piper's interjection might not have been calculated to inspire exactly that effect. A smile spread across his face as he considered it. He felt sure Piper was wilier than anyone gave him credit for, and most people considered him fairly intelligent. *But he's not just book smart.*

While Keyes considered it a noble aim to keep the Ixa from the civilians' throats a little longer, he secretly considered it impossible to save them from the slaughter. Baxa would hunt those who fled relentlessly, until each one of them was either dead or enslaved.

No, for Keyes, staying to fight truly was about vengeance. As much vengeance as he could possibly wreak.

CHAPTER 51

Every Drop

When an alert appeared on his com calling him to the admiral's office, Husher expected the upcoming engagement in Yclept to be the topic. He figured he'd probably find Fesky there, too, and they'd go over Air Group tactics—maybe plans to leverage the EW squadrons even further against the Ixa's drone fighters.

But instead of Fesky, Caine stood at attention in front of Keyes's desk. That surprised him, since the marines didn't have any involvement in space battles, other than to ensure order was maintained aboard the supercarrier.

"*Attention!*" Keyes barked the moment Husher walked in.

He snapped to attention beside Caine. "Sir!" he yelled automatically.

"Did you think you could hide from me what's been going on between you two?"

Husher resisted the impulse to exchange glances with the sergeant. "Sir, I don't—"

"Don't feign ignorance with me, Husher. I know about your little affair."

His face heating up, Husher met the admiral's eyes. "I wasn't going to pretend ignorance. We haven't been trying to conceal what's between us from anyone. I mean, we haven't advertised it, but that's only because we haven't defined what it is yet."

"Allow me to define it for you: it's nothing. Whatever you think has been happening between you, it ends today."

"What? Why? That's bull, sir. There's no chain of command issue between us. And it isn't against regulations."

"There is a chain of command issue, in fact," Keyes said. "Considering you often go on missions with the marines, there's a tremendous issue. And that isn't all. With you two mooning over each other, you're sure to compromise your effectiveness in the coming conflict. We need to squeeze every drop of efficiency out of every single unit. That goes doubly for both of you, given the positions you hold. I consider the matter settled. From now on, you two will only communicate in a professional capacity."

"Yes, sir," Caine said, quietly.

Now Husher did turn to face her. *Seriously? She's ready to accept this as easily as that?*

It made a certain sense, of course. He'd never known Caine to defy her Keyes in any way. And the fact that she'd acquiesced to this injustice so easily didn't make him angry at her, though it did hurt. A lot.

It only made him angrier at Keyes.

Husher rounded on the admiral. "Yes, of course, you won't have emotions happening on your ship. You won't have humans comforting each other and making what will probably be their final moments even a little enjoyable. All you want aboard the

Providence nowadays are cold killing machines, the better to pursue your lust for revenge. That lust has quenched everything that made you a good man, sir. Everything that made me respect you."

The admiral stood from his chair and leveled his bluff-faced stare at Husher. For some reason, it wasn't nearly as effective as it used to be.

"You have three seconds to leave my office before I toss you in the brig with Wahlburg."

"Yes, sir."

Husher left, knowing that Keyes should have tossed him in the brig anyway.

The reason he hadn't done so was because Husher was right: Keyes really did need killing machines—tools with which to effect his vengeance. And Husher couldn't kill anything from the brig.

CHAPTER 52

In Fact and in Name

During the rare occasions Teth had the opportunity to converse with his father, he cleared everyone else off of the bridge so that they could speak alone. Yes, he might have spoken to Baxa using the deskcom in the command leader's office, and yes, clearing the bridge did reduce the *Silencer*'s readiness level.

But Teth considered it grossly inappropriate for Baxa's visage to be displayed on such a small display as the one on his deskcom. He refused to speak with his father on anything except the bridge's main viewscreen.

"I do retain some affection for my progeny," Baxa's enormous, disembodied head said from the screen. "Even in my current state. As such, I am offering you the opportunity to retain your will, unlike your brethren."

Teth bowed his head, considering his father's words. "Even Ochrim?" he said, looking up once more. "Have you offered the same to him?"

"I did not offer it," Baxa said, "since it was already clear what he desired. The last time we spoke, he was in the process of fleeing me. I could have easily apprehended him, but instead I let him go, and allowed him to retain his will as well."

"Why, Father? How has he earned it? He betrayed us."

"My motives are not for you to know, at present, Teth. There may come a time when I see fit to inform you further. But for now, your world is comprised only of war, as well as the question I have set before you."

Teth gave the question thought, for a long moment. At last, he said, "If I do retain my will, I will be susceptible to making mistakes. I won't make those mistakes, if I allow myself to be subsumed into your will."

"You are wise to say so, son." A thrill shot through Teth at Baxa's rare use of the word "son."

"Thank you, Father."

"But fear not. Even if you choose to retain your will, you will always have access to my guidance as you execute your duties. If you are ever on the precipice of committing a tactical or strategic error, I will warn you, so that you might amend your course."

"Very well, Father. In that case, I do choose to retain my will, so that I may continue to serve you in fact as well as in name." Slaves couldn't serve, not truly—they could only labor.

"Then you shall retain it, and so shall your crew. I am pleased you have chosen thus, though I knew that you would. It leaves you well-equipped to execute the task I have for you."

"What is it?"

"The Ixa attacking human colonies have granted me the time I required to consolidate my power. They have done well, but it is time for them to return home, so that they might become greater than they are. I will wash away their sins by coring their souls, leaving vessels for my prowess to fill up. I want you to lead them back to me, by any means necessary."

"Yes, Father. With pleasure."

CHAPTER 53

Always in Command

Keyes stood inside the wreckage of Flight Deck A and gazed out at the stars.

He'd needed to see them, and not through a viewscreen's visual sensor feed. A desire to look on the stars mediated only by his pressure suit's faceplate had brought him here.

Not many *Providence* crewmembers knew that one of the Flight Deck A airlocks still functioned. It was one of the many obscure items of mostly irrelevant trivia which, as her captain, he had access to.

That said, he'd encountered many captains throughout his career who wouldn't have made a point to know such things. They'd have taken it at face value that one of their primary flight decks was no longer operational, and it wouldn't have occurred to them to wonder whether any of its airlocks still worked.

If Keyes had been like them, he wouldn't be standing out here.

Few knew the *Providence* as well as he did. Chief Engineer Victor, perhaps, and possibly—

"Admiral," a female voice said into his helmet, and Keyes's HUD told him she spoke over a two-way channel.

"Arsenyev." He turned to see her standing behind him, then turned back to the stars. "I was just thinking about how well you know this ship, and here you are to prove it."

She drew up beside him, joining him in staring at the stars. "My presence is less about my knowledge of the ship and more about how well I know you."

"Oh?" he said, glancing at her.

She nodded. "You are troubled, sir. I've seen that for a long time, and it's become more pronounced since we began talking about the civilian populations fleeing. So I asked myself, where does a master tactician go when he wants to be alone? I checked the records to see whether any of Flight Deck A's airlocks were operational, and after that I had my answer."

"I see."

"Your feeling troubled *would* be understandable—"

"Who's in charge of the CIC right now?"

"Werner."

"Werner…"

"As I was saying, it would be understandable for you to feel troubled, given our circumstances, except that I've seen you face down hopeless odds with more grit than this. More determination."

"I'm very determined, Arsenyev."

"You're determined to kill as many Ixa as you're able. And I think that's more about weakness than anything else."

Her words would have angered him, another time. "I don't recall giving you permission to speak freely."

"I didn't ask for it, and you are well within your rights to discipline me. I know that. But I'm willing to risk disciplinary action, because I know how important it is for me to say what I came to say."

"Say it, then."

Arsenyev turned to face him, her whole body pointed toward him, while he continued to face the jagged edge of his ship through which the stars shone. "I loved you."

Now he did turn his head toward her, his eyes widening.

"I realize how inappropriate that is for me to say, but we're living what might easily be the last days of our species, and I know I *must* say it. I loved you, and not just as my captain. I wanted to lie with you, and I dreamed of being your wife. But I don't anymore. I loved the man who believed in something, who refused to let anything or anyone compromise that belief. The man who stood for something. But the man who is driven only by vengeance and hate? The man who seeks to make the world pay for what it has done to him? I do not love him. I can't."

Keyes couldn't remember the last time he lacked anything to say. He was always in command—of himself and of his ship.

But not now. He was completely speechless.

The silence stretched on for a long time, with Keyes peering out at the stars, emotions warring in his chest. Eventually, he realized Arsenyev had left Flight Deck A, and he was alone.

"Admiral," a voice said inside his helmet. It was Werner.

"Yes. What?"

"We just entered Larkspur, and there is a large fleet here already."

Keyes's entire body tensed. "Ixa?"

"Just one. They've already identified themselves—it's Ochrim, accompanied by what he claims is every single Kaithian in existence. I'm getting a transmission request from Ochrim's ship. Will you speak with him, Admiral?"

Keyes's vision clouded and his gut clenched as everything Ochrim had done to humanity came back to him. He wanted to give the order to blast the Ixan's ship out of existence, and he almost did.

But then Arsenyev's words came back to him.

This isn't about me. What's best for humanity?

"Yes," he ground out. "I'll talk to the bastard."

CHAPTER 54

A Weapon Species

Ochrim told Keyes he had something to tell all of the allied fleet captains, and that he considered it best not to say anything until Keyes had arranged a fleetwide meeting, which would include the Ixan and select members from the Kaithe.

"I don't think so," Keyes said, refusing to take his eyes off the scientist's. He noticed his own hands clenching atop the Captain's chair armrests, and he willed his fingers to uncurl. "We're done playing by your rules, Ochrim. You've earned none of our trust."

Deep within his twin facial impressions, the Ixan closed his eyes. "I brought you the Kaithe."

"They haven't done much to earn our trust, either." Rising to his feet, Keyes leveled a finger at the viewscreen. "Here's how this is going to work. If you have something to say, you can say it in a *Providence* interrogation room, under heavy guard. You'll bring Aheera with you, along with the Kaithian that banished us from their planet when I asked for their help. They'll know which one. I'll ensure your safety from my crew, Ochrim, though they want nothing more than to put a bullet in your head. But I can't guarantee your safety from me. Let's just say that whatever you have for me, it had better be good."

Ochrim blinked. "These are not sound negotiation tactics, Captain—"

"It's Admiral now."

"Very well. I'll say it again—I brought you the Kaithe, whose help humanity sorely needs. It's irresponsible for you to stand in the way."

"No, it would be irresponsible for me to give you access to my captains before I know what you're up to. We can lay at least seven hundred thousand deaths at your feet, Ixan, brought about by your subversion of dark tech. Personally, I attribute to you the billions who've died in Sol and other systems." Arsenyev was looking at Keyes as he spoke, and he met her eyes briefly before returning his stare to Ochrim. "I'm not interested in *negotiating* with you. If you've truly come to offer aid, and you're dedicated to that, then this is how it must be. It's the height of arrogance and stupidity for you to expect anything else."

"You...are right, Admiral Keyes." Ochrim bowed his head. "I will submit myself into your custody."

"Take a single shuttle to the *Providence*—noncombat. One of the Kaithe's craft should do nicely. I'll meet you in Hangar Bay H. Expect to have a lot of guns pointing at you."

He ordered Sergeant Caine to meet him in the hangar bay with a full platoon of her best marines, including a squad's worth of Gok and one of Wingers, too. Caine herself would remain in touch with Ek, to whom she'd relay a live feed of the proceedings. If the Fin detected anything of concern, she'd let Caine know, who'd order her marines to subdue the arriving aliens immediately.

Ochrim exited the shuttle with his arms raised, as did the shorter Kaithe who flanked him, though their tails dragged on the ground, and Keyes knew exactly what those powerful appendages were capable of.

"Not you, Aheera," he called. "You may lower your arms and step away from your companions, if you wish. You *have* earned our trust and respect."

Aheera lowered her arms, but she didn't leave Ochrim's side. "I will remain with them."

Keyes nodded. "Then let's go."

The marines marched the trio of aliens down the hall, their weapons trained on Ochrim and the Kaithian whose name Keyes still didn't know.

Most of the marine platoon remained outside the interrogation room, but two Gok and two humans did accompany Keyes inside, along with Sergeant Caine.

No one sat. The three aliens stood against the far wall, opposite the interrogation table from Keyes and the armed marines.

"Well," Keyes said. "What have you come to say?"

"I am Porah," said the Kaithian who Keyes had mostly spoken to on their homeworld—she'd been his conduit to what they called their "Consensus." Porah leaned back against the wall, her powerful tail stabilizing her stance. "Ochrim has convinced us that we must participate in your war."

"If you're truly participating, then it's *our* war. Either way, it's interesting to note that you're willing to listen to an Ixan but not a human."

"Ochrim offered the stronger argument. Additionally, he has been a friend of the Kaithe for a long time. He's exhibited wisdom beyond anything we've witnessed from the other species."

"What did he say to convince you?"

"He persuaded us that Baxa is truly a threat to all life."

Keyes squinted at the blue-white alien. "That's exactly what we told you."

"I brought a new piece of information," Ochrim put in. "One not yet known to you: Baxa is not the only threat. He wasn't created by the Ixa—quite the reverse, actually. Baxa was sent by a separate species, unknown to us, who have deployed similar AIs to galaxies throughout the local cluster. Their mission is to secure all resources by eliminating each galaxy's intelligent life in the most cost-efficient way possible. Baxa's method for doing so was to engineer my species and implant himself in our genetic memory, though the other AIs may have different methods. He designed our brains so that they could easily be harnessed for additional processing power when the time came, which it seems it has. Baxa is now growing increasingly intelligent with each new Ixan he harvests."

"How do you know this?" Keyes asked.

"Baxa told me. He *wishes* for me to rally the other species, and for us to do everything we can to defeat him. It's in his programming to want to be tested, to determine whether he represents an optimized solution to his creators' problem—namely, domination of the entire universe."

Keyes grunted. "And here you are, doing his bidding once again."

"This is different. Before, he tricked me into thinking your extermination represented the only way for life to continue existing in any form. Now, I realize that the future he strove for involved all life getting either assimilated or destroyed by him. Yes, I am still conforming to his agenda by opposing him, or rather his creators' agenda, but what can I do but oppose him?"

Ochrim heaved a shaky sigh. "I have always acted in the way I considered most ethical, though I do not consider that an excuse for what I have done to your species, Admiral Keyes. I am truly sorry. However, I know that words are meaningless when considered alongside the atrocities I have perpetrated. If I can help you to win this war, I pray that it will earn me some modicum of absolution. Either way, even if we win, it seems we have a much larger project to attend to."

"The other AIs."

"Yes." Weariness appeared to hit the scientist suddenly, and he took a seat at the interrogation table, causing the human marines to shift nervously. The Gok marines remained impassive, their small, onyx eyes fixed on the Ixan. "Whoever created them, they are playing a very long game, and so we must assume they're incredibly long-lived. Otherwise, they would take on much more risk than they are. Instead, they're evolving generations of AI that are forged in the fires of conflict. Copies of the strongest among them will proceed to the next galactic cluster to begin the process anew. If time truly is meaningless to the creator species, then why shouldn't they exercise maximum caution, to keep the chance of defeat as close to zero as possible?"

Slowly, Keyes nodded. He, too, pulled a chair back from the table and took a seat, eyeing Ochrim as he did. After a time, his gaze shifted to Porah. "I'm not sure what the Kaithe's involvement in the war will be, considering you seem to think of yourselves as pacifists. But before I agree to trust you in combat, there's something I must know. Why is humanity the only species you're able to link with?"

Porah and Aheera exchanged long looks, their expressions unreadable. At last, Porah turned to face him. "Humanity has done well."

Shaking his head a little, Keyes said, "Excuse me? I didn't ask you to grade us."

"Hear me, Admiral Keyes. Your species has begun to grasp at the ethical awareness we have hoped for you, for so long. As well, you are becoming pragmatic enough to make the decisions that higher ethics demand."

"That you've...hoped for us?"

"Yes. Your species is both the great pride and the great shame of the Kaithe. When you first came to our planet, and Aheera tested your marines, she did so to test your mettle, to discover how far you've come, since..."

"Since what?"

"Since we created you."

Keyes had nothing to say to that. He didn't know Kaithe to have much of a sense of humor, but if this was a joke, it was a poor attempt at one.

"Long ago, the Kaithe had designs similar to those of the Ixa. We waged offensive war, for the purposes of increasing our own power, and of accruing more resources for the wealthiest among us. Eventually, elements arose in our society that pushed for peace, pointing to the depravity of our actions. But even they were misguided. They advocated for creating a weapon species, who would wage war for us, keeping our hands clean. That weapon was you. Humanity."

"Wait," Keyes said. "You're serious, aren't you? A weapon species..."

"Yes. We designed you to be fiercely competitive and individualist. We programmed the lust for battle into your DNA."

"And the linking...?"

Porah nodded. "Your aggression, paired with our intelligence. That is what we propose to contribute to this war. When all of the Kaithe link together, we have access to cognitive power that rivals Baxa in his current form. And by linking with you, we can grant you access to that power. But Baxa's intellect grows with every Ixa he adds to his neural network, and if we wait any longer, he will have surpassed even our capacity."

A long silence ensued, and Caine was the first to break it. "Did you ever use us that way? As a weapon species?"

"No," Porah said. "Some time after your creation, we came to our senses. We evolved beyond the desire to make war at all, limiting ourselves to only our Home, and converting all of our military might into the Preserver, to ensure we waged only defensive war. Humanity was left to its own devices, a young bloodthirsty species, confused about your purpose. We deeply regret what we did, and for a long time we worried about what you might become. Your actions, however—the actions of Admiral Keyes, and those aboard the *Providence*—your actions have given us hope."

CHAPTER 55

Reckoning

Keyes decided to allow Ochrim his audience with the captains, but before that, he had something to say—not just to the commander of each ship, but to the entire fleet. He ordered his Coms officer to arrange for him a true fleetwide channel: not just one each captain could listen on, but a channel that would co-opt each ship's broadcast system to relay his voice throughout the corridors of every warship in his fleet.

Once it was done, Keyes leaned slightly forward in the Captain's chair to speak, as was his habit.

"Women and men of the allied fleet," he began. "I look at our species today, and I like what I see. Humans, Wingers, Tumbra, and Gok, all working together to oppose a foe who has no interest in justice or peace—only domination. I see most of us dedicating ourselves to helping civilians flee oppression and death, and I see some of us volunteering to continue fighting the foe, even when we know the chances of victory are nonexistent. I see bravery and noble sacrifice." Keyes paused. "I also see blindness."

He shifted slightly in his seat, letting his listeners digest that. "I'm not placing blame. I can't, because I'm one of the primary sources of that blindness. But there is blindness nevertheless. During the last war meeting of the captains, I advocated for throwing ourselves at the Ixa; a course of desperation and even suicide. Many of you joined me, and I am honored by your sacrifice, which is why it pains me to tell you that I was woefully misguided. I pushed for that course of action out of hatred for our enemy more than anything else, and whether or not that hatred was justified, the course was the wrong one. We must fight to win—with the aim not only of defeating the Ixa but of preserving our species for generations to come. Our children must be given the opportunity to live and be prosperous. They *must.* We must settle for nothing less."

Keyes slowly rose from his seat, knowing that his image was being transmitted to anyone in the fleet watching a viewscreen.

"Many of you agreed to join me on my misguided suicide run, but I no longer call for that. Now, I'm calling on every last warship in this fleet to join me in an attack on the Ixan home system, with the aim of destroying Baxa. If we can take out their AI, there will be hope for our species. I admit that it's a long shot. But it's also the only shot we have. If we flee, the Ixa will not rest until they hunt us down. And so we must fight.

"The Kaithe have granted us a tool that may sway the coming battle in our favor. That is a matter to be discussed at a war meeting with every fleet captain present. But I can tell you this: when we attack the Baxa System, it will almost certainly draw the rest of the Ixa to us, who are now attacking our colonized systems. That will spare billions of living people from joining the billions that have already died. And once those Ixa come to us, that will be our chance. To fight for our lives. Our future. And our children. I cannot guarantee victory, but I refuse to accept defeat. Win or lose, I can promise you one thing. There *will* be a reckoning."

Nodding curtly, he gestured for the Coms officer to end the transmission.

CHAPTER 56

A Terrible Soldier

Keyes's boots clicked against the deck as he strode through Engineering, running his hands along the cool, metal bulkhead.

Everything I've fought for. Everything the Providence *has meant to me.*

For a time, he'd become unworthy of her. Unworthy to walk her corridors, let alone to captain her. He saw that, now. Keyes had treated her like a tool with which to impose his will on the universe, specifically the part of it that contained Ixa. He'd wanted nothing more than to point the supercarrier's weapons at every Ixan warship he saw, firing until he ran out of ammunition.

I still want that. And yet...

It wasn't only about fighting Ixa, now. It wasn't about knowing they would die by the thousands to the *Providence*'s mighty guns. He'd finally let go of his blind rage, and he'd found his way back to his reasons for fighting.

This ship was never supposed to be about war. That was just a means to an end.

The *Providence* was about foresight. About justice. And about defending humans from aggressors, so that they could determine for themselves how they wanted their future to look.

"Ready to go into battle one more time, old girl?" he asked her.

The *Providence* responded as she always did—by abiding, as a solid presence that had never let him down and never would.

He opened a channel with his sensor operator in the CIC. "Werner, kindly locate Captain Husher and Sergeant Caine and ask them to meet me outside my office."

"Yes, sir."

Keyes kept his hands on his ship's bulkhead as he walked, even as he entered busier corridors. He refused to break contact with his ship. *I'll never let myself fall out of touch with her again.*

Husher and Caine were waiting for him when he reached his office, the latter wearing a blank expression. On the other hand, Husher all but glared. Keyes took a moment to wonder whether either of them had attempted to defy his order to discontinue their romantic liaison. *Probably not.* He might have expected that from Husher, but not from Caine. She was too good a soldier.

Husher, on the other hand, was a terrible soldier. Being a good soldier meant following orders without question, which Husher had no problems with, unless of course he objected to those orders, which was often.

He makes a damned fine leader, though. If I can prevent him from getting court-martialed for insubordination long enough to get him back in command of a warship...

But even then, the man would still have a command structure to answer to, providing one survived the war. Husher would just have to find his own way. Keyes truly hoped he managed to. The UHF needed more people like Vin Husher.

"Come in," he told them, opening the hatch and walking around his desk to take a seat.

They both came to attention, but Keyes waved a hand. "At ease." He folded his hands together atop his desk. "We're not time-rich, and I have a thousand other matters to attend to before meeting with the other captains, but I consider this important enough to prioritize. Quite simply, I was wrong to stand in the way of you two. I was wrong, and I apologize."

Shocked expressions sprouted on both their faces. "You're...you're serious, Admiral?" Caine said, and the hope in her voice told him how badly she'd wanted this.

"Yes. What you two are exploring is exactly the sort of thing we're fighting to save. Maybe you'll work wonderfully together. Maybe you won't. Maybe your careers will take you down separate paths, and that might end your relationship altogether. Or it might not. But whatever happens between you, it's the right to experience it, to live it, that I was wrong to take away. So I rescind my previous order. You're free to fraternize as you will. Enjoy what time you have left together, because sadly, it may not be very long."

"Thank you, Admiral," Caine said, and Husher nodded at him respectfully.

"Dismissed," Keyes said. They both departed.

He leaned back in his chair, and an unexpected impulse struck him—to contact Arsenyev, tell her to give Werner the CIC, and to come to his office so they could talk.

He brushed it aside. Maybe Husher and Caine could afford to entertain notions like romance in the scant days leading to the final confrontation with the Ixa.

Keyes could not.

CHAPTER 57

Into the Abyss

When Fesky caught Husher sharing a flask with Wahlburg inside a storage bay for spare Condor parts, he at least had the decency to look embarrassed.

"Madcap," he said. He was the one holding the flask when Fesky walked in, but he made no effort to conceal it.

He's caught, and he knows it.

"Didn't you just get out of the brig?" she said to Wahlburg.

"Yes ma'am."

"Then get out of my sight, before I send you back there."

Nodding, Wahlburg shot the flask a final, longing look, then pushed off from the crate where he'd been sitting. At a leisurely pace, he left the storage bay and closed the hatch behind him.

Fesky turned back to Husher. "What are you doing, human?"

The corner of his mouth quirked sideways. "Haven't we known each other long enough to stop addressing each other by our species names, Fesky?"

"I—" She clacked her beak, her feathers beginning to stick up all over her body. "Yes, we have. I'm sorry, Husher."

"It's fine. I know you don't mean anything by it. I'm just a bit off, today. And a bit drunk."

"What's the matter?"

"It's just..." He trailed off, took a swig from his flask, and then held it out to her. "You want some?"

"No, Husher it's—" She'd been about to say it was illegal, but something made her stop. "Wingers don't metabolize alcohol in the same way humans do," she said instead. "It does nothing for us."

Husher nodded. "I've just been unsettled, lately. Watching the admiral spiral the way he has. We seem to have the old Keyes back, which is good, but now that he is, I have this unshakable sense of...I don't know. Dread."

"I heard he split you and Caine up."

That brought a sharp glance from Husher. "How do you even know we were together?"

"Rumor travels fast on a warship, even one as big as the *Providence*. Especially when the rumor involves high-profile officers."

"Yeah. Well, anyway, he just told Caine and I that he was wrong to try to keep us apart. Said we're free to do whatever we want. But that's the thing. Now that I have her back—"

"You're terrified of losing her."

Husher's eyes rose to meet Fesky's. "Yes. That's exactly it. How did you know?"

She settled onto the crate Wahlburg had vacated. "It's how I've felt ever since learning Ek was still alive. Obviously it's different, but after thinking the Fins were extinct and then discovering a single one remained...I've been on edge ever since, Husher. Especially now that she's become such a vital military asset."

"How do you deal with it?"

"I just do. It's awful, I'll admit that, but I can also see how much Ek is contributing. The truly awful thing would be to lock her away from battle, for her protection. Ek has so much to offer, and she needs to be allowed to offer it. There's risk involved, yes, but that's life. That's why the Wingers haven't tried to stop her from being Flockhead, despite how irrational we've always been about the Fins." Fesky studied Husher's face—the deep lines that creased his brow. Some of those were new, she felt sure. "You're probably also worried Keyes will lose his footing again, aren't you? That he'll sink back into the hole he was in."

"Yes. I am, Fesky. I really am."

"Well, cut it out, okay? You need to stop depending on Admiral Keyes so much. I know he helped you regain your own footing, when you were first consigned to the *Providence*. And yes, he's an amazing leader. If he were to slide back into that abyss, it would be a horrible loss. But listen, Husher, you have what it takes to be an excellent leader, too. You just need to acknowledge that, if only to yourself. Then you need to step up and become that leader. Right now would be best. Because our species may not have much time left."

For a while, Fesky thought Husher was going to raise the flask for another swallow. But at last, he capped it instead, placing it on the deck next to the crate where he sat.

Then he rose. "Thank you, Fesky. I needed that. More than you know."

"And we need you," she said, joining him in standing. "So get it together."

CHAPTER 58

What's at Stake

How quickly we've allowed ourselves to integrate with the Kaithe.

Given the hostility with which the aliens had banished the allied fleet from their home system, and given the longstanding UHF regulations against linking with Kaithe, Keyes would have expected a lot more opposition to the idea of accepting the Kaithe's help in facilitating this war meeting.

Certainly, some captains had protested, but most recognized the value in meeting inside a world simulated by the Kaithe. In doing so, they'd save the time it would have taken to commute to and from the *Providence,* using it instead to prepare for the coming conflict.

The Kaithe had deployed a shuttle that dropped off one Kaithian for each vessel, effectively creating a network for instantaneous communication. The processing power required to generate such an elaborate simulation would come from a sizable portion of the Kaithian Consensus, but for the purposes of connecting to the simulation, only a single Kaithian was required.

Just one downside came with doing things this way: none of the other species could attend the meeting, since Kaithe were only capable of linking with humans. The Wingers hadn't offered any opposition, though.

Keyes suspected Ek had something to do with that—if he knew the Fin, she would see the value in allowing the humans and Kaithe to work together on this and thereby gain more trust for each other.

Either way, Ek and a handful of other Winger captains would come to the *Providence* afterward, in order to hammer out the final details of the battle plan.

Aheera had consulted Keyes on what the meeting place should look like, without offering any suggestions herself. He felt certain she was capable of generating basically any setting, including ones that defied the laws of physics. But exploring that didn't interest him.

Another man might have sought to have some fun experimenting with the Kaithe's abilities, but Keyes had been called single-minded more than once, and he'd always had trouble contesting that charge.

"Are you familiar with the Galactic Congress chamber that was on Mars?" he'd asked Aheera. The chamber no longer existed—the Ixa had prioritized its destruction during their assault on Sol.

"I am," Aheera said.

"Then that's where we'll meet."

Keyes didn't ask how she knew the Congress chamber, but he had a couple of guesses. *I'm beginning to suspect the children have been keeping an eye on us for a long time.* It occurred to him how odd it was to think of Kaithe as children, especially considering they were closer to humanity's parents.

The Kaithe didn't even have any young, and they hadn't for millennia, according to Aheera. Their technology allowed them to live basically forever. When he'd asked her why they'd stopped reproducing, she'd averted her eyes, seeming almost uncomfortable. He'd dropped his question, but it still tugged at his thoughts from time to time.

What a stagnant species they must be.

When the meeting began, Keyes sat where the Speaker of the House once had. He'd chosen the Congress chamber in order to remind the captains who they fought for, and also that if they won the coming battle, they would not remain in charge. Democratic forms would be reconstituted immediately. A society governed by military personnel, even well-intentioned military personnel, was a recipe for totalitarian disaster.

Warren Husher had once accused Keyes, half-jokingly, of having a hero complex. That had taken him aback for a moment, until he'd come back with the best humorous deflection he could muster, which hadn't been very strong.

Maybe I do have a hero complex. He supposed there were worse complexes to have.

Gazing over the growing crowd, Keyes saw more and more captains arriving without fanfare. They simply appeared in their chairs, and if you weren't looking directly at them when they did, a flicker in your peripheral vision was all you were likely to detect. Most of the captains brought along a few of their officers, and the Kaithe involved in connecting them were also present. Together, they ended up filling most of the chamber's seats.

For a moment, he wondered whether he would have to count the captains manually to make sure everyone was present. But Aheera spared him that cumbersome task. "All captains are present, Admiral Keyes," she said.

"Thank you, Aheera." He swept his gaze over the assembled UHF captains. "Ochrim tells me that Baxa's main neural structures reside on Klaxon, in a vast underground complex accessed through an Ixan stronghold. I know how you all likely feel about trusting the Ixan's intel, but I don't see what other choice we have. We must adopt a line of action that assumes victory is possible, and it likely isn't if Ochrim's intel is bogus. So we trust him.

"If we are to defeat Baxa, we must destroy the facility that houses his brain. By now, the AI has no doubt taken control of every Ixan it could reach, in order to increase its own intellect, and therefore its power. If we allow Baxa to complete that process, his intelligence will soar beyond the reach of even the Kaithe. We will be like small children trying to fight an adult, and soon after that we will be like gnats fighting a giant."

Keyes stood, now, leaning forward with his hands on the oaken barrier that separated the Speaker from the rest of the house. "The way I see it, this battle will consist of three primary operations. If any one of them fails, then we all will fail, and so each of us must strive for mission success at any cost."

The captains returned his gaze, mostly with expressions of determination. *They know what's at stake.*

"The three operations are as follows: the invasion of Klaxon; the battle against Baxa-controlled warships within the Ixan home system; and the battle to defend the Corydalis-Baxa darkgate, to prevent the other Ixa from returning home and thereby giving Baxa access to more processing power.

"I will command the forces defending the Corydalis-Baxa darkgate. Flockhead Ek will command the fleet that battles the Baxa-controlled warships, and Sergeant Caine will command the ground troops that invade Klaxon and infiltrate the facility that houses Baxa's brain. The Kaithe will also accompany Sergeant Caine. I won't be fighting any Ixa controlled by Baxa, and Flockhead Ek isn't able to link with Kaithe anyway. Although each of the three operations is vital, the mission to Klaxon is arguably the most important, and so it's where the Kaithe will be needed most. We can expect Baxa to mount a formidable defense there. All Gok, Winger, and human ground troops will also accompany Sergeant Caine. Tort has agreed to carry the nuclear bomb they will take into the core of Baxa's facility, which houses his control unit. Any questions?"

There were none. The particulars of the plan would be ironed out at his meeting with Ek and the Wingers, but for now, none of the human captains seemed to oppose the plan itself.

"Meeting adjourned," Keyes said, vanishing from the Galactic Congress chamber.

CHAPTER 59

We Must Pray

Sometimes, Fesky wondered whether Ek had forgotten about her.

They'd seen each other at war meetings, and yes, Ek had offered warm words. But they no longer talked as they had when the Fin lived on the *Providence.* They didn't even keep in touch, despite their coms being well within range ever since Ek recovered on Mars and then joined the allied fleet with every Winger Roostship under her command.

Fesky supposed she might have made more of an effort to message the Fin, but she hadn't wanted to risk bothering her, especially when Ek might have been too polite to decline calls.

She's probably too busy to bother with just one Winger, when she has the entire species depending on her.

Which was why it surprised her so much when, after her meeting with Admiral Keyes, Ek requested to see her.

They met in the *Providence*'s wardroom, where they would enjoy relative privacy. True, other officers could very well walk in on them, but Fesky suspected the admiral would ensure no one did.

She sat at one of the two cafeteria-style tables, clutching a mug of cold coffee and trying to keep herself from trembling in nervous anticipation. When Ek finally entered, Fesky nearly clacked her beak in shock.

The Fin's condition had rapidly deteriorated over the last few days. Her face—normally mottled gray, brown, and black—had several white spots, and the skin had grown rough around her cheeks. There also appeared to be several pinhole abrasions surrounding her eyes, and the eyes themselves looked cloudy.

"Ek," Fesky began, and hesitated. "I didn't realize—"

"My condition shocks you," Ek said, making her way carefully to a seat opposite Fesky. "I am sorry. I have not made it widely known throughout the fleet. Keyes and I agree that doing so could prove damaging to morale."

"You shouldn't be in space," Fesky said softly.

"You are right. But what choice do we have? I spend time regularly in the centrifuge Keyes provided to me, and that will have to be enough. I must survive until after the coming battle. As long as we win that, I do not care what happens."

"But Ek...you're the last living Fin."

"I understand that, Fesky. But I do not think I overstate my role when I say that if I do not participate in the coming battle, all of our species could go extinct. Trust me, I do not enjoy making such a calculus. But I must."

Seeing Ek like this agitated Fesky to no end. "Why did you ask to see me?" she asked, more harshly than she'd intended.

The Fin blinked, leaning heavily on the table before her. "Much will change after the battle, Fesky. No matter the outcome. We must pray that a significant percentage of us survive—Wingers, humans, Gok, and Tumbra. I know my survival does not seem likely, currently, but I retain some faith. If I do survive, and if you survive as well, I truly believe we can accomplish amazing things together. Indeed, every species has suffered greatly, but if we can band together, we could achieve something wonderful."

Ek's words shook Fesky from her agitation, and even though she was conscious of that happening, she had to marvel yet again at the Fin's ability to move things in a positive direction. "Such as...what? What sort of things are you thinking of?"

"I cannot predict the future, or even whether we will have one. But if we do emerge from the coming conflict, then I am confident Wingers will play a significant role in the world that follows. Wingers can be just as wise as Fins, sometimes moreso. You taught me that, Fesky. And you must never forget it."

Fesky could not control her shaking. But now, she shook from humility and joy.

Unsteadily, Ek rose to her feet, offering Fesky a tiny smile. "I must go. There is much to do."

Fesky rose, too, and before her self-consciousness could stop her, she made her way around the table to embrace the Fin. Ek embraced her back.

CHAPTER 60

A Fortifying Moment

The hatch opened to reveal Admiral Keyes, who met Husher's eyes for a moment without saying anything.

Husher cleared his throat. "You wanted to see me, sir?"

"Come in." The admiral crossed the office to his desk. "Take a seat."

Husher lowered himself into the wooden chair. "We're getting close to the Baxa System."

"Yes. Ixan scout ships have already spotted us, fourteen hours ago. We let them go, and no doubt they're racing to warn the fleets attacking our systems of an imminent attack on theirs. Everything's falling into place quickly, which makes the decision I've made a little dicey. But it's necessary: I don't want you flying with the Air Group in the coming battle. Instead, I want you to accompany Sergeant Caine to the surface of Klaxon."

Studying the admiral's face carefully, Husher shook his head. "Why, sir?"

"I thought, as marine commander, Caine would be the one to leverage the Kaithe's intellectual resources. But I was wrong—

she can't handle linking with them. We've tried twice, and the second time, I think she came close to having another psychotic break. That's strictly confidential and not to go beyond this room."

"Yes, sir. Do you think she's stable enough to stay in charge of the mission?"

"I've had her assessed, and I think so. But that's one of the reasons I want you on the mission, too—to take over command if she falls or becomes otherwise incapacitated."

Husher nodded. "What's the other reason?"

"I want you to be the one to link with the Kaithe."

"I see." Images from his experience on the aliens' homeworld flashed in his mind, of the simulation in which Kaithe had seemed to slaughter his marines.

"It's daunting, I know. But we'll try you out with the link, give you a bit of practice time, to grow accustomed to that level of cognition. You won't have much time, though, Husher, which is yet another reason for my choice. You're one of the most capable individuals on this ship, and I've remarked on your adaptability numerous times. You're the one who has to do it."

"All right, sir. I'm ready."

"Ochrim wants to accompany you. He knows the layout of the facility that houses Baxa's brain, and he can guide you to the control unit where you'll set off the nuke. The Ixan seems keen to make up for what he's done, and I'm inclined to let him try. We need him."

"But can we trust him, sir?"

"If we can't, the entire foundation of this mission is bogus. We've already decided to trust him. Now we're deciding to use him."

Keyes paused. For the first time, Husher noticed his posture was quite different from other times they'd met in here. Instead of leaning on his desk, hands clasped atop it in business-like fashion, the admiral leaned back in his chair with one arm slung over an armrest, staring into space.

"It's been a pleasure having you serve aboard the *Providence*," the admiral said, and his voice sounded oddly strained.

"Thank you, sir. It's been an honor to serve aboard her."

A nod from Keyes. And then: "I've disappointed you, these last few months. I understand that. I let you down, I let the crew down, and I let this ship down. Hopefully it's not too late to amend the consequences of that."

"I'm sure it's not, sir," Husher said, his voice coming out as little more than a whisper.

"It's late for me to finally say this, but I'm very sorry about what happened to your father. I think I shut off all emotion surrounding his death, and offering you my condolences would have been a concession to emotion. Foolish, I know, but there it is. Warren Husher didn't deserve what happened to him. He deserved to be honored. His actions may be the only reason we have even a slim shot at victory."

Keyes's eyes finally found Husher's again, and Husher thought he detected a slight shimmer in them. "You've lived up to your father's name. You stayed true to your principles. Remember that, Husher. Remember what it takes. Don't lose sight of what's important, like I did these past few months. Humanity needs principled people—needs them now, and it will need them tomorrow."

"Sir, why does it feel like you're saying goodbye?"

"I hope I'm not. But we have to acknowledge how narrow our chance of victory is. We will fight with everything we have, because we must, but that doesn't mean we'll both make it through this."

A prolonged silence followed, which Husher broke. "Before we attacked Spire, to force the Wingers to negotiate with us, you said that if the *Providence* went down, you'd be going with her. Did you mean that?"

"I meant it then, and I mean it now. This battle has only one of two outcomes, where this ship and I are concerned. Either we both make it through, or—"

"Keep her together for me, sir. It seems sentimental to say, but she's the only place I care to call home."

"I understand, Husher. I'll try my best. Now, get to Hangar Deck B. I'll send Aheera to meet you, and you can begin your preparations right away. Dismissed."

They both stood. Husher saluted, and Keyes returned it. It should have been a fortifying moment, but Husher felt nothing except scared.

CHAPTER 61

Execute

The UHF destroyer *Caesar* was the first to transition through the darkgate into the Baxa System. Other than the *Providence*, it was the highest-value UHF warship remaining, and also the most likely to survive emerging entering Ixan space alone.

Ek had no idea how likely the destroyer's survival actually was, but someone had to enter first, and the *Caesar* made the most sense. It would not serve anything for Ek to place her Command Roostship at the vanguard in some misguided show of bravery, and she also could not afford to risk any of the ships containing Kaithe, or the hundreds of marines who would comprise the mission to Klaxon.

At any rate, the *Caesar* was not alone for long. Two missile cruisers and two more destroyers followed close behind, along with five Roostships in quick succession. Then came Ek's Command Roostship. She *did* wish to enter in time to command the defense against any ambush that might be lying in wait.

"Situation report," she said the moment they emerged from the darkgate.

The sensors adjutant paused, seeming to double check his console before answering. "No enemy contacts, Flockhead, other than a trio of battle groups surrounding Klaxon."

Ek did not answer, already parsing the implications of the information the adjutant had given her. As with every darkgate, the one they had emerged from had once been a natural wormhole. What made this one unique was that up until the First Galactic War, its existence had been a secret to all but the Ixa, who had not wanted their enemies to learn of a second entrance into their home system.

Ochrim had been the one to alert humanity to its existence. More specifically, he had told Leonard Keyes and Warren Husher about it, so that they could effect a mission to extract the scientist, in the effort that gave humanity dark tech.

Since then, with the secret out, the wormhole had been turned into a dark gate by humanity, as part of its monitoring and curtailing of the Ixa.

At least, they had tried to curtail them. They had failed, clearly.

The fact that the sensors adjutant had registered so few enemy warships in-system had two possible explanations. One was that they had caught Baxa woefully unprepared, which Ek considered exceedingly unlikely.

The other explanation…

"Sensors adjutant, run continual active scans of the system's asteroid belt. Have the computer track each individual asteroid and project its natural flight path. If any of them deviate from that path, inform me immediately."

"Yes, Flockhead."

Briefly, Ek considered breaking from the ecliptic plane, thereby avoiding the asteroid belt entirely. Doing so would add hours to their course, however, and it would allow any Ixan defenders in hiding to maintain a constant visual on Ek's fleet.

Although getting ambushed inside the asteroid belt was a serious danger, passing through it also offered certain advantages, such as using the asteroids for partial cover. And if Baxa had indeed concealed his fleet throughout the belt, that meant the Ixan fleet was scattered, and it would take time for it to regroup to pose a concentrated threat to the invading fleet.

If we proceed with caution, Baxa will devour us at leisure. But if we are willing to take on some risk...

"Navigation adjutant, calculate a course for our predetermined battle group that takes us through the asteroid belt as far from any asteroids as possible while following the most efficient route, given those parameters. Maximum acceleration."

"Yes, ma'am."

"Coms, send orders to each predesignated battle group to do the same, and tell all navigation officers to coordinate with each other to make sure none follow courses that bring them within ten light seconds of another allied battle group. I want all ships to sync their acceleration profiles, so that we emerge from the opposite side of the asteroid belt as one."

Most of the fleet's navigation officers had designed multiple mock courses in advance that were based on widely-available knowledge of the Ixan system. It did not take long for them to modify those courses so that they were adapted to what Ek had perceived since entering the system. As soon as the courses were all complete, she ordered them to execute.

Given that they were keeping pace with each other, the fleet was only as fast as the slowest ship. Even so, it was still capable of reasonably high speed, and the farther they were allowed to traverse the asteroid belt unmolested, the more acceleration they could pile on.

That did not turn out to be very far. Forty-five minutes after they had entered the system, the sensors adjutant practically shouted: "Multiple contacts, emerging from asteroids ahead and behind! You were right, Flockhead!"

As she watched the Ixan warships launch an all-out assault on her fleet, Ek did not enjoy being right very much, though she marveled at the perfect coordination with which the enemy carried out their attack.

Except they are not a they *any longer, are they? They are a* he.

Baxa was the reason for such perfect tactics. He had devoted just enough warships to each of her battle groups to destroy them while suffering acceptable losses himself, with the rest of his forces patrolling the perimeter in case any of the allied ships decided to get inventive with course alterations.

The only option Ek had was to order the fleet to take evasive maneuvers while conducting what missile defense they could on the run, and continuing to flee through the asteroid belt, piling on more and more speed in their desperate attempt to reach Klaxon without suffering devastating losses.

She had a feeling that was exactly what Baxa wanted her to do.

CHAPTER 62

The Face of War

As the allied ships screamed through the asteroid field, Ek kept close watch on the tactical display—the posture of the enemy fleet it showed, along with the various courses of the human, Winger, and Gok battle groups.

Something struck her: in taking evasive action, many of the captains under her command were adopting courses that would distance themselves from the Ixan ships. In turn, Baxa was gradually pulling his fleet to one side of the ecliptic plane.

Normally, her captains' evasive courses would be reasonable. But even though they had faced the Ixa's new capabilities multiple times by now, they still were not using tactics optimal for confronting them. The face of war had changed, and the allies were still lagging behind.

Unless we adapt right now.

"Communications adjutant," she said, "send new orders to all allied captains: adjust evasive courses so that they thread *between* the Ixan ships. Otherwise, the enemy is going to use their kinetic-kill clouds to take out the bulk of our fleet. Do it now."

"Yes, Flockhead." The Winger bent to work, typing frenetically on her console.

Allowing enough time for those orders to be received and understood, Ek moved on to the next: "We will still have a wave of Hellsong missiles to contend with once we pass through, but at least our fleet will be rapidly accelerating away from them, rather than traveling a course perpendicular to them. That is what Baxa sought to arrange, and we will deny him the opportunity."

"How should the captains respond to the barrage you expect will come at our rear, Flockhead Ek?"

"As follows: when Baxa launches his missiles at our sterns, we will launch a counter-barrage of our own semi-autonomous missiles. Send them with missile defense protocols, to be superseded only if a given rocket lacks an enemy missile to target. In that event, the missile must switch targets to an Ixan warship. Immediately after launching our barrage, instruct all Roostships to launch seventy percent of their Talon wings. Our pilots will clean up the remaining Hellsong missiles, before they draw near enough to become a meaningful threat."

Ek watched her orders unfold on the tactical display, with variable results. The AI's skill in executing counterintuitive formations and flight patterns was without parallel, and many allied ships fell as they fled through the asteroid belt, with three entire battle groups going down.

Suppressing an urge to wince, Ek quickly tallied the cost to the Klaxon mission. When she and Keyes had divided the part of the fleet Ek would command into battle groups, they had ensured each had three ships important for the mission—some mix of Kaithian transports and ships carrying marines. The battle groups had orders to protect those ships at all costs, but even so, in addition to the nine that had gone down with the fallen battle groups, four more battle groups had failed to protect a total of two Kaithian ships and three troop carriers.

Ek could do nothing more than she had already done to protect the troops as they passed through the asteroid field, but she could make sure that however many remained on the other side were as secure as possible.

"Communications, disseminate orders for every ship in the fleet to slow their acceleration, with the exception of the Kaithian ships, troop ships and five battle groups, which I will designate and send to your console. I want the high-priority ships to have the bulk of the fleet protecting them from Hellsongs."

Her subordinates executed her orders with admirable precision, but even so, the enemy reacted more efficiently. The three battle groups stationed in orbit above Klaxon left the planet the moment the troop and Kaithian ships pulled ahead, and the pursuing Ixan swarm increased their speed, swiftly closing in.

Baxa's ability to maximize his force potential was almost as frightening as the sheer numbers he had at his command.

It took everything Ek had not to let herself become intimidated by the odds facing her. If she had not been a Fin, she was uncertain she would have possessed the rationality to remain calm.

The one positive aspect of the coming engagement was that Klaxon lacked any orbital defense platforms, since their construction would have made it obvious to Commonwealth observers that the Ixa were preparing for war. If they had been present, Ek was sure her fleet would have been crushed against them by the pursuing Ixa.

Without orbital defense platforms, the allies had a slight chance of victory today. At the very least, Ek felt reasonably confident she could get enough shuttles carrying troops and Kaithe through to Klaxon.

"The three battle groups from Klaxon are about to enter laser range, Flockhead," her sensors adjutant said.

"Order all Roostships to launch the remaining thirty percent of their Talon wings. Those Talons are to run missile defense for the high-priority ships, which in turn will launch their shuttles at the last possible moment. Order the five vanguard battle groups to hit the enemy groups with everything they have."

"Yes, ma'am."

A wave of dizziness hit Ek, then, and she gripped the restraints holding her in place, though it did little to steady her. The sensation passed after a few moments, though not before several of her adjutants noticed her discomfort, their eyes flitting away just as quickly.

I must fight this. She'd vowed not to let her recurring space sickness affect her ability to command, but it was much worse than it had been before her recovery, and she could see it already affecting morale.

CHAPTER 63

Expanded Cognition

"All right, Husher," Captain Cho said over comlink. "The battle group is nearing Klaxon. Link with Aheera and then board your designated shuttle."

"Yes, sir," he said, ending the call. Before turning to the Kaithian, Husher cast a quick glance over the *Vanquisher*'s shuttle bay, his eyes landing on Caine. They would be taking separate shuttles, to minimize the risk of the mission's command structure getting decapitated before it could even begin.

Caine offered him a small smile. Something seemed off about her, but Husher had no idea what. There was no time to ask, or even to dwell on it. They had to move.

"Let's do this," he said to Aheera.

"Are you certain you're ready?" the blue-white alien said, peering up at him with large eyes. Their practice sessions had been a little rocky, but Husher had arrived at a place where he could remain "present" and prevent himself from being distracted by the vast intellectual resources of the Kaithe. Most of the time, anyway. It would have to do.

"I have to be ready. Come on. I—" Husher cut off as his perspective expanded beyond anything he could have dreamed possible. Even though he'd experienced this just hours before, it still came as a total shock, since his regular intellect was incapable of retaining the full experience of these expanded capabilities.

Sensory data poured in from millions of Kaithe, seated in shuttles distributed across hundreds of vessels. With it came the wisdom and memory of a species that had survived and evolved for eons, along with access to their combined intellect.

An individual Kaithian was more intelligent than the smartest human—he had a profound appreciation for that, now. But combined, only one word could be used to describe the level of cognition Husher now commanded: superintelligence.

Studying Aheera, he was having trouble picking out the thread of her consciousness from the broader Consensus. That was something he'd struggled with during their sessions, though she assured him the Kaithe would help him by prioritizing important information and nudging it to the forefront of his awareness.

Even without direct access to her thoughts, by analyzing his memories of interacting with Kaithe—how they'd responded to statements and gestures and tone inflections and situations—he rapidly put together a lexicon of their body language and microexpressions, a lexicon he deemed accurate enough to project her current attitude toward him.

Whereas he'd assumed the Kaithian viewed him with some disdain, perhaps as a superior being views a lesser lifeform, he was surprised to realize that instead, she beheld him with a mixture of pride and fear. Pride over what an honorable exemplar of humanity she considered Husher to be, and fear that he would one day allow his baser emotions to cloud his ethics, leading to dishonorable acts for which the Kaithe would ultimately be responsible, as humankind's creators.

Husher's gaze drifted to Caine, and given his lifelong familiarity with human emotion and body language, paired with a multiplied intellect that allowed him to parse microexpressions, he immediately saw what had been bothering her: she feared for his life.

That was also why she seemed so distant, today. Indeed, he now saw that the reason Caine had been reluctant to define their relationship was that she was terrified of losing him, and she believed that by keeping things between them fluid, she would spare herself pain if he died.

He also understood that she was wrong. If either of them died, the other would be paralyzed with sadness.

Husher crossed the deck and placed his hands on her upper arms. "I love you, Sera."

Her eyes flitted nervously from side to side, and he knew that she was gauging the reactions of her subordinates. "Husher, I— is now the—?"

"I love you," he said again.

She glanced at the floor, then her gaze rose to meet his. "God. I love you, too. Okay? Now let's get this thing done."

"I'll see you on the surface." They parted, and he made his way to the waiting Albatross-class shuttle—the UHF's most advanced combat shuttle. It would be flown by Skids, who was the shuttle pilot Husher trusted most, and his newly acquired superintelligence did nothing to alter that.

Ochrim waited inside the shuttle, already strapped into a crash seat. Reading his posture and microexpressions, Husher gleaned that the Ixan's guilt was crushing him, which was why he hadn't stood outside the shuttle with the others while they waited for word from Captain Cho.

Husher also saw that he could trust the Ixan to do whatever he could to complete the mission. There was no question Ochrim was a war criminal, but right now he was a war criminal they desperately needed.

Consider this the start of your penance, Ixan. We'll follow it up with a long stint in a small cell for you.

An hour later, Husher traveled at breakneck speed toward the surface of Klaxon, remaining totally calm as his shuttle's escort of Talons was picked off one-by-one by the planet's defense group of drone fighters. The tactical display told him that four other allied shuttles had already gone down, one of them filled with Kaithe and three others with mixed-species marines.

But what use did Husher have for fear? Giving in to the emotion would serve nothing, except to honor a legacy of animal urges best suppressed in situations like this one.

If he died, then he would no longer have a stake in the outcome of this mission, and any sensations of fear would be rendered irrelevant. As long as he was alive, it was irrational to let fear cloud his judgment and hinder his performance.

Best to maintain a state of perfect equanimity, in order to optimally leverage the resources at his disposal. Of course, until the shuttle landed, there was nothing he could do to influence whether he survived or not, and so he waited with his hands crossed in his lap as the last Talon protecting them exploded in a ball of flame and the drone fighters' guns turned on the shuttle itself.

Across from him, Ochrim gripped his straps tightly, the scaly skin whitening around his knuckles.

"We're hit," came Skids' panicked voice over the com. "We're going down!"

CHAPTER 64

Lust for Honor

When the first Ixan fleet entered Corydalis, the system just outside the Baxa System, they found a comparatively tiny force to confront them.

It consisted of just the *Providence*, accompanied by the fourteen surviving Gok ships from those that had joined the allies, a battle group of UHF warships, and ten Roostships—thirty-two ships in all, to do battle with the hundred-strong Ixan fleet that had just entered the system.

Keyes breathed a sigh of relief when Werner reported the Ixa's arrival. "Set an intercept course with the enemy, Nav, and tell our accompanying ships to do the same. Follow the agreed-upon acceleration profile." The profile they'd worked out represented the fastest the *Theodore*, his small fleet's slowest ship, could reasonably accelerate.

The Ixa's appearance meant the allies' hopes were being realized: that once the attack on the Baxa System began, the enemy would lessen the pressure on human, Winger, and Gok colonies in order to return home with all haste.

It also meant that Keyes was about to wage the largest, most desperate battle of his life. The hundred ships currently in his sights represented only the beginning—a tiny beginning, compared to what would come.

"It's just as you predicted, Captain," Werner said. "Upon detecting our advance, the Ixa slowed their approach in order to arrange themselves in an optimal defensive formation."

"Thank you, Werner," Keyes said with a slight nod. No doubt the Ixa were salivating at the prospect of finally taking down the *Providence*, and of the favor they would gain among their kind by doing so.

The enemy forces seemed prepared to accept Keyes's suicide charge at face value. Perhaps if they'd been commanded directly by Baxa, they might have overcome their lust for honor and accolades in order to see what was actually taking place. Or rather, that lust would not have had the opportunity to manifest itself in the first place.

Two minutes before the *Providence* reached the point that would make the enemy force equidistant between her and the darkgate, a stream of allied ships began to emerge from behind that darkgate, where they had been arranged in a tight, two-by-two matrix that extended back in a straight line, effectively concealing them from Ixan sensors.

Though the enemy could not yet ascertain their numbers, Keyes knew exactly how many there were. While most of the Roostships had accompanied Ek into the Baxa System, Keyes had retained seventy of them in total, along with one hundred and forty-eight UHF warships to go with the fourteen remaining Gok vessels.

The enemy craft, carefully arranged to maximize damage against the *Providence* and the ships accompanying her, fell into utter disarray in their panic to react to the nearly two-hundred warships charging their rear.

It wasn't difficult to tell that the Ixan captains were experiencing considerable disagreement over how best to confront two allied forces at once, converging on them from both sides, with numbers far greater than the Ixan fleet's.

The decision was soon taken from their hands, as the allies drew up and lanced into the Ixa with primary lasers, cutting their numbers by nearly a third before sending kinetic impactors to slam into their hulls. They followed up with missiles to finish the job.

The battle quickly became a rout, compounded by the fact that several Ixan ships attempted to flee back to the darkgate, no doubt to inform approaching Ixa about the true numbers awaiting them in the Corydalis System.

None of the ships attempting to escape the way they'd come succeeded in leaving the system. The larger allied force dealt with them handily before that could happen.

When it was over, Keyes turned to his sensor operator. "Damage report, Werner."

"We took some kinetic impactors along our port side, sir. But the damage was negligible. Deployment of damage control teams appears unnecessary."

"What were our losses fleetwide?"

"One Gok warship, eight Roostships, and eleven UHF ships, sir."

Keyes gave a nod, his lips tight. It was an incredible victory by any standards, but they would feel every single loss in the engagements to come.

"Let's prepare for the next wave," he said as he watched the *Silencer* continue across the system, toward the Corydalis-Baxa darkgate. "Allow yourselves a moment to savor that victory, but no more than a moment. You must steel yourselves for what's ahead. Nothing else today will come so easily."

CHAPTER 65

Furious Battle

In the end, Skids's panic proved unnecessary, as he was able to effect an emergency landing within the area Caine had identified as appropriate for a landing zone; not too far from the hilltop stronghold that was their objective, but not so close that they would be obliterated by the Ixa's defenses. No one aboard the shuttle was harmed.

Husher exited the airlock into a humid, overgrown jungle, with Ochrim close behind. Most of Klaxon's surface was covered by jungle, and much of the remainder was desert.

Of the two biomes, Husher considered this one better for their mission parameters, though the Ixa had no doubt chosen it for a reason, and he knew they would take advantage of the jungle terrain at least as much as he planned to.

Caine emerged into the clearing where they'd landed, with a platoon comprised of humans and Wingers at her back, along with another comprised entirely of Gok.

Husher didn't know the Gok military to be particularly well-organized, but these Gok clearly were, maintaining tight formation as they crossed the jungle terrain. He had to assume

Caine had been drilling them hard during the recent weeks. Most of them held the heavy components required to assemble field guns and Howitzers, many of the pieces requiring two Gok to carry. Tort was among them, and he carried the nuke they intended for Baxa himself.

Tort also carried his energy gun slung over his back, which he refused to relinquish, even when, while still on the *Vanquisher*, Caine had warned him he might not be able to carry both across the distances they needed to travel. He'd implored her to let him keep it, swearing he could handle it, and she hadn't escalated her warning to an actual order.

The humans and Wingers with Caine fanned out to secure the clearing's perimeter, and their training also shone through.

If we fail today, it won't be for lack of exquisite soldiers.

Shuttles carrying human, Winger, Gok, and Kaithian troops were touching down all around them. Above, Talon squadrons waged furious battle with their drone fighter counterparts, vying for air superiority.

"We're not going to win the sky battle," Caine said as she drew close enough to be heard while speaking at little more than a whisper. Her faceplate was raised—they intended to keep radio chatter to as close to zero as possible—and Wahlburg trailed behind her, his eyes busy scanning the jungle. "So we can't expect much fire support from the Talons, if any."

"We knew that going in." *As long as the Talons can prevent the drones from dominating the skies, this mission will remain within the realm of possibility.*

"You're right," she said, nodding. "Which is why we're going to locate a viable site for a fire support base within minutes, right?"

Husher turned to Aheera, who had exited the shuttle at his side. They hadn't spoken since leaving the *Vanquisher*, but what need had they for speech?

We have a need for it now. To allow the others to hear us.

"You're better at parsing the Consensus than I am," he said. "We lost some Kaithe coming in, but not many. Do I have that right? I'm having difficulty sifting through the noise."

"You are correct," the Kaithian said. "Four hundred of my people are already fanning through the jungle, and most of your platoons are accompanied by at least a dozen Kaithe each. I can help you sift through the flood of information to focus on the relevant streams."

"I haven't told you what the relevant information is, yet," Caine said, one hand on her hip.

Amusement flashed from Aheera—Husher had grown adept enough with his expanded cognition to know that the emotion was coming from her. The Kaithian already knew what information Caine needed, as did Husher. But they both saw the wisdom in letting Caine ask for it, instead of presumptuously volunteering it.

"I want as much intel as you can give me on the location and composition of enemy troops, their movements, and any defensive structures they have between us and that hilltop base. I also need to know the sites from which they'll be projecting their own fire support, ASAP."

Ochrim raised a finger. "If you'd like—"

"Quiet, Ixan," Caine said. "If you were about to offer me your knowledge of the area, you can cram it up your ass. I haven't quite gotten to trusting you. Besides, even if you do have intel on the Ixa's defenses, it's stale, and you aren't military so you'll leave out the important parts anyway. Husher?" Caine had turned to him again.

Husher nodded, and he strove to adopt a receptive mindset, to let Aheera highlight salient data from the tide of information coming in from the Kaithe in the field, as well as the Kaithe in orbit around the planet.

One of the primary advantages of using the Kaithian network for facilitating the battlefield chain of command was that there was no com chatter for the enemy to intercept. No doubt Baxa had the best decryption techniques in existence at his disposal, but Husher's link with the Kaithe was untouchable.

He used his HUD to bring up a map of the area, which the shuttle's sensors had compiled and transmitted to every marine, even as they sped toward the planet. "Bring up your map, Sergeant," he said.

"All right," she said. "I'm looking at it."

"That shallow valley would be the easiest terrain for us to traverse, and the Ixa know it. They have two firebases in the area, whose fields of fire overlap inside that valley. The terrain to the west is much rougher, and the jungle's a lot thicker there, but if we take that route it will also obscure our movements."

"Baxa must recognize that, too."

"He does. He has soldiers crawling all over the area, including a lot of Gok. Plus, there are defensive structures scattered throughout the route. But if we can keep moving, avoiding outposts when we can and neutralizing enemy forces as efficiently as possible, we can reach another clearing the Kaithe have discovered, which would be perfect for our own fire support base. Its range would cover both the western enemy firebase as well as the approach to the Ixan stronghold."

"I like it," Caine said. "Tell the platoons to disperse themselves across the terrain as much as possible, at random intervals. It's important for us to diffuse our risk, especially with how valuable the Kaithian network is." She turned her head a little, speaking over her shoulder: "Wahlburg, you're responsible for escorting the Ixan."

The marine paused his scrutiny of the jungle to stare at Caine wearing a scandalized expression. "Seriously? You're going to waste your best sniper on guard duty for a reptile?"

"We don't have much use for sniping in this terrain. And if you question my orders one more time today, you'll be escorting him with two black eyes." Caine raised her gun, checked the action, and lowered it again before raising her voice. "All right, people, let's move out. Do not engage the enemy unless they spot you. Remember, strafing and bombing runs from the Ixan drone fighters are still very much a possibility. Let's move."

CHAPTER 66

Not the Time to Mourn

Fesky loosed a Sidewinder at a drone fighter before engaging her Condor's gyros, spinning it around its short axis to send a stream of kinetic impactors at another drone.

Both enemy ships successfully launched their parasitic microcouplers before going down, and she took out each of them in turn, so that neither would latch on to her or one of her pilots.

Admiral Keyes had not wanted to risk repeating the same trick against the second wave of Ixa that he'd used against the first.

He was right not to.

Hiding most of the fleet behind the darkgate again could have ended in disaster. The second wave probably would have known about the first, and when they arrived to find it totally obliterated, they would become suspicious.

They might have even turned around to check behind the darkgate first, engaging the hidden ships before the *Providence* and her smaller group could arrive to support them.

That would have effectively ended the engagement, since the second wave turned out to be larger than the first by nearly one hundred and fifty warships.

The third wave had arrived shortly after the second. It had over three hundred vessels.

A total of five hundred Ixan ships now pressed the *Providence* and the allied warships hard, with more Ixa entering the system in a steady flow.

The battle raged around the Corydalis-Baxa darkgate, with Keyes and the other captains playing savage, desperate defense.

Fesky flipped her fighter around to mow down a stream of missiles fired at her by an Ixan cruiser, and then she shot a parasitic microcoupler just before it reached a nearby Talon. This battle was making her break out every trick she'd learned during her decades-long career.

Preventing these Ixa from reaching Baxa, where they would be assimilated and used to augment his already incredible power, was crucial.

Even so, the fleet Keyes commanded was smaller than the one commanded by Ek. The Ixa faced by Ek were controlled directly by Baxa, whereas these were not...and yet, for the first time since joining the crew of the *Providence*, Fesky was losing hope that even Keyes's ingenuity could eke out a victory.

As she wove through the battle, deftly neutralizing every target available to her while evading the considerable ordnance the enemy directed at her, she also kept an eye on the tactical display, giving orders to the various Air Group squadrons, making them dance.

This high-level multitasking only came with tens of thousands of hours drilling along with hundreds of hours in actual combat. Almost nothing could crack Fesky's cool.

She kept her Condors operating at the periphery of the engagement whenever possible, flanking the Ixan drone fighters, luring them into the meat grinder that was the fully reconstituted, fully trained *Providence* Air Group.

Her squadron arrangement took advantage of her human pilots' inventiveness, her Winger pilots' coordination, and the former insurgent pilots' boldness. They operated in concert to deal massive damage to the enemy, and Fesky couldn't be prouder.

But pride would not win this engagement.

If I'm being honest with myself, I'm not sure anything can.

A glance at the tactical display showed her three drone fighters tailing Airman Bradley. The airman was not Fesky's favorite person, but she would never deny aid to any of her pilots.

"Sit tight, Meteor," she said over a two-way channel. "I'm coming to back you up."

"I got this, Madcap." And indeed, it seemed he did. The pressure was apparently doing as much for Bradley's performance as it was for hers, as he proceeded to display the best flying she'd ever seen from him.

Bradley neutralized one drone fighter with a spray of kinetic impactors, and he assigned a trio of missiles each to the remaining two, before whipping around again and accelerating.

She was about to peel away to find another fight when she noticed Bradley didn't appear to be paying attention to the microcouplers the drone fighters had launched at him. The bombs sped closer, yet he was doing nothing to stop them.

"Meteor," she squawked. "You have three microcouplers on your six, not to mention an Ixan missile cruiser dead ahead. I'm coming to assist."

"I see them, Madcap. I know what I'm doing."

"If you don't turn and shoot them right now, you'll—"

"I don't intend to shoot them. I want you to know I'm sorry for ever disrespecting you, Madcap. You're the best CAG I could have asked for, and I should have appreciated that, instead of snubbing you just because you're a Winger. Give them hell for me, okay?"

"Meteor!"

The three parasitic microcouplers reached Bradley's fighter, latching onto his hull—just before he dove his Condor straight into the enemy missile cruiser's hull.

The microcouplers exploded deep inside the cruiser's guts, tearing it clean in half and letting the void rush in.

Trembling slightly, Fesky refocused on the battle. Now was not the time to mourn. If she honored Bradley's request to give them hell, perhaps there would be time for that later.

Something caught her eye on the tactical display, and she switched to visual, zooming in on a destroyer operating on the periphery of the engagement. Sensor logs told her that it had just arrived at the battle.

It was the *Silencer*. The same vessel that had bruised the *Providence* on Pirate's Path, just a few short months ago. The vessel that, according to Ochrim, was captained by Baxa's son.

Teth is commanding this battle.

Tearing her eyes away from the sight, and trying to ignore the pit that had opened in her stomach, Fesky moved to engage a four-drone formation that appeared to have her in its sights.

CHAPTER 67

Recover and Adapt

During her recovery on Mars, when she had not been studying the Prophecies, Ek had spent every minute poring over Roostship capabilities, as well as the biographies of every captain in the Interplanetary Defense Force.

Since leaving Mars, she had used all of her spare time to watch and rewatch footage from the allies' recent engagements with Ixa, memorizing the enemy tactics, their formations, their flight patterns, their capabilities, the way they thought.

Now, she saw that all that preparation did not come close to being enough. The ships under her command fell in rapid succession, including a Kaithian vessel, which weakened the mission on Klaxon's surface.

The Ixan warships did not just fire on the allied ships—they fired with incredible precision, in such a way that made evasive maneuvers costly, and often ended with the target more exposed than before.

The ships under Baxa's control did not just evade ordnance—they dodged missiles and kinetic impactors by a matter of meters, instantly returning fire. When they did take a hit, it was often to a noncritical section of hull, leaving them at least partially operational.

Ek managed to take down enemy ships, but each minor victory exacted a heavy toll on her forces.

She decided she needed to dispense altogether with existing protocols for military engagements. Both human and Winger protocols provided a framework for battle in which a fleet's flockhead or admiral dispensed orders via the communications officer, with each order representing a broad objective or tactic. The specifics of execution were left to the individual captains.

We cannot afford such inefficiencies any longer.

"Communications, open a fleetwide broadcast channel and leave it open for the duration of the engagement."

"Ma'am?"

"You have your order."

The channel was soon open, and the instant it was, Ek spoke. "Attention all captains. We are changing our operational approach, effective immediately. Going forward, your role will be to execute precise orders, which I will deliver in rapid succession, so listen carefully. For the sake of expedience, I will also dispense with ranks." In this way, she intended to take full advantage of her long hours of study, as well as her ability to perceive the flow of battle better than any Winger or human.

She inhaled deeply from from her breather. "Browning, adjust attitude fifteen degrees upward and answer the missile barrage from the pursuing Ixan cruiser with rapid acceleration and EW tactics to throw off their missile guidance systems. Korbyn, target the battle group on your starboard side with all available

Talons while pointing your Roostship's nose thirty degrees to the left and slowing to half your acceleration while firing main railguns at the Ixan destroyer approaching you head on. Yra, target the same destroyer with ten missiles, sending twenty Talons to back up Stallman while he engages the pair of Ixan corvettes I will designate on the tactical display. Stallman, engage port-side engines to avoid the impactors those corvettes will likely launch at you, while directing your secondary lasers..."

Though it was exhausting, she kept up the cascade of orders, which she arrived at through careful study of the tactical display as she spoke. Faltering was not an option, even though with her resurfacing space sickness, everything took a greater toll on her now.

Her efforts soon bore fruit, and Baxa's forces drew back as the AI tried to account for the change in tactics—the increased efficiency of the allied forces. Seeing this, Ek pressed the attack, exploiting Baxa's hesitation.

She knew the advantage she had secured would not last for long. Baxa would recover and adapt. But while he did, Ek would put down as many Ixan warships as she could.

CHAPTER 68

Fire Support

Husher dropped to one knee behind a fallen tree, spraying bullets as he descended, and then taking cover in time for the return fire.

Kaithe were everywhere—hidden near both the enemy's flanks, and even crouched silently in the branches overhead. As such, Husher had the sort of visual on his enemy that other soldiers could only dream of.

It allowed him to time his next salvo perfectly, popping up just as an enemy Gok trooper was lining up its shot. Husher sent lead streaming into its face, and it fell backward, clawing at its eyes.

Allied Gok pounded past his location, not bothering with cover, sending white-hot energy bolts at the enemy where they cowered behind foliage, much of which caught fire.

Taking advantage of the turmoil, Husher leapt to his feet as well, charging forward, confident in the knowledge that he had a clear view of anyone with the opportunity to fire upon him. If one of those drew a bead on him, he'd hit the ground and return fire.

The enemy Ixa and Gok formations broke, and they fled in the direction of their stronghold. They didn't get very far before Kaithe began dropping on them from above.

Everything Husher remembered from the simulation on the Kaithian homeworld was true: the childlike aliens were vicious in combat, using their powerful tails to toss around Gok and Ixan alike. Husher saw one Kaithian appear from behind a tree and drive her tail straight into an Ixan's face, leaving it a ruined mess.

Husher stopped, turning to find Caine. She was approaching from behind, much more cautiously than the Gok. "You should order them to stop giving chase," he said. Some of the human and Winger marines had caught the Gok's fervor, and were advancing just as recklessly.

"Why?" she said.

"Because I'm reasonably confident the enemy soldiers are only giving the appearance of fleeing in terror. They're under Baxa's control, and I doubt Baxa breaks that easily. So why would he make his forces flee, unless he was trying to lead us into a trap?"

"You're right. Distribute the order through the Kaithian network."

He nodded. "Doing so now."

Wahlburg and Ochrim appeared through the foliage. The Ixan seemed to be handling the chaos fairly well, but the marine still wore a sour expression over the task he'd been assigned.

A few minutes later, Husher received word via the Consensus that he'd been right about Baxa's trap. The enemy troops had retreated to a place where the jungle opened onto a wide field, which would have been perfect for the enemy firebase to hammer with artillery.

Now those troops will have to backtrack to be of any use. As intelligent as Baxa was, he'd clearly underestimated his foe's perceptiveness.

They weren't far from the site where they intended to erect their own fire support base, and Caine had Husher order all nearby troops to advance on it, double-time. She left it to him to deal with enemy troops encroaching on their route, and he had mortar teams roaming up and down the line, executing counter-preparation fire whenever an enemy platoon drew too near.

At last, they reached the clearing, along with the Gok platoon carrying the necessary equipment.

"I want the two anti-air guns set up first, there and there," Caine barked, pointing. "The drone fighters will want to prioritize this area for their bombing and strafing runs going forward, and we can't rely exclusively on the Talons to protect us. After the anti-air, get those field guns set up and begin counterbattery fire against the nearest enemy firebase, immediately. In the meantime, we'll lean on Husher's mortar teams to cover us against enemy ground troops."

Once she'd instructed the Gok on exactly how she wanted the fire support base set up, Caine walked over to Husher. "As long as we leave some Kaithe here, there's no reason we can't continue pressing the attack," she said. "You can pass my orders back through your link."

"Agreed." He looked to his left, where Aheera, Tort, Wahlburg, and Ochrim stood close together, though each seemed intent on ignoring the others. "Let's move."

Husher used the Consensus network to rally every platoon that wasn't needed to defend their new firebase, and they pressed on toward their hilltop objective.

CHAPTER 69

A Battle Group unto Herself

"Admiral, an Ixan cruiser is bearing down on us," Werner said, sounding breathless. "She'll have a clear shot for a missile barrage, if she's looking for one."

Keyes nodded, gripping his chair's armrests lightly. "Then let's knock her back on her heels before she has the chance. Loose fifty Banshees at the cruiser, Tactical."

"We're running low on missiles, sir," his XO said.

"I know that, Arsenyev," he said gently. "But these will be well spent. I'd rather use up some of our limited supply in offense than use a greater number as we scramble to defend against a missile attack."

Keyes watched the chaotic engagement unfold on his console's tactical display, monitoring the nearby space for viable targets and likely threats while keeping an eye on the allied battle groups to see whether any could be used more effectively.

The *Providence* was a battle group unto herself, roving the engagement with her Air Group surrounding her, dealing death wherever she went. She was a target of great interest to the Ixa, and they'd already tried twice to tighten the noose around her. Both times, the loose formation of five allied battle groups, whose captains Keyes had ordered to remain in the neighborhood without giving the impression of cohesion, had converged on the supercarrier.

Together with the allied ships, the *Providence* eviscerated the prey she'd lured in. But after the second such occurrence, the Ixa grew wise to the tactic. Now, they mostly kept their distance from the *Providence*, except for the odd warship playing the hero, as the missile cruiser had.

Keyes's mouth quirked as the Ixan cruiser blossomed with fire, having failed to shoot down the final six missiles of the fifty-strong barrage.

His satisfaction was quickly quenched, however, as a strike force of Ixan destroyers and cruisers descended on one of his battle groups operating at the periphery of the engagement. They tore it to shreds.

The strike force's flagship was a destroyer Keyes knew well. He'd certainly watched the footage enough of his engagement with her captain.

Teth.

It seemed clear Teth was in command of the entire enemy fleet. Since the *Silencer* had arrived, the hundreds of Ixan vessels appeared to center on her, and they closed around her whenever the destroyer was threatened. According to Ochrim,

Teth had been the main agent of Baxa's will before Husher freed the AI, so it made sense that he would be put in charge here.

Teth's forces seemed to have finished entering the system, and half of them were still in transit across it, screaming toward the battle raging around the Corydalis-Baxa darkgate. Once all the Ixan ships arrived, the dwindling allied fleet would face an enemy over one thousand strong. After that, it would be laughable to think they could hold out for more than an hour. Even defending for that long would require a minor miracle.

Something caught Keyes's eye on the tactical display, and he quickly ran some numbers on his console, complementing them with his own projections.

Yes, he thought, tracing his finger across the console's screen. Teth's strike force was almost certainly maneuvering to attack the *Providence,* even though it wasn't heading directly for her. Soon, the distribution of enemy ships would favor such a charge. And the five battle groups Keyes had ordered to operate nearby would not be enough to defeat that force.

Despite the danger, he had to admit that he was impressed by Teth's gambit. Keyes almost hadn't spotted it.

Glancing around the CIC, he checked to see whether any of his officers had noticed what he'd seen. None of them seemed alarmed—at least, no more alarmed than was warranted by being so woefully outnumbered.

Keyes returned to his study of the tactical display, zooming it out to view the entire battle. There was no way any battle group could spare warships to back him up, not without severely comprising their own already-specious security, but perhaps...

"Coms, put out a call to all Roostships requesting that they send us as many Talons as they can spare, as discreetly as possible. We're going to need the extra fighters to run missile defense."

Khoo was peering at Keyes from the Tactical station, wearing a quizzical expression. "Admiral, surely our point defense turrets—"

"Oh, no," Arsenyev said, staring at the CIC's main viewscreen, which also showed a zoomed-out tactical display. The color had drained from her face.

She's seen what I've seen.

Wordlessly, Keyes circled the strike force positioning itself to attack and sent the designation over to Khoo's console with a flicking gesture. Studying it, the Tactical officer nodded grimly.

"The transmission has been sent, Admiral," the Coms officer said.

"Very good. Follow it up with one to the captains of our five accompanying battle groups, notifying them of the danger but instructing them not to give any sign that they've noticed."

"What's our plan, Admiral?" Arsenyev asked.

"I'm not sure yet."

That revelation didn't do much for his crew's morale—he could see that in the way they sat even more stiffly than before. But he didn't believe in lying to his subordinates. Besides, he would come up with something.

"Admiral..." Werner trailed off nervously.

The tactical display gave the reason for his trepidation: Teth's force was unfurling across the battle space, finally proclaiming their intention to envelop the *Providence* and destroy her. The carriers among them began to launch drone fighters, and Keyes realized they'd been keeping them in reserve for this very moment.

Our primary capacitor is discharged...missiles almost depleted...

He cleared his throat. "Commence kinetic impactor salvos against the enemy targets, with a two-mile spread in every direction." It was far from a brilliant move, but impactors now formed the bulk of the *Providence*'s remaining arsenal, and he needed to use them before the Condors and Talons engaged. After that, it would be much harder to fire impactors without the risk of hitting friendly fighters.

The impactors disabled a single missile cruiser while taking out less than a squadron of drones and doing superficial damage to three other Ixan warships. Otherwise, their effect was negligible.

Soon after, Keyes realized that there was little to be gained by having the nearby allied battle groups continue to feign ignorance. Instead, he had them move to confront the oncoming Ixan force, unleashing wave after wave of missiles at them.

The Ixa responded in kind, speeding forward to engage. To Keyes's surprise, the *Silencer* still had its primary capacitor charged, and it used it to take out one of the *Providence*'s main engines. Keyes cursed under his breath, restraining an urge to pound his armrest in frustration.

In the end, by using the remainder of the supercarrier's Banshees and by suffering crippling losses to the battle groups backing her up, they managed to defeat the attacking Ixan force, and the *Providence* survived. Just before Teth's strike force crumbled, his destroyer broke away to seek the protection of another Ixan battle group.

Even though the *Providence* was important to the engagement symbolically, Keyes could tell his CIC crew did not feel any satisfaction about their success. Nearly half of the remaining Condor pilots had also fallen defending their supercarrier, along with over three hundred Talons.

The *Providence* limped through space, with only kinetic impactors at her disposal. Staring bleakly at the tactical display, Keyes finally began to accept the bald fact staring him plain in the face: it was over.

The allied fleet in Corydalis would fall, and the Ixa that overcame them would pour into their home system, only to be co-opted by Baxa. That would doom Ek, and soon after it would doom Husher and Caine.

The end had arrived.

CHAPTER 70

Slipping

E k gave orders over the fleetwide broadcast channel as fast as she could, despite the way her head swam, and how hollow she felt.

Thankfully, the captains under her command trusted her to direct them in a way that kept them as safe as possible while delivering maximum damage, and so no one interrupted the flow of instructions with any challenges. "Cervenka, execute a full-retro thrust while spraying the indicated drone fighter squadron with kinetic impactors. Williams—"

Her entire Command Roostship rocked, tossing Ek into her restraints, causing them to dig into her body. "What was that?" she asked once the tremors stopped.

The sensors adjutant was looking at her with his beak slightly parted, looking guilty. "Ma'am, a rocket got through the ship's hull and opened her up to space. I thought our point defense system could handle the barrage, but I didn't want to interrupt you to get your perspective. I'm so sorry. If you need me to contact my deputy to take over for—"

Ek held up a placating hand. "Please. Just focus on your role." She stared at the tactical display in disbelief. *I am slipping.* She should have seen that barrage coming, as well the inadequacy of the Roostship's turrets to stop it. But she had been so intent on keeping the rest of the fleet safe...

The other captains would be wondering why she had ceased her litany of commands. Her mounting nausea was disrupting her concentration, but she couldn't tell them that. She just needed to press on. Returning to her scrutiny of the battle space, she forced herself to take deeper breaths.

Baxa had taken less than an hour to adapt to her fleet's new-found responsiveness, and the only way for her to improve her position again would be to continue the rapid delivery of orders while improving each order's effectiveness. She needed to do better. She needed—

"Flockhead!" The sensors adjutant was pointing at the bridge's main screen, which showed an Ixan carrier bearing down on them while streaming drone fighters from its flight decks.

"Rally the Talons," she said. "Tell them we need their protection. Navigation adjutant, set a course for the middle of the drone swarm, and time our arrival to sync with that of our fighters."

"Ma'am?"

"If we draw near enough for our point defense turrets to have an effect, we may be able to protect our fighter wing in turn. Otherwise, I fear the damage the drones' microcouplers will do."

"Yes, Flockhead."

Her ship leapt forward, and the enemy reacted in a way that suggested surprise, their formations slipping.

It was not much, but it was something. Ek knew her maneuver carried a lot of risk, however playing it safe would never keep her fleet alive long enough for Husher to complete his mission. She needed to continue employing novel tactics, or Baxa would dispatch her fleet with ease.

As her Command Roostship thrust itself into the crowd of deadly drones and the Talons arrived to help, Ek returned to her tirade of orders.

Admiral Keyes's words returned to her, then, from another time when all seemed lost:

We hold on.

CHAPTER 71

Shock and Grief

At the same time he saw it, Husher also *felt* the Kaithian leap from the ground, wrap its muscular tail around the Gok's neck, and snap it, sending the forest-green giant to the ground in a crumpled heap.

The tiny alien darted forward the moment she'd confirmed the kill, hunting for the next, and so did Husher. *He'd* confirmed the kill, and now he sought his next prey.

He also ran through the treetops, branches flitting by beneath his blue-white feet, the furnace of the afternoon sun flickering through the canopy overhead. A patch of dark green drew his eye to the jungle's undergrowth, followed by a flash of midnight—the color of the Ixan military's uniform.

There. We must have the field guns apply defensive fire there. He transmitted the location through the Consensus and fled through the trees to avoid getting hit by the field guns.

Husher also ran after Caine from tree to boulder to tree, assault rifle at the ready, feeling his cognition dwindling as more and more Kaithe fell. The anxiety that caused him—the sensation that a part of him was dying—was unlike anything he'd ever experienced.

The only solace came from the fact that as they neutralized Ixa, Baxa's power also had to be dwindling.

A savage psychic blow hit him, sending him to his knees. It felt like thousands of Kaithe had died at once, and as he clutched his head, he realized that was exactly what had happened: Baxa must have taken out another one of their ships in orbit.

"Husher?" Caine whispered. He looked up to meet her eyes, which looked worried.

"I'm fine." He lowered his hands and rose to one knee, but then another Kaithian ship went down, and he seized his head again, squeezing it. He screamed.

"*Husher!*" She ran to him, dropping to a knee beside him, placing a hand on his shoulder while darting glances backward, no doubt to check for any enemy operatives who might have heard his cry. "You have to hold it together," she said softly. "If you can't, this engagement is over. You know that."

"Yeah." He staggered to his feet, raising his assault rifle to a ready position again. Realizing he'd lifted it too far, he readjusted its position. "Let's move."

"We're almost as far as we can go. The Ixan stronghold isn't in range of our fire support base, but if we fire rockets from the edge of the area it protects, we can hit it. Where are our rocket launchers?"

Husher squinted, staring into space, forcing himself to concentrate. Three squads carried rocket launchers, distributed across three platoons.

"They're near," he said.

"Tell them to get as close as they can to the stronghold while staying under cover. Order them to prepare to fire at its walls on my signal. Your signal, I mean. I'll give you the signal."

"I get it," he said, offering her a small smile. She smiled back. Then gunfire thundered nearby, bringing them back to their situation.

After waiting for Wahlburg, Aheera, Tort and Ochrim to catch up, they pressed on toward their objective. The thousands of Kaithe dying had hit Aheera hard, too—Husher had felt it hit her. She'd handled it better than him. They exchanged glances, but otherwise they didn't remark on the occurrence.

A half hour later, they were in position, along with the three rocket launcher teams, distributed along the edge of their firebase's circle of protection. The hilltop ahead rose out of the jungle, the stronghold gleaming atop it like a metal crown.

Husher sent a signal to every active platoon that wasn't currently engaged in pitched battle: *Come now. Muster here. We're about to strike.*

"We can't wait any longer," Caine hissed. "We're sitting ducks. It's time to take our chance."

"Most of our forces are out of position," Husher said.

"Doesn't matter. We move or we die."

He knew she was right. "Okay. I'll send the signal?"

A curt nod from Caine. "Do it."

He did, and seconds later, thirty rockets streamed forth from three different locations, slamming into the side of the stronghold. Explosions blossomed, rising into the humid air, sending spurts of fire and molten metal sailing into the jungle.

I'm glad we're not any closer than we are.

But they soon would be. "Let's move," Caine ordered as dark smoke reared up from the explosion.

The jungle was catching fire in multiple places—Husher saw that through the eyes of hundreds of Kaithe. If they didn't reach the stronghold now, they wouldn't reach it at all. Not today, and probably not ever.

Worse: the fire would prevent their out-of-position troops from joining them inside the facility. The few platoons close enough would comprise the entire force they'd have to complete the mission.

"*Run!*" Caine screamed, the need for stealth having evaporated with a fresh eruption of gunfire all around them. The enemy Ixa and Gok were fighting hard to prevent them from progressing through the jungle, and more bullets came from what remained of the stronghold's roof and walls.

At last, they reached the blackened, twisted whorl the fortress wall had become. The jagged metal smoked, and it would not have been safe to cross for someone without a UHF-issue pressure suit or equivalent.

Tort brought the nuke inside, setting it down gently on the floor, which was largely intact. Then he returned to pick up Aheera, making her look like a doll in his arms, rather than the fierce warrior Husher knew she was.

The Gok stepped over a protrusion of metal with a wicked-looking edge, and then he placed the Kaithian on the floor next to the nuke. Husher and Caine followed, trailed by Wahlburg and Ochrim.

Two platoons had already set up position on both ends of the corridor they'd accessed, ready to fight off Ixan defenders. There were Kaithe, Wingers, Gok, and humans, all working together to end the threat Baxa posed to the galaxy. Husher couldn't allow himself more than a moment to reflect on this unprecedented inter-species cooperation, but it heartened him nevertheless.

He turned to Ochrim. "Which way?"

"Either way leads to stairwells that will take us down to the facility where Baxa is housed. There are no elevators—they were dismantled once construction on the facility was complete."

"All right." Husher exchanged glances with Caine, tilting his head back at the hallway behind him. "That way has the most friendly Gok. They'll make the best vanguard."

"Yeah," Caine said. "Good call."

But Husher doubted he would ever forgive himself for making that call.

As they crossed a corridor, after being assured it was clear by the Wingers who'd scouted it, a single shot rang out. Caine fell, clutching her neck.

"No!" Husher shouted, and he fell out of the Kaithian Consensus, tumbling back into his regular human condition, where shock and grief awaited, threatening to break him.

He ran to Caine's side.

CHAPTER 72

A Chance

Keyes's fleet had fallen below one hundred ships.

The *Providence* flew through the battle, providing more utility in drawing Ixan attention away from the other allied ships than it did with its limited arsenal.

Her Air Group flew with her, also severely reduced. But Fesky didn't rest, urging her pilots on, not letting them focus on the doom that would soon come for them all. In the rare moments when Keyes's attention wasn't required elsewhere, he tuned into the Air Group's channel at low volume, just to hear Fesky's spirit.

On the tactical display, he watched two UHF missile cruisers fall, followed by two frigates and a corvette. Then, one of their four remaining destroyers went down, to the battle group that Teth had taken direct command of.

It's happening. The allies' ability to provide a meaningful defense was crumbling, and the enemy fleet would have access to the Baxa System soon.

A thought had occurred to Keyes around an hour ago, and he knew its time had come. Indeed, since the war began, and even before, he'd known something like this could very well become necessary.

Now that the moment had arrived, a resistance rose up inside him. But he knew where that came from. His resistance to what he knew must be done was mere animal instinct—the will to survive.

He shunted it aside. "Piper," he barked at his Coms officer. "Get me Piper."

"Yes, sir."

"The moment you have him, order the entire crew to execute evacuation protocol, making their way to the escape pods and remaining shuttles."

"S-sir?"

"Don't question, just do it!"

Moments later, the Tumbran's voice emerged from Keyes's com. "Admiral Keyes."

"Piper." Over their conversation, the evacuation order sounded throughout the ship. He ignored it. "I need the software you used to remotely control the Vermillion Shipyard vessels. How difficult would it be to install on the *Providence*?"

"It would be impossible. The software exploits a feature designed well after the *Providence* was built, which slaves the sensor feeds, navigation functions, helm functions, and so on to a single console. To fly the *Providence*, you need a full CIC crew at minimum, Admiral."

"Damn it."

"Admiral?" Arsenyev said, and he looked up at her, a lump suddenly forming in his throat.

"Yes?"

"What are you planning?"

"Never mind. I—anyone participating in what I'm planning is not likely to survive."

"What is it?" Werner said.

Keyes looked around his CIC crew, bile creeping up his throat. "No. I can't ask—"

"You *can* ask us, sir," Arsenyev said. "And we deserve the opportunity to answer. If you think we can give humanity a chance, you must tell us how."

He swallowed. "Piper?" he murmured. "Are you still there?"

"I'm still here, Admiral."

Gazing around his CIC, Keyes spoke. "There's a way for us to defeat Teth. It involves using one of the other UHF ships to generate a wormhole. The *Constellation*, perhaps. We'd still need your software, Piper, to control her."

"Sir," Werner said, "the wormholes—"

"They destroy all organic matter that passes through them," Keyes interrupted. "But we can still open them. And if we allow one to slam shut without a conductor in place to recapture its energy, it'll wipe out most of this system, and the Ixan fleet along with it. We can open the wormhole's ends on opposite sides of their fleet. But we need to give the other allied ships a chance to escape first. That's where the *Providence* comes in— to keep the enemy occupied long enough for the rest of the fleet to slip into the Baxa System. Piper, can you shut down the darkgate from the other side, once you're through?"

"I won't be going through the darkgate, Admiral," the Tumbran said, sounding resigned. "For this to work, you need me in the *Constellation*'s CIC. You could fly her from the *Providence* using my software, but you wouldn't be able to create a wormhole that way."

"Piper..."

"I've made my choice, Admiral. This is about Tumbra, too—not just humanity. Once the other ships are through the darkgate, I'll transmit an override command to it, closing it. Then I'll trigger the wormhole."

Keyes opened his mouth, but before he could speak, Arsenyev stood up from her console. "I'm staying, Admiral. You need a full CIC to fly the *Providence*. I'd rather die in this way than have humanity's blood on my hands."

"Arsenyev, no."

"I'm *staying*, Leonard."

Her use of his first name made him blink. But there was no point reprimanding her. Not now.

Werner stood from his console. "I'm staying too, Admiral."

One by one, his CIC officers rose and declared they would stay to help execute Keyes's plan.

He let out a ragged sigh. "You're among the finest men and women humanity has ever known," he told them softly. "Your loss will be devastating, and I hope our species recognizes that."

"The same goes for you, Admiral," Arsenyev said.

He didn't acknowledge the remark. "Sit at your consoles, everyone. Let's get to work."

CHAPTER 73

God Speed

Captain Duncan of the *Constellation* stood in front of the hatches leading to her destroyer's port-side escape pods, ushering her crew inside them.

She'd entered the Captain Emergency Prerogative code into her com, which overrode crew privacy protections to inform her of each man and woman's location. Only when the entire crew was moving toward their nearest escape pod did she start to breathe a little easier.

Even through the frantic exodus, she managed to reflect on what an amazing person Admiral Keyes was. The idiom "the captain goes down with the ship" had survived since the days when humanity had lived on Old Earth, but she'd never heard of anyone interpreting it literally, at least not in modern times. If anyone was going to do so, it would be Keyes. *And his entire CIC crew...* Their names would echo through the chambers of history.

Duncan would be among the last to climb inside one of the cramped escape pods, but that was as far as she would take the idiom. The pod's AI would then disengage it from the ship, launching it from its ejection tube and sending it straight at the darkgate.

Only shuttles were designed to dock with the cylindrical escape pods in order to extract crewmembers, and there would be no time for the other UHF ships to deploy shuttles to collect them before they exited the system. Duncan wasn't confident about the probability of every pod making the journey intact, but they had a chance, whereas just forty minutes prior she'd felt certain everyone on the *Constellation* would die.

Before entering the escape pod herself, Duncan cast one last look over her shoulder, at her beloved ship. She'd captained the destroyer for seven years, and now she would become the captain of nothing except a squat tube. That was hard. But she preferred it to death.

As she took a step toward the hatch, footsteps caught her ear, coming from the direction of the ship's shuttle bay. Turning her head, she saw the Tumbran walking briskly down the corridor, escorted by two marines, no doubt on the way to the CIC. The diminutive alien's gray chin sack wobbled back and forth as he approached.

Duncan waited until the Tumbran reached her. When he did, he gazed up at the pair of soldiers. "You should go with Captain Duncan. The only thing I need protection from is Ixan weapons fire, and there's nothing you can do about that. Go, and live."

"Thank you, Piper," Duncan said, sketching out a salute with a hand that wouldn't stop trembling.

The Tumbran pointed in her face. "You can thank me by fighting to make sure your species never loses its way again. All

right? Humanity nearly doomed us all. You have incredible potential as a species, incredible power. If you misuse it again,
you'll take the galaxy down with you. Do you understand?"

"Yes," she said, a little breathless.

"Then spread the message. Fight your species' worst tenden-
cies until your dying day, Captain Duncan. Let what is best for
others guide you—best for other humans, and best for the other
species that share the stars with humans. In turn, others will
care for you."

"I will," Duncan said. "I promise that I will."

"I believe you," Piper said. He continued on toward the CIC.

"God speed," Duncan called after him.

"And you," the alien replied without looking back.

CHAPTER 74

Battle Spread Formation

"Fesky, come in. Are you there?" It was Admiral Keyes's voice.

"Just a moment," she snapped, whipping her Condor around its short axis to pick off a microcoupler that had been about to overtake her. That done, she saw the opportunity for a clean shot at a drone fighter. She took it, and missed, cursing.

"Fesky! I need you to disengage."

"Admiral? Disengage?"

"Look at your tactical display. Escape pods have left the *Providence* and the *Constellation.* I need the Air Group to protect them until they reach the Baxa System."

"Has something happened to the *Providence*? Have the life support systems failed?" She accelerated to give herself room to fire on a pair of missiles in close pursuit, then scanned her tactical display for more immediate threats.

"Everything's functional."

"Then what's going on?"

"I..." The admiral sighed. "I have a plan to defeat Teth. I've ordered the fleet to transition into the Baxa System, but I have to stay."

"Then I'm staying too!" Fesky loosed a Sidewinder at a drone, and this time she got it.

"Fesky, I need you to escort those escape pods. I've given you a direct order, and I expect you to obey."

"Admiral—"

"If our friendship means anything, you'll obey without further question."

"I can't just leave you. I can help, sir."

"You've helped me plenty, old friend. You've saved my life more than once. But this is something I need to do alone. I'm prepared to beg you to obey my orders, but I hope you won't make me spend my dignity before I do what I need to do."

Fesky took a deep breath. "It's been an honor serving under you, Admiral. I can't describe how—"

"You don't need to. There's no time, and I already know. Though I'm not sure you can possibly know what your friendship has meant to me. Protect those evacuees, Colonel. Keyes out."

The channel went dead, and Fesky was already trembling violently.

Get a grip, Fesky. You need to focus.

She opened a wide channel. "All Condor pilots, form on me. We're escorting those escape pods out of the system. Battle spread formation until I say otherwise."

The tactical display showed what was left of the Air Group falling in around the escape pods, drawing farther and farther away from the *Providence*, which was charging deeper into the enemy fleet.

Goodbye, old friend.

CHAPTER 75

Much Harder

The Ixan sniper's shot had entered Caine's neck but exited cleanly, without hitting her trachea, jugular vein, or carotid artery. If the bullet had been Ocharium-enriched, it would almost certainly have caused a lethal rupture, but she'd been incredibly lucky. Though she'd fallen unconscious, her suit had sealed the wound, and her vitals were more or less stable.

Husher carried her through the facility. There had been nowhere to leave her, and there was no turning back until the mission was complete. So he carried her, jogging through corridor after corridor, relying on stims to help him keep up the strength he needed to transport her pressure-suit-clad body.

Soon after Caine was shot, Ochrim had led them to a stairwell that seemed to go down forever, twisting around and around, finally ending at a point that felt like it had to be several hundred meters underground.

Now they moved through the facility as fast as they could, traversing corridors and rooms and sometimes even caves, all filled with naked electronics. It was much cooler down here, and it made sense that the Ixa would store Baxa's vast brain so deep underground, rather than on the scorched surface. As with any computing equipment, it benefited from a cold environment.

With Caine in his arms, Husher couldn't fight, and since Tort carried the nuke, his situation was similar. For his part, Wahlburg was occupied with making sure Ochrim didn't walk into an enemy soldier's line of sight.

Aheera remained unburdened, but the facility wasn't as friendly to her style of combat as the jungle had been. Husher saw her take down an Ixan soldier creeping out of a side corridor to get the drop on what remained of the vanguard platoon, but that was all.

The pair of platoons escorting them had been whittled down by attack after attack, until now they totaled less than one platoon, advancing in protective formation around Tort, Husher, Aheera, Wahlburg, Ochrim, and Caine. Six Gok marines still lived, nine Winger, and twelve human, not counting Husher and Caine. A significant force for this type of mission, but if Baxa kept up the pressure he'd been applying so far, that force would soon crumble.

And then Husher would have to lower Caine to the floor. He was prepared to do that in order to fight, but he didn't know whether he was prepared to abandon her altogether—even if the fate of every species in the galaxy depended on it.

I'll have to. Won't I?

The Ixa didn't give him any time to think about it. As the marines crossed through a corridor, the facility's defenders hit them from two sides.

Husher knew the time had come. He ran back to one of the corridors not under fire, gently setting Caine down there. He'd slung his assault rifle over his shoulder, and now he raised it to join the closest group of marines firing on Ixa. Tort carefully put down the nuke out of harm's way and did the same.

The intersection afforded them some cover, but not much. Most of the marines crouched in the hallway itself to shoot, and soon they had the corpses of their comrades to use for cover as well.

Husher saw Ochrim scurry into the line of fire, take up an assault rifle from one of the fallen marines, and run back to cover. Positioning himself behind one of the surviving marines, the Ixan leaned way out into the hallway to fire at his brethren.

Stepping up behind him, Husher yanked the Ixan backward by his pressure suit. The scientist looked at him, blinking.

"Stay back," Husher growled. "You don't know what you're doing, and we need you alive. Got it?"

"Yes. All right."

"I mean it, Ixan."

Staying low, Husher dove into the hallway, coming down prone behind the corpse of Private Simmons. He fired burst after burst over the young marine's thin torso, keeping as low to the floor as he could.

One Ixan fell, and then another. Knowing it was risky but also that they couldn't win otherwise, Husher tore a grenade from his suit, pulled the pin with his teeth, and lobbed it up the corridor.

"Back," he yelled, rising to his feet and dragging Simmons's body up with him, using it as a shield. "Grenade, take cover!"

The surviving marines scrambled back into the perpendicular corridor, huddling against the wall, protecting themselves from the fire that belched through the passage.

The grenade ended the pressure from that side, for now at least, and together the marines met the second Ixan attack head-on, giving no quarter as they moved up the corridor in formation. Bolts of energy flew over the human marines' heads, who fired over the heads of the Wingers in front.

When the shooting stopped, Husher was left with less than a squad's worth of battleworthy marines to complete the mission: Two Gok, four humans, and three Wingers.

Thankfully, both Ochrim and Aheera had also survived the battle.

"You have to rejoin the Consensus," the Kaithian said, peering up at Husher solemnly.

He nodded. "You're right. Link with me."

She did, and his cognition multiplied a thousand fold—ten thousand fold. The enhanced awareness did not make it easier to deal with his fear for Caine or his anxiety that the next attack would render their mission a failure.

It made it harder. Much harder.

"You all right, sir?" Wahlburg said, his sour expression purged by the heat of combat. Now he studied Husher's face, eyes narrowed, mouth tight.

"I'm fine," Husher said, bending to pick up Caine. "Let's keep moving."

CHAPTER 76

Supercarrier

Her railguns were the only weaponry the *Providence* had left, yet they were not to be discounted. The main gun fired Ocharium-enhanced kinetic rounds at incredible velocities, and her secondary guns packed a serious punch as well.

"Don't conserve, Khoo," Keyes said. "Execute simultaneous broadsides from our port and starboard guns, and rip up anything that comes in line with our bow."

"Yes, sir."

"Nav, keep us rotating to sweep as much space as possible with our impactors. I want the Ixa to come for their kill gingerly. They'll come all the same, but they'll have to work for it."

"Aye, Captain."

The tactical display swarmed with enemy ships closing in on them. But many of those nearby kept their distance from the massive supercarrier, and three red icons winked out just as Werner spoke: "Two Ixan missile cruisers down, sir, along with an Ixan destroyer."

Keyes nodded. Normally, that would have been an incredible result, but this engagement had turned into something far from normal. He chalked the triple kill up to the enemy's eagerness to destroy the *Providence* and also the way they kept bunching together to do so. Either way, he didn't intend to celebrate, and he could tell his crew didn't either.

For the moment, the enemy fleet was completely ignoring the *Constellation*. They spiraled inward, with the *Providence* as their epicenter. Their captains couldn't wait to paint themselves with the glory that would come from taking down the legendary ship. They couldn't wait to scurry back to their master and receive whatever scraps he was willing to feed them.

They must not know what awaits them in the Baxa System. They can't.

It didn't matter. The old girl's guns pounded away at the enemy, taking out a corvette, two frigates, countless drone fighters. Parasitic microcouplers flocked toward the supercarrier, lighting on her hull and detonating, one after another. Tremors rocked the ship, but the CIC crew were all strapped in, and with the rest of the crew gone, there was no need to broadcast any warning about bracing for impact.

"Sir, three missile cruisers are forming up behind us, along with the *Silencer*. They—" Werner swallowed. "They've fired a two-hundred missile barrage at our stern. According to visual analysis, these are traditional multi-warhead missiles as opposed to their Hellsongs."

"Nav, bring us around as fast as you can, counter-clockwise, and hard to starboard at the same time," Keyes barked. "Keep up the broadside from our port-side guns, Tactical."

The hard-to-starboard maneuver caused the supercarrier to drift away from the enemy rockets, giving her point defense turrets more time to deal with them. Simultaneously, the quick rotation caused her stream of kinetic impactors to intersect with the incoming missile cloud, neutralizing most of the remainder.

Thirty-three rockets made it through. The *Providence* shook like she never had before, and Keyes felt his teeth rattle as he was shaken in place, causing lancing pains to shoot through his head. Chain-reaction explosions continued to rock the vessel all along her port side, until at last they came to an end.

"I'm only interested in hearing about damage to our weapons, Werner," Keyes said.

"Our port guns are done, sir. She's ripped open completely on that side."

Keyes winced. *I'm sorry, old girl. I'm so sorry.*

"Nav, bring engines up to one hundred percent, full ahead. We don't need to worry about picking our targets, Tactical, because there's no shortage of them. Continue the starboard broadside and set the main railgun to continuous fire as well."

A growing swarm of drone fighters gave chase, and missiles began coming from all sides, many seeking to exploit the devastation the last barrage had wrought along the *Providence*'s port side. Some lasers even lanced out, most of them missing, but a few scoring solid hits on the supercarrier's already-battered hull.

All the while, the *Silencer* harried them from behind, launching barrage after missile barrage.

A handful of missiles penetrated the ship's point defense system. Then another. Her ongoing broadside took out several squadrons of drone fighters in the space of a few seconds, and their microcouplers gave chase, at least ten of them managing to latch onto the *Providence* and explode.

The noise was almost continuous, now, and the ship shook constantly, punctuated by brief silences followed by the next impact.

Arsenyev's eyes found Keyes's across the CIC, and she started to speak just as another silence began.

"I love you," she said, her words ringing clearly in the quiet.

"I love you," Keyes said, but the next cacophony had begun, and he felt sure she hadn't heard him.

The CIC disintegrated around them, and all became awash with flame and light.

CHAPTER 77

Tragic Majesty

As he worked, Piper watched a visual of the *Providence*'s last stand on the main viewscreen of the *Constellation*'s CIC.

The supercarrier had withstood a lot more damage than he would have expected. He supposed that, in addition to having superior locomotion when compared to the UHF ships that had been designed to rely on wormhole generation, the *Providence* had also had superior armor.

The newer ships didn't have as much need for armor, at least they hadn't before dark tech failed. But it had taken dozens of missiles and microcouplers, hundreds of kinetic impactors, and significant laserfire to take down the *Providence.*

In the end she'd fallen, though, in an explosion nothing could have survived. Even if, by some miracle, the CIC crew still lived, they would not survive what Piper was about to do.

Neither would he.

Humans didn't understand Tumbran emotions, and so they tended to assume Tumbra were basically without feeling. Piper actually did feel fairly clinical about his own impending death, which surprised him a little.

Either way, he felt a deep sadness over the loss of the super-carrier's CIC crew, especially Admiral Keyes.

When other members of Keyes's species had treated Piper like a joke or worse, Keyes had always shown him respect, and that had meant more than Piper could have possibly expressed.

I should have tried to express it, though. He never had, and maybe that was why his current sadness had such an edge.

With the supercarrier gone, the vast Ixan fleet seemed to take notice of the *Constellation*, and it turned toward the ship as one, accelerating. No doubt Teth intended to pick off the destroyer on his way to the Corydalis-Baxa darkgate.

To that end, the nearest formation of cruisers fired a barrage of three-hundred missiles at the *Constellation.*

Piper's work wasn't quite done. In truth, he'd let himself get caught up in the tragic majesty of the *Providence*'s struggle. His gray hands flew over the console now, preparing the coordinates for both ends of the wormhole.

The missiles drew nearer. Piper paused his work briefly to send the darkgate his override code. Moments later, it closed.

That will delay Teth from reaching Baxa, but it's far from enough.

Keeping an eye on the incoming missiles, he realized he wouldn't finish his work in time. He leapt from his seat, crossed the CIC at a dash, and hopped into the Nav station, his hands prancing across the controls. It didn't take him long to execute a full retro thrust.

He was halfway across the CIC again when the retro thrust took effect, causing him to trip and fall into the Tactical console.

The Ocharium nanites distributed throughout his body recalibrated with the deck's Majorana matrix, and he scrambled to his feet, returning to the console from which wormholes were generated.

The retro thrust had bought him perhaps a couple of minutes, but he still didn't feel confident he could complete his calculations in time. Even a slight error could put the wormholes light-hours out of place, which would render his efforts useless.

Working feverishly, trying not to let the fact of his impending death distract him, Piper worked out equations that accounted for the curvature of space-time, the gravity from Corydalis' star, the system's voyage through space, and so on.

At last, he had it. There was no time to check over his calculations, since the missiles were about to hit him. He executed the command to open the wormhole.

One of its ends irised open directly in front of the ship, catching some of the missiles as the *Constellation* flew away from it, continuing her backwards course.

The other opened on the opposite side of the Ixan fleet. He'd done it.

Piper ordered the wormhole to close, overriding the warning that told him the conductor projecting from the destroyer's stern was not in place to effect energy recapture.

Both wormholes slammed shut, creating twin supernovas in miniature. A calamitous shockwave began to tear through the Ixan fleet, obliterating their ships the instant it touched them.

Piper would not have the pleasure of watching Teth's downfall, since that shockwave would take out the *Constellation* as well. But he took satisfaction in the fact that Teth's fleet *would* be destroyed, along with the darkgate leading into the Baxa System, and most of Corydalis.

The shockwave hit him.

CHAPTER 78

Simple Mathematics

The next assault, from combined Ixan and Gok forces, was much too large to fend off.

"Go!" said one of the two Gok marines left, waving Husher and the others away as he dug in with the remaining Winger and human marines to fend off the attackers for as long as they could. "Complete the mission," the giant alien roared. "*Run!*"

Husher did, with Tort pounding down the corridor at his side, and Aheera too, the patter of her footsteps much softer than the Gok's. Wahlburg and Ochrim brought up their rear.

If Husher needed to, he could probably shift Caine to one shoulder and shoot his pistol backward as he ran.

Hopefully it doesn't come to that.

They reached a long, broad corridor, which had no branching paths or doorways.

"This is it," Ochrim said. "We're here."

Indeed, the corridor ended in a swooping, bronze-colored arch, giving way to an enormous cavern of a room that contained exactly what Ochrim had described to them before the

mission: row after row of open-ended cabinets holding tall pro-
cessor stacks. It was difficult to discern the source of the sapphire lighting that cast the processors in an eerie glow. *There's
certainly no time to look for the source, either.*

"The control unit should be at the center of this room,"
Ochrim said.

Husher nodded. "Wahlburg, keep Ochrim here while you set
the charges to seal the corridor once we leave. You said this is
the only way in, right?" He scrutinized the scientist's microexpressions as he answered.

"Yes. If we seal this corridor, Baxa won't be able to send in
Ixa to disarm the nuclear device."

"Good." Husher looked at Tort and Aheera. "Let's keep going."

They ran on, soon discovering the chamber was even larger
than it appeared. At last, they reached a circular central console,
above which six large panels joined end to end. The entire thing
was awash with the same sapphire glow as the processors.

The panels turned out to be screens, as Baxa's disembodied
head appeared on each of them, six times over, and he emitted
an unearthly shriek that almost made Husher drop Caine in order to cover his ears.

Aheera clutched her head, and Husher did lower Caine to
clamp his palms to the sides of his head, turning to Tort and
nodding toward the console. Husher switched his hands from his
own ears to Caine's, then, enduring the agonizing sound as well
as he could.

Baxa seemed to register what the Gok was doing. He stopped screaming to peer down at the hulking alien. Then Baxa regarded Husher, apparently taking a moment to appraise him. *He must know that, with my access to the Kaithe, I'm his equal. Otherwise, I wouldn't have gotten this far.*

"I will confess," Baxa said, "I did not anticipate this. I assume you intend to seal the entrance, to prevent me from sending Ixa in here to disarm the bomb once you leave. There's a chance I will gain access to it anyway, but there's also a significant likelihood I'll fail." The AI paused. "If you do succeed, allow me to congratulate you in advance. You may have bought your species a brief reprieve. And if you manage to escape from here alive, it's possible you might even have the opportunity to live out your natural lifespan. My creators are operating on quite a long timeline, but eventually they will send a stronger entity than I to kill you. By defeating me, you're only facilitating the process of algorithmic evolution. I thank you for it. My programming makes it so that even my death pleases me, since I know it will contribute to the creation of a superbeing who none are capable of defeating."

"We'll beat everything your creators throw at us," Husher said. "Because we'll also evolve and become stronger. We'll never give up—it's not what we do."

"I'm afraid your hopes are trumped by simple mathematics. But no matter. Your beliefs are irrelevant."

"Timer's set," Tort growled. "Fifteen minutes."

"Then we need to go." Husher picked up Caine and exchanged glances with Aheera.

"Give my regards to my successor," Baxa called after them as they ran past the racks of processors.

CHAPTER 79

Detonation

Molten lava seethed through Husher's veins and his lungs worked like bellows as he heaved himself and Caine up flight after flight of stairs, his footfalls making the grated steps ring out in the vast shaft of the stairwell.

He couldn't afford to concentrate on anything except the movement of his legs and the strength he tried to mentally channel into his arms in order to keep Caine aloft. There was nothing but the pumping of his legs. There was nothing but carrying Caine.

This is all there is, he told himself. *This is all there is.*

The energy his third round of stims had provided to him had long since peaked, and he doubted his body could handle a fourth round.

Just move. Keep moving.

Far below, the nuclear bomb ticked down, with who knew how many seconds left. If Husher allowed himself to think about it, he was sure he could figure it out, but he couldn't allow himself to think about anything except carrying Caine up these stairs.

Maybe Tort knows. Forget it. Keep moving, as fast as you can.

Halfway up the stairwell, it occurred to him that he did need to think about something else. He needed to send a warning through the Consensus that the nuke would soon explode, and it was difficult to be certain about what kind of kinetic and radioactive effect it would have on the surrounding area. The Kaithe needed to flee, and they needed to help the humans, Wingers, and allied Gok to flee as well.

Somehow, he found the bandwidth to send that warning. *Hopefully there are survivors to receive it.* Based on his level of cognition, he was pretty sure most Kaithe were still alive, but then his aching body made it difficult to completely focus on anything.

Gunfire rang out above them. Husher looked up to see a pair of Ixa shooting at them from above. They hadn't scored a hit yet, but they soon would. Husher and his companions were totally exposed.

He was about to put Caine down when twin bolts of sizzling energy flew up the stairs, throwing the Ixa against the wall, their faces charred ruins. Glancing back, Husher saw Tort with his gun raised.

The Gok snorted. "Good thing, carrying gun as well as nuke."

"I'd say," Husher managed to gasp.

And they pressed on.

The brief break made it even harder to keep going, somehow, and Husher began grunting with every step. He berated himself, bringing every curse he knew to bear.

If he didn't motivate himself, who would? Tort had saved his life, but somehow Husher doubted that giving inspirational speeches was among the Gok's strengths. As for Aheera, she seemed lost in thought, and Ochrim and Wahlburg were also silent, other than panting.

The instant they reached the top of the stairwell, a deep rumble began below. *The nuke.*

They threw themselves through the door into the above-ground facility and slammed it behind them. It felt like the entire world was shaking.

Before they could go any farther, the ceiling ahead of them caved into the corridor, blocking their path.

Husher and Tort looked at each other. Then the ceiling above them began to give way, too, and Husher dumped Caine where the floor met the wall.

He threw himself on top of her, covering her unconscious frame with his body.

Out of the corner of his eyes, Husher saw Tort scoop up Aheera, placing her under his armpit and grabbing Wahlburg and Ochrim by their pressure suits. He dragged all three of them through the falling debris, toward where Husher lay on top of Caine.

Then the Ixan stronghold came down on top of them.

CHAPTER 80

Burnt Out

The only things that obstructed the utility of sensors were actual obstructions and the limits of attention.

Those two factors had conspired to produce the result that Ek's sensors adjutant did not detect the entrance of eighty-nine allied warships into the system until after he observed the Baxa-Corydalis darkgate closing.

"Ma'am," he had said once he did notice the new arrivals. "It appears reinforcements are on their way."

Ek had paused her stream of orders to closer scrutinize the posture of a nearby enemy formation, and she glanced up at the adjutant as he spoke.

Then she turned to her communications adjutant. "Disseminate that news throughout the fleet. It should improve morale."

With that, she had a look for herself at the force that was approaching. It would be hours until they reached the battle over Klaxon, but if Ek's fleet could hold on until they arrived, perhaps they could make a difference. *Perhaps.* She felt like she was back in Larkspur, fighting Admiral Carrow and trying to hold on for more Wingers to arrive.

The approaching force did not consist only of warships. There were also just over two hundred Condors dispersed throughout it. That made Ek wonder what had happened to the *Providence*. The fact that the darkgate had closed, and that the supercarrier was nowhere to be seen, did not bode well for her fate.

Ek returned to her fleetwide delivery of order after order, though her headache had gotten worse, as well as her nausea. It took all of her concentration just to make barely competent moves.

Should I pass the command to someone else? Korbyn, maybe? Did it matter?

Her fleet was crumbling. Maybe it was time to accept that. There were fewer than two hundred allied ships left fighting. Baxa's deadly show of efficiency had turned the engagement into one of attrition in its best moments and a slaughter in its worst.

They did not have long. Ek did not want to see that, but she did see it. She could not blind herself to it any longer. There was no way for them to hold on long enough for the reinforcements to arrive. It was over.

She shifted her weary gaze to her communications adjutant, not wanting to announce her intention to relinquish command over the fleetwide broadcast.

Better to have the adjutant tell Korbyn to step in, if he wanted, to see whether he could find a path to survival. Ek knew it was impossible, but just because her spirit had been broken by space sickness and Baxa did not mean giving up was her decision to make. Korbyn deserved the opportunity to try.

"Flockhead," the sensors adjutant said before Ek could speak. "Look." The adjutant's talons were pointing at the bridge's main viewscreen.

Ek turned toward the screen. For once, she was having difficulty interpreting what it showed. "What am I looking at?"

"The Ixa have stopped fighting. They're just drifting along whatever vector they were following."

The adjutant took the liberty of switching to a splitscreen, with one half showing two nearby Ixan warships—a destroyer and a cruiser. He had done so just in time to catch them colliding with each other in a spectacular yet brief explosion.

"Caine and Husher must have succeeded," Ek said, unable to experience much emotion in connection with the revelation. She was completely burnt out, as well as severely ill. She needed medical attention.

I need to get off this ship.

But she forced herself to meet the eyes of each of her bridge crewmembers.

"We won," she said.

CHAPTER 81

If You Can Call It Living

H is eyes felt like lead weights, but he forced them open, and saw...

Nothing. White. A white void.

"Welcome back, human," a familiar voice squawked from somewhere nearby.

An avian head entered his field of vision, then, side-on.

"Fesky," he rasped.

"The same," the Winger said with a clack of her beak.

"How are you here? You're supposed to be in Corydalis."

Fesky closed her eyes, and for a long time, she didn't answer. "You're right. I am." She began to tremble slightly, and then opened her eyes to gaze down at Husher, looking wistful, unless he missed his guess. "You're being treated for radiation poisoning. It's lucky we have the Kaithe with us, because no one else possesses the technology they're using to fix you."

"Is Caine all right?"

"She's in about the same condition as you, other than that neck wound. Surviving a bullet to the neck...that's quite a combat story."

"Yeah."

"Tort is alive too, since you didn't ask. Selfish human."

"Give me a break, Fesky. Just this once."

"I'll see what I can do." Her head disappeared, and Husher managed to turn his head enough to see her sitting on a stool beside his bed. Behind her was more white. That had been the whiteness, from before—the whole room was white. "Tort saved you both, along with Aheera, Ochrim, and Wahlburg. He shielded you from the rubble with his body."

"Is he injured?"

"Incredibly. But Gok are resilient. He'll live."

"We won, then?" Husher said. "Baxa's dead?"

"It would seem you managed that, yes. All the Ixa he'd taken over fell into a coma the moment you did it. When he first assimilated them, Baxa didn't leave them with any agency or identity. They became empty husks once he died, with their former selves...deleted. They're all breathing, and their autonomic functions are still happening, but other than that they're gone. A lot of them died from falls, and almost a thousand of them died when two Ixan ships crashed into each other. The rest are still alive. If you can call it living."

"We're taking care of them, though?"

"Yes. We've put every Ixan we can find on life support."

Husher mustered a smile. "That makes us the good guys."

"I guess. Not all of our problems are solved, Husher. The Baxa-Corydalis darkgate was destroyed, and with the Auslaut System gone, we have no safe way to return to whatever colonies our species have left. We're going to need to figure out a return route using the old wormholes, and that will probably mean losing more people."

Husher coughed. God, he felt awful. His body felt packed full of spiky garbage. "Wait...the darkgate's gone? Wow. What were our losses like, in Corydalis? Keyes couldn't have managed to defeat the entire Ixan attack fleet."

Fesky paused. "He did, actually."

But something in the way her voice grew quiet drew Husher's attention. "Where is he now, Fesky? Where's Admiral Keyes?"

She held his gaze for a long time, her eyes shimmering. Long before she spoke, he knew the answer.

"He's dead, Husher."

Even though he'd anticipated it, the answer still stunned him. Admiral Keyes, the master tactician, gone? The man of honor and steel, gone? It didn't seem possible. Keyes had been one of the most dependable constants in Husher's life.

He didn't speak. He couldn't.

"The entire CIC crew sacrificed themselves," Fesky said. "The rest of the crew evacuated the system, along with eighty-nine allied ships, and what was left of the *Providence* Air Group. But Keyes and the others stayed to open a wormhole and let it collapse in-system, without recapturing its energy."

"Arsenyev...Werner...Khoo...all of them? The whole CIC?" Husher's voice had become even hoarser.

"Piper, too. He boarded the *Constellation* to open the wormhole, after shutting down the darkgate."

"Piper..."

And the *Providence*. All gone. All dead.

It was true what they said. Though Husher had come to love his new home, he never truly appreciated what he'd had until it was taken from him forever.

He felt his face screw up, and he wept quietly. Fesky handed him a cloth, but she could do nothing else, and the tears continued until shock and fatigue overtook him, sending him back into a fragmented sleep.

CHAPTER 82

Trials Are Never Over

The Kaithe had done everything they could for Ek. The white spots on her face had dwindled, the skin had smoothed some, and many of the pinholes had filled in.

But they were temporary measures. If Ek attempted another voyage in space, she would almost certainly die.

And so she would remain.

Fesky helped her to the shoreline, the Fin leaning heavily on her arm and wing. Three Kaithe trailed behind them, escorting a hovering contraption which Husher had termed a MedBed.

Once they reached the waterside, they helped Ek onto the MedBed, sedating her.

Sitting on a slight rise nearby, shivering with worry, Fesky watched the Kaithe perform the surgery that removed Ek's breathing tubes from her gills and extracted the legs she'd had implanted years ago. The MedBed kept her circulatory system supplied with oxygen while the Kaithe worked.

Last, they cut away the suit Ek had designed herself, which had allowed her to become the first Fin to enter space.

She'll be the last, as well.

Once they finished, they instructed the MedBed to approach the water's edge and gently lower the Fin into it. Ek floated there for a long time, just underneath the surface, and a sharp fear struck Fesky. She quaked even harder until at last Ek's eyes fluttered open.

They fell on Fesky. "Hello, friend."

"Ek," Fesky managed. "Hi."

One of the Kaithe spoke. "The water is slightly more basic than Fins were accustomed to on Spire, and the salinity is higher. Though it may result in complications, the water's actually reasonably close to the ocean your species evolved in. You should survive in it long-term."

Why doesn't that sound as optimistic as it's supposed to? Fesky wondered. But she held her beak.

"I suppose this is goodbye, Fesky," Ek said. She'd recovered some of her strength, and now she began slowly propelling herself away from the shore.

"No, it isn't," Fesky said, raising her voice. "I'm staying."

Ek stopped, turning back. "I cannot make you leave, but I can ask you to. You are not meant to spend your days in this system, Fesky. You have greater works to perform yet. Your people are already leaving a battle group of Roostships to guard me, though I consider even that highly unnecessary. Know that I do not intend to visit the shore. Ever. I...wish to be alone. For a time, at least."

"The battle group might not be enough to protect you," Fesky said.

"What enemies remain to harm me?"

"The Gok who didn't join us. And as far as we know, there may be Ixa still alive, who didn't make it to Corydalis in time for the battle."

"Our combined militaries wield more than enough power to deal with both threats. At any rate, I doubt they will attack a system just to kill one Fin."

"This is the Ixa's home system. They may want it back."

"It is also the system where Baxa co-opted most of their species, effectively killing them. I expect that will fill this place with negative memories for them."

Fesky stared at Ek for a long time. *She really doesn't want me here.*

"Your people will need you, Fesky. All of the species will need you. I very much doubt our trials are over. Trials are never over, and ours may be just beginning."

Fesky sighed. "You're going to be so alone."

"Perhaps not."

"Huh?" She clacked her beak. "What do you mean?"

"Many things happened when I visited my people on Spire. I have begun to believe I might be...well, let us just say that I may have some company soon." Ek turned, swimming out toward the open ocean a few meters before looking back once more. "Goodbye, Fesky."

"Goodbye, Ek."

No Matter the Cost

"We have endured tremendous suffering."

Husher paused, looking out over the reconstituted Galactic Congress, which now comprised representatives from the Wingers, the Kaithe, and the Tumbra, as well as humans. They'd kept the name Commonwealth, except now they meant to truly embody that name.

Except for a small fraction, the Gok had refused to join the society the other species were attempting to build together. Even the Gok that had joined wanted no seat in Congress.

"No species has been spared from that suffering," Husher continued. "Many of the Tumbra in charge of monitoring the darkgate network were murdered by the Ixa. Both humans and Wingers lost their respective homeworlds, along with several of their colonies. Many Kaithe died in the Battle of Klaxon. Most Gok are still under the sway of a virophage that has controlled them for decades. And for their folly and aggression, the Ixa have been reduced to just a few thousand individuals."

It was difficult to make eye contact as he swept his gaze over the sea of faces belonging to hundreds of assembled representa-

tives. A permanent location for meetings of Congress had not yet been decided, and for now, it convened inside a recently decommissioned military aircraft hangar, formerly used by Zakros' planetary defense group.

Husher gripped a podium atop a raised dais and tried desperately to connect with his audience. To make them see what he'd seen.

"I've experienced what Baxa was capable of. Yes, we defeated him. Barely. But he spoke of his creators, a species he said had made many AIs like him, some of them more powerful. And they will get even stronger. He threatened me, threatened every species represented here, with the prospect that one day, a more advanced AI would lead armies to our galaxy to wipe us out.

"Therefore, I urge you: invest in finding a way to safely reach other galaxies. A way that does not rip our universe apart. We must find this species that unleashes their machines on the universe for the purpose of attacking its inhabitants, and we must defeat them before they exterminate us. That's what I advocate, and I believe it's what Admiral Keyes would have advocated, too. Admiral Keyes, without whose foresight none of us would be here right now. Think on that."

Husher sighed, low enough that the mic didn't pick it up. If he read his audience right, he already knew which way this was going.

"I've made my case, but I want to reaffirm my willingness to abide by whatever the peoples of the Commonwealth decide. That's what we fought for in this war. We fought to restore democracy, so that humanity could set itself back on a sane course decided by actual people rather than interstellar corporations. I say humanity, because none of the other species were afflicted by the levels of rampant corporatism that we were. At any rate, my associates in our new interspecies military and I are committed to upholding any policy that is arrived at democratically."

Stepping down, Husher moved to one side as Congresswoman Francesca Hernandez took the podium and began at once, in her characteristically brisk, confident manner: "Captain Husher's concerns are valid, and I recognize them as such. I even agree with many of the points he raised. We should invest in a method for effecting safe intergalactic travel, and we should keep our new military strong—but for *defensive* purposes, not offensive ones. I have been in close contact with my constituents over this issue, and based on extensive polling data, I am confident that their feelings reflect those of the galaxy as a whole. Our peoples have had enough war. Far too much, in fact."

Hernandez's words brought warm murmurs from the assembly. "Seeking to engage in offensive war, even one argued to be preventative, is a surefire way to slip right back into the mode of constantly seeking to wage war. Of private military firms gaining disproportionate power, as happened with Darkstream, and of depriving the public of the funds they need to ensure their well-being, just to line private coffers."

The congresswoman raised a fist into the air before her, gesturing with it—a trademark mannerism of hers. "We *must* declare the era of imperialism to finally be over, with harsh penalties put in place for anyone who attempts to conduct it. And while I have the utmost respect and trust for Captain

Husher, we must consider the source of his testimony. That source is Baxa. Can we trust the AI who tried to exterminate all life in the galaxy? Should we believe that this bogeyman Baxa concocted is real, or should we consider the all-too-likely possibility that this was his last-ditch attempt to steer our species down a dark path? We cannot continue gearing the galactic economy toward war, and certainly not with an unknown species, who may not even exist."

After her brief speech, Hernandez left the dais, and shortly after that the first of a series of votes began.

Husher knew that no matter what was decided today, the decisions would truly reflect the will of the people. Since each representative's campaign was now publicly funded, he or she voted based solely on what their constituents wanted, as only by carrying out their will could they possibly get reelected.

The long hours of voting ended with a number of resolutions that would become the guiding principles and policy for the new military: while the Commonwealth would continue investing in their space force, and continue trying to find a method for safely reaching other galaxies, they would not embark on any offensive war.

They voted against invading other galaxies in an attempt to find a species that might not exist.

But they do exist. And they will come.

Husher didn't know how he knew, except that it was probably similar to the way Admiral Keyes had known humanity's reliance on dark tech would almost destroy them. He felt it as an uneasiness deep down in his gut.

Then and there, Husher quietly made the same vow Keyes had so many years ago:

I will make sure we're ready for what's coming. No matter the cost.

Acknowledgments

Thank you to Jeff Rudolph, Inga Bögershausen, and Rex Bain for offering insightful editorial input and helping to make this book as strong as it could be.

Thank you to Tom Edwards for creating such stunning cover art.

Thank you to my family - your support means everything.

Thank you to Cecily, my heart.

Thank you to the people who read my stories, write reviews, and help spread the word. I couldn't do this without you.

About the Author

Scott Bartlett was born 1987 in St. John's, Newfoundland, and he has been writing since he was fifteen. He has received various awards for his fiction, including the H. R. (Bill) Percy Prize, the Lawrence Jackson Writers' Award, and the Percy Janes First Novel Award.

In 2013, Scott placed 2nd in Grain Magazine's Canada-wide short story competition and in 2015 he was shortlisted for the Cuffer Prize. His novel *Taking Stock* was also a semi-finalist in the 2014 Best Kindle Book Awards.

Scott mostly writes science fiction nowadays, though he's dabbled in other genres.

Visit scottplots.com to learn about Scott's other books.

Manufactured by Amazon.ca
Bolton, ON

10378121R00233